THE DEVIL'S MOON

The Fourth Brighton Mystery

Peter Guttridge

severn
House

This first world edition published 2013
in Great Britain and the USA by
SEVERN HOUSE PUBLISHERS LTD of
19 Cedar Road, Sutton, Surrey, England, SM2 5DA.
Trade paperback edition first published
in Great Britain and the USA 2013 by
SEVERN HOUSE PUBLISHERS LTD

ISBN-13: 978-0-7278-8225-7 (cased)
ISBN-13: 978-1-84751-485-1 (trade paper)

All Severn House titles are printed on acid-free paper.

Severn House Publishers support The Forest Stewardship Council [FSC],
the leading international forest certification organisation. All our titles that
are printed on Greenpeace-approved FSC-certified paper carry the FSC logo.

Typeset by Palimpsest Book Production Ltd.,
Falkirk, Stirlingshire, Scotland.
Printed and bound in Great Britain by
MPG Books Ltd., Bodmin, Cornwall.

THE DEVIL'S MOON

A Selection of Recent Titles by Peter Guttridge

The Brighton Mystery Series

CITY OF DREADFUL NIGHT *
THE LAST KING OF BRIGHTON *
THE THING ITSELF *
THE DEVIL'S MOON *

The Nick Madrid Series

NO LAUGHING MATTER
A GHOST OF A CHANCE
TWO TO TANGO
THE ONCE AND FUTURE CON
FOILED AGAIN
CAST ADRIFT

* available from Severn House

For Terry Dean (1947–2012)
Musician, writer, artist and friend

'I am Wrath.'
Christopher Marlowe: Dr Faustus

PROLOGUE

The shape at the edge of the rippling water was at first indistinct. Beyond it the sea was unnaturally placid, the waves sluggish. Then, as the first fingers of the sun spread across the morning from the east, the shape took form.

The keenest runners along the promenade glanced and noted it and continued on their way. The early-morning dog walkers kept half an eye on their unleashed dogs and the other half on the shape taking form with the coming of light. In Brighton, curious structures sprouting up overnight were nothing remarkable. Yet another art installation, though the skateboarders would have a difficult time turning this one into a practice loop.

Others had more time to reflect, if they were not too drunk to do so. The all-night revellers staggering on to the beach from the clubs under the arches. The just awaking homeless, the ones who preferred sleeping on the steep bank of shifting shingle to huddling on hard concrete in the city's streets and alleys.

The dawn revealed a giant, faceless man. Some twenty feet high, legs planted hip-width apart, arms stiff down his sides but at a slight angle away from his body. Those who had seen the cult movie or its unfortunate remake, or who knew something of paganism, knew it was a Wicker Man.

Individuals and groups were drawn towards the faceless figure. As they approached, the top rim of the sun bobbed on to the horizon and flames sprouted from the Wicker Man's ankles and gushed over his legs and torso.

To scattered applause the crackling, roaring flames engulfed the structure. People drew near to warm themselves against the chill of the morning. Those who were pagans at heart looked towards the sun rising beyond it and back at the burning effigy, its head now wreathed in vivid fire, and took significance from it.

Seagulls, clamouring at the dawn, wheeled towards and then away from the shimmering tower of flame. A pall of black smoke rose from the conflagration and drifted lazily in the brightening sky towards the collapsed ruins of the West Pier.

The heat grew more intense, the raging of the flames louder. Those nearest moved back a few paces. And so they could not be certain that they heard screams above the racket of the fire and the screech of the gulls.

Those who were sure took the screams as proof that this was indeed an installation or a performance of some sort. Four clubbers skirted the side of the effigy and looked round the back for the sound system producing the terrible cries. There wasn't one.

Two of them later insisted that just before the screams were swallowed in flames they heard an agonized voice shriek out: 'Why hast thou forsaken me?'

ONE

As the rain pelted down, Sarah Gilchrist splish-splashed along the narrow passage of Meeting House Lane, focused on avoiding a poke in the eye from one of the jumble of umbrellas around her. That meant she was off guard when the large fish fell on her head and almost knocked her down.

Not that she would normally be on her guard against fish. She stopped and looked down at it, dead in the puddle at her feet. She looked up at the rooftops to find the joker who had dropped it on her. Another fish slapped her in the face and slid away.

Shielding her head with her hand, she looked around. People were crying out and ducking as a hail of fish of all shapes and sizes rained down on them.

What the hell? The fish were not being dropped or thrown by anyone. Hundreds, maybe thousands of them were falling out of the sky.

Gilchrist pushed through to the junction with Union Street, fish pelting her as she went, and ducked into the Bath Arms. The staff and the early-morning drinkers were all at the window, gazing out open-mouthed or filming the surreal sight with their phones. One alert staff member pulled on the pub door and hooked it open.

The others laughed as he called into the street: 'Don't you even know enough to come in out of the fish?'

Gilchrist laughed too, though her neck and her head ached. Ludicrous as it sounded, those fish hurt. They were heavy and hit with force. The hail of them was doing real damage. People were being beaten to the ground. Some people just slipped and slithered as the lane filled up with fish. There was panic in the confined space.

The fish were all shapes and sizes, all colours. They were already dead as they dropped from the sky. All except for these long, writhing creatures with heads the size of water-melons and fearsome-looking jaws.

Conger eels.

Gilchrist watched, horrified, as a shower of them plummeted on to the crowded lane, jaws snapping, tails thrashing. They crashed through umbrellas and bore people to the ground beneath their weight. There was terrified screaming.

One eel, about four feet long, dropped like lead on to the shoulders of a teenage girl and sent her reeling into the window of the jeweller just across from the pub. The glass shattered and girl and eel both fell into the window display.

A jangling alarm blared out as jewellery fell into the street. Girl and eel sprawled, half in, half out of the window. Gilchrist could see jagged shards of glass sticking up from the base of the window frame but hoped the girl's thick waterproof was protecting her.

Gilchrist watched, stupefied, as people ignored the fish falling on their heads to grab at the jewellery in the window and on the lane. She was astonished when the girl who had fallen into the window reared up, screaming, but with fistfuls of jewellery in her hands. She stumbled away, clutching her loot, blood streaming down her face.

The jewellery shop manager came to the shop doorway to remonstrate with those people scrabbling for his silver watches and brooches and necklaces. He tried to snatch the jewellery back. Someone pushed him in the chest and he fell into the shop.

Gilchrist barged out of the pub and over to the shop, her boots slithering on the fish and the slick of water in the lane. 'Police officer!' she called. 'Make way.'

'Go fuck yourself,' a fat man snarled. As she looked towards him he shouldered her away. She lost her footing and fell towards the broken window. She reached out a hand to stop her fall. It landed on the slick skin of the eel. She grabbed the door frame with her other hand and steadied herself.

As Gilchrist did so, the eel whipped its head round and sank its teeth into her hand. She snatched her arm back and stood looking in horror at the eel dangling from the web of her skin between thumb and first finger. She shook her arm feebly to dislodge the eel but all it did was lash its tail. Blood dripped off Gilchrist's hand. The pain was intense.

Gilchrist shrieked. The alarm shrieked. Fish fell from the sky. Looters jostled each other for a share of the jewellery shop spoils.

Gilchrist prised at the jaws one-handed. She was surprised the eel, out of water, showed no sign of expiring. It was strong and every time it writhed it dragged at her flesh. She had a sudden thought that an eel might be like those dogs whose jaws remain clamped shut even after death.

Gilchrist looked at the jagged glass sticking out of the window frame. She swept her hand towards it, dragging the heavy fish with her. She tried to impale it on the broken shard. The eel, as if sensing what she was trying to do, released her hand. It thrashed its tail and slithered to the ground.

Gilchrist fell back against the doorjamb. The hubbub continued around her. Holding her throbbing hand, she let her head fall back and looked up at the roiling sky. At least it had stopped raining fish.

'You're listening to Simon Says on Southern Shores Radio, in case you thought you'd died and gone to heaven. Well, talk about being slapped in the face with a wet fish. The people of Brighton were stunned earlier this morning when fish rained down on them from a clear sky. But it's no laughing matter. So far, three people have died and at least forty people have been treated at Sussex County Hospital for cuts and bruises and shock as the fish – some weighing up to twenty-five pounds – plummeted down on the centre of town. One man had his skull crushed by a conger eel weighing seventy-five pounds; another of the dead was hit by a bass and a third was killed by a falling pollack . . .'

Kate Simpson looked into the studio. Simon was corpsing. He'd spun on his chair away from his microphone and was trying to control his giggles. Inevitably that meant there was going to be a big explosion when he failed to do so. She flicked a switch and spoke into the microphone on her producer's desk.

'Hi everyone, apologies for the sudden silence here at

Southern Shores Radio but Simon is having a coughing fit. As he said, the lethal fish fell from a clear sky and included pollack, bream, cod, mackerel, bass, ling, thornback rays, tope and smoothhound.' She stopped for a moment then gasped, 'Excuse me . . .'

She'd forgotten that giggles, like yawns, are catching.

Sarah Gilchrist, listening to Southern Shores Radio in the waiting room in A&E, laughed at the silence that followed. It was clearly a Jim Naughtie moment. Watts had heard Naughtie's famous fit of the giggles when the *Today* programme presenter had made a classic spoonerism in his introduction to Jeremy Hunt, Culture Secretary, in the days before the politician became Minister for Murdoch and it didn't seem quite such a spoonerism.

Gilchrist could imagine first Simon then her flatmate, Kate Simpson, suffering in the same way. She looked down at her crudely self-bandaged hand and grinned. There *was* something inherently funny about being killed by a fish falling out of the sky.

This weather. The River Ouse, which ran through Lewes, had broken its banks and the meadows outside the town were lakes. Cliffe village, at the bottom end of town, was in danger of being flooded again as it had been in the nineties. All around Brighton there were posters from the Water Authority advising that despite the rain there was still a drought. 'Please be careful with our water' the posters said. Most had been defaced by the same graffiti in various styles: 'We will if you will.'

Marble and tiled floors in shopping centres and restaurants were so slippery they had turned into ice rinks. There were large puddles and small lakes on every road and street. Most sensible women had abandoned fashion raincoats and boots for rainwear that was actually waterproof, giving them all a certain bulky uniformity.

Of course, in Brighton, that still left a lot of not-so-sensible women – and men – getting soaked through on a daily basis.

Gilchrist had never had much vanity when it came to clothes – not much point in the days she was a uniformed copper weighed down with clobber – and she was tall enough never to need high-heeled boots and shoes except when she really wanted to intimidate.

The man sitting next to her gave her the slightest of nudges. 'Bloody biblical, that's what it is,' he said. 'It'll be frogs next.'

The man on the far side of him leaned forward to address them both. 'Long as it's not cats and dogs,' he said. 'If it rains the Rottweilers and bull terriers from the Milldean estate we've no bloody chance.'

Gilchrist smiled awkwardly. Milldean held only bad memories for her.

The man next to her nodded at her hand. 'Looks nasty, that hand. What did it?'

Gilchrist couldn't really be bothered but she didn't want to be rude. 'A conger eel bit me.'

'Nasty things them eels,' the other man said. 'They're quite the predator. Ugly looking things too. Expect you'll need a tetanus jab.'

She frowned. 'Not sure how tetanus from fish would work – it's usually linked to farms, isn't it?'

'You never heard of fish farms?' the man said, and Gilchrist couldn't work out from his expression whether he was being funny or not.

She looked at the gash on the side of the head of the man beside her. 'What clobbered you?' she asked.

He shrugged. 'Damned if I know. The only time I usually see a fish it's got batter on it.'

Gilchrist's mobile rang. 'Excuse me,' she said and stepped away.

'The chief constable wants to see you,' said the voice on the other end of the line. 'Tomorrow. Nine a.m. prompt.'

TWO

Ex-Chief Constable Bob Watts wandered aimlessly from room to gloomy room of his late father's Barnes Bridge house. His father, Donald Watts, aka bestselling thriller writer Victor Tempest, aka thorough bastard.

The house had a sour, old person's smell but it also smelled still of his father's bay rum aftershave. Watts looked in his father's wardrobe where the suits and jackets and shirts and trousers were all hung in neat rows. He examined at random cufflinks in surprising numbers in a leather box that also contained dress shirt studs, tiepins and even a worn brass ring. He wondered if it was his wedding ring. His father was of the generation that tended not to wear a wedding band.

Although he had loved his mother more, he didn't remember feeling this depth of emotion when she had died many years earlier. Given the tangled relationship he had with his father, this surprised him.

He walked over to the bookshelves and ran his fingers over the spines of the books. He had been working his way through his father's library, sorting out which books to sell and which to keep. His own small library of books was in store until he figured out where he wanted to live.

He glanced to his left out of the long window at the heavy rain and watched for a moment the brown tide of the Thames washing over the towpath. It had been raining solidly for a month.

He could live here, he knew, if he bought out his brother and sister. But he was a Brighton boy at heart and a river was no substitute for the sea, even if that river was the Thames.

Many of the books on the shelves were signed first editions with personal dedications to his father. Margot Bennett was most effusive in her inscription in her 1958 crime novel, *Someone from the Past*. Watts thought he could probably guess why.

His father had been a womanizer, no getting around that. His mother had been stalwart for the sake of the children although she must have felt so wretched at her husband's infidelities.

A recurring, puzzling memory was of a beautiful, enigmatic woman coming to their house once when the family was in the back garden. Watts, a teenager at the time, had been sent to let her in. He remembered vividly how sensual she'd seemed. How, back out in the garden, he saw her at the window and how she slowly faded as she withdrew into the room. How his mother looked up from her book and saw the woman at the window then looked fixedly back at her book again.

He wondered again who the woman was and what part she had played in his father's life. A mystery he would probably never solve.

A number of books surprised him. There were several signed by Albert Camus, the French existentialist philosopher. R D Laing's anti-psychiatry works, once so influential, had personal inscriptions.

Watts could understand the signed copies of the novels of thriller writer Alistair MacLean. MacLean had been his father's friend as well as rival. There was a scrawled card tucked in MacLean's *The Guns of Navarone*: 'Victor – scopolamine – use in moderation! Affectionately, Alistair.'

On the title page of *Where Eagles Dare* MacLean had written: 'Truth drug all used up. Maybe you've still got some. Admiringly, Alistair.'

Watts had come across the tropane alkaloid scopolamine as a truth serum during his army career but had been dubious about its value. His father had referred to it two or three times in his thrillers. People strapped to a chair, injection in the arm, helpless blabbing of things supposed to be kept secret, and so on. He deduced MacLean had done the same in these two novels.

Dennis Wheatley was fond of Victor Tempest, judging by the affectionate inscriptions in his books *The Devil Rides Out*, *To the Devil a Daughter* and *They Used Dark Forces*. The inscriptions were all variations of the message in the first of them: 'To Victor, *mon semblable, mon frère.* Yours ever, Dennis.'

Watts frowned. He didn't really understand the French. *The Devil Rides Out*, he noted, had been published in 1934, the same year as the Brighton Trunk Murders.

There were half a dozen of Colin Pearson's books. There was his precocious first work, *Outside Looking Out* which, in the sixties, when Pearson was in his early twenties, had made him a philosophical *wunderkind*; four of his famously didactic novels; and a copy of his biggest seller, *Magic*.

Watts drew *Magic* out. According to the blurb on the back this was the seminal work on the occult as a pathway for what Maslow had called meta-motivated people. Whatever that meant.

Watts read the inscription: 'Victor, let the search continue, *mon semblable*, *mon frère*. Salutations, Colin.'

The same French phrase. And the search for what?

Watts was puzzled to think of his father befriending such men as Wheatley and Pearson. He didn't think that black magic mumbo-jumbo had been his father's thing. At Halloween, when his mother got out the Ouija board, his father would play along, depending on his mood, but it was jokey, never sinister.

That was about the extent of it as far as Watts knew. But, as he'd been discovering in recent months, there was a lot he didn't know about his father.

A friendship with Wheatley he could understand – two professional writers talking shop. Watts went over to the roll-top desk where he'd set up his laptop and Googled Wheatley. A well-educated, prolific author whose eighty or so novels, especially in the fifties and sixties, sold in their millions around the world. He wrote mostly adventures but there were some novels dealing with Satanism, often featuring a wealthy aristocrat, the Duc de Richleau.

Wheatley and Victor Tempest had the war in common, of course, although Wheatley – like Tempest's other writer friend, Ian Fleming – had been in the Navy. Tempest had been a commando.

Watts read about Wheatley's admiration for Mussolini.

Perhaps that was also something the two writers had in common. Victor Tempest had been one of Mosley's Blackshirts for a while.

Pearson, though, was more of a puzzle. Sure, he was a writer, but he was better known for his eccentric philosophizing. Pearson's take on existentialism had soon been ridiculed and he had sidelined himself by heading into eccentric waters in pursuit of his theories about people fulfilling their true potential.

By that, as Watts recalled from various discussion programmes over the years, Pearson meant accessing the ninety-nine per cent of the brain people don't use to raise their levels of consciousness and live at the peak of experience. Watts shook his head. He was impatient of such New Age stuff. As far as he was concerned, every morning he needed to figure out anew just how to get through the day.

Pearson was also almost two decades younger than Victor Tempest. On its own that didn't preclude friendship. Watts knew that women of Pearson's age hadn't had any trouble relating to the older man. Still, it was strange.

Watts went back to the shelves. Next to Pearson's books was a novel called *Moonchild*. The author was Aleister Crowley.

Watts had heard of Crowley but as a charlatan occultist rather than a novelist. The novel had a winsome-looking woman on the cover with an even more winsome child behind her. It seemed an odd cover for a book by the self-styled Great Beast, who had been dubbed by one newspaper 'the wickedest man in the world'.

The inscription was undated but the book's frontispiece gave the book's publication as 1917. The publisher was The Mandrake Press at an address in New York. Even odder was the fact that Crowley had signed the title page, in a shaky hand: 'This in honour of you, *magister* Victor, *mon semblable, mon frère*, from a mere acolyte. Aleister.'

There it was again, the same bloody French phrase. And his father had known Aleister Crowley? Watts hadn't read all his father's novels but he didn't recall that any of the ones he had read dealt with black magic. In the Wikipedia entry for Dennis Wheatley it stated that he too had known Aleister Crowley. He had based the character Mocata in *The Devil Rides Out* on the occultist.

Watts knew Crowley called himself 666 but he had no clear idea what that meant. The anti-Christ? He had a vague memory of seeing *The Omen* in which a devil child also had the 666 tag. He remembered Gregory Peck searching through some child actor's hair for the numbers etched somewhere on his scalp.

Watts Googled Crowley. The magician seemed to be nothing more than a bombastic poseur, albeit one who had destroyed a number of people's lives. The creed of his church – *Do what thou wilt is the whole of the law* – was an excuse for degeneracy of every sort.

In one way, Watts felt a little sorry for the man. He had set up his own church and wealthy people had occasionally funded it. But he had ended his life in poverty in a Hastings nursing home, his health shattered by heroin and morphine addiction.

Others after him had followed his model of starting new spiritual movements and made a mint. Such movements had proved licences to print money in the confusing and troubled modern world. Crowley had been ahead of his time and so not for him the millions of dollars with which gurus and cult leaders had been showered since.

Watts took the book over to the window. He looked at the inscription again. What the hell was Crowley doing inscribing a book to Victor Tempest and referring to him as *magister*? And how come all the books had the same French phrase?

There was a sudden crack of thunder and Watts looked up at the sky, at the sudden gust of wind and the swill of dark clouds above his head. He laughed. Spooky.

THREE

Sarah Gilchrist did a double-take when she turned a corner and saw a poster outside the imposing Saint Michael and All Angels Church with crime scene tape all across it. The statement on the poster was: SOMEONE IS DEAD AND THE BODY IS MISSING. It took a moment for her to realize it was a now-out-of-date advert for Easter services. She shook her head and laughed.

She walked round the church, trying each door in turn, embarrassed that it had been so long since she'd been here that she didn't know where the entrance was. Eventually she reached some steps that led up into the large vestibule. She went through that and into the church.

She was nervous about her next-day meeting with the chief constable but that wasn't why she was here. Nor did she think the fish falling from the sky had any religious significance. She wasn't a believer. For her God was Absence. She was here to try to make a connection. Or rather a re-connection.

She looked slowly around. She'd been a child the last time she'd been here and it had seemed vast. It was still impressive, the size of a cathedral, high-ceilinged and broad though not particularly long.

Someone in jeans and a T-shirt was fussing with the flowers beneath the carved altar, showing what seemed like an indecent amount of bum crack for a church.

'Excuse me?' Gilchrist called. 'Is the vicar around?'

The person – Gilchrist couldn't immediately see if it was a man or a woman – remained bent over but pointed to the right.

'Thanks,' Gilchrist said, muttering, 'Don't put yourself out.'

Gilchrist walked over to a narrow door halfway along the wall. It opened on to a small office over-stuffed with filing cabinets and a broad desk covered with papers. There was an ancient computer on the desk. An electric fan heater was rattling away in the corner but the room remained chilly.

There was another door in the corner behind the desk. Gilchrist squeezed between the edge of the desk and a bulky filing cabinet and tried the handle. This door was locked. As she turned away she thought she heard movement behind it.

'Hello?' Gilchrist said, rapping on the wood.

'Someone has locked me in,' a female voice said.

Gilchrist looked back at the desk. 'Where is the key usually kept?'

'In the door.'

'It isn't here. Give me a minute to look.'

'Hurry.'

Gilchrist opened drawers and filing cabinets but found no key. She went out into the church to get the help of the person who'd been by the altar. She couldn't immediately see him or her. 'Is anybody there?' she called.

'A question I often ask myself,' a voice close beside her said.

She jumped and turned.

'Forgive me for startling you.'

It was not the person she had seen at the altar. This was a tall, slender, middle-aged man in a dark suit and a dog collar.

'I believe God is in this place but sometimes it feels like a hope rather than a certainty.' He held out his hand. 'I'm David Rutherford, one of the vicars here.'

'I thought certainty came with the job,' Gilchrist said as she briefly shook his hand.

'Most definitely not. Death and taxes are, I believe, the only certainties in life. In your profession, you must deal every day in uncertainties and the contingent, surely?'

'Is it so obvious what I do for a living?'

'It is if you are recognized, Detective Sergeant Sarah Gilchrist.'

She examined his face. 'Do I know you?'

He shook his head. 'Not really. For my sins, I've seen you in the newspapers.'

'For my sins,' Gilchrist corrected him.

Rutherford gave her an inscrutable look. 'But how can I help you?'

'Well, for one thing you have a woman locked in your office store and the key is missing.'

He raised an eyebrow. 'Isn't that a children's rhyme?'

'I think that's a lavatory occupied by three old ladies.'

He smiled. He had good teeth. 'You're right.' He gestured for her to precede him into the office. He rooted in a small wooden cupboard on the wall and produced a key. 'The spare,' he said.

He unlocked the storeroom door and a near-hysterical, middle-aged woman came rushing out, pulling the door closed behind her. As the vicar calmed her Gilchrist wondered if she was claustrophobic. She couldn't think why else the woman was so distressed. She had not been attacked. She had simply been looking for something in the storeroom when she heard the door close and the lock turn.

Gilchrist went round the desk and pushed the door open again. When she saw the pool of liquid in the corner she understood the woman's distress. Being locked in the lavatory would have been more appropriate.

She left the vicar comforting his secretary and wandered back into the church. She was thinking about the person who had been at the altar. Had he or she locked the door on the woman?

She walked to the centre aisle and looked up at the altar. It had been overturned. Spray-painted in red across the wall were the words: THIS IS NOT THE PLACE.

She moved nearer. A crucifix had been torn down from the wall and now leaned, upside down, against it. Something was impaled on it. Something bloody. Gilchrist peered. It was a heart. She counted the thorns sticking into it. Thirteen.

Bob Watts took a sip of his scrumpy cider and looked at a pleasure boat chugging past the pub heading west towards Hampton Court. He was in Ye Old White Hart by Barnes Bridge. It was his father's old local. Well, one of them.

People on the boat waved at him – he was the only one on

the balcony – and he half raised his arm in a self-conscious gesture of acknowledgement.

The river was high. He'd been unable to do his riverside run earlier that day because the towpaths on both sides of the river were flooded.

London hadn't had the deluge as badly as Sussex but it had been raining pretty steadily and it seemed the Thames was in flood whether it was high or low tide. He looked up at the sky. Black, brooding clouds hung low.

He'd brought the Aleister Crowley book down with him and a paperback biography of the black magician he'd found elsewhere on his father's shelves.

On a whim he telephoned Oliver Daubney, his father's elderly literary agent. While the number was ringing he looked at his watch. Daubney was old-style publishing; he was probably at lunch.

But Watts was wrong. Daubney himself answered on the fifth ring.

'Expected you to be lunching,' Watts said.

'Everybody else is out at lunch,' Daubney said in his pleasant voice. 'I'm manning the phones and eating sandwiches.'

Daubney always reminded Watts of an old Hollywood actor called Louis Calhern. Watts had seen him in some black and white movies on late-night TV. Same relaxed charm and affability, same timbre to his voice.

'I assume with a glass of decent red,' he said.

'I did manage to find something quaffable in the back of my drinks cabinet. How can I help you, Robert?'

'Was my father good friends with Dennis Wheatley, Colin Pearson and Aleister Crowley?'

Daubney chuckled. 'There's an unholy trio. He did know the first two, yes. Crowley is a bit before my time – he died in the late forties, didn't he?'

'Cremated in Brighton, 1947.'

'Ah. As always, all roads lead to Brighton.'

Watts heard Daubney take a glug of his wine. He could picture him at his desk, white linen napkin tucked into his shirt collar. ('Never seen the point of putting the napkin in your lap – too many other things for your sauce or wine to stain on the way down.')

'I can root through my files, ask around, if it's important to you.'

'Would you mind? It's only curiosity but . . .' Watts tailed off.

'I'll get on it after lunch. Not much doing at the moment. I deal with more dead authors than live ones these days. In fact I need to talk to you about your father's literary estate sometime soon.'

'How soon? Tomorrow?'

'Tomorrow? And it's only curiosity you say?'

Watts laughed but said nothing.

'How would the British Museum suit? I've got a meeting with Faber and Faber nearby. I haven't had a chance to see the Picasso prints yet. We could see those and then, after, we could lunch in the restaurant up in the rafters in the Great Courtyard.'

'I didn't know there was one.'

'Not bad. Decent wine list.' Daubney laughed. 'You feel somehow more cultured just breathing in the atmosphere.'

They arranged to meet at noon in the Print Rooms and Watts hung up.

Frankly, he was at a loose end. For years he'd thrived on getting things done but since he'd lost his job he'd found it hard to find an outlet for his energy. Hence his almost obsessive interest in his father's secretive, complicated life.

A man in a paint-splattered jumper came on to the balcony at the far end. He looked like an artist rather than a decorator. In a vaguely fastidious way he took off his jumper and folded it neatly on the chair. Before he picked up his pint he laid out on the table in front of him an asthma inhaler, a mobile phone and a packet of cigarettes.

The deliberation with which he did this reminded Watts of his friend and comrade-in-arms, Jimmy Tingley, recuperating from more than just physical injuries somewhere in Italy. Watts had been keen to visit the ex-SAS man but Tingley had discouraged him, saying he needed time alone and would be back in touch when he was ready.

Although close, the two men had never been in each other's pockets, so Watts had accepted this, albeit reluctantly.

Watts drained his glass and stood as the man took a sip of his beer, a puff from his asthma inhaler and a drag from his cigarette. He coughed as he smoked. Watts glanced back at the swirling river and listened to the low rumble of distant thunder.

He took his empty glass back to the bar. As he turned to leave a man standing a few yards along the bar beckoned him over.

He was an ageing rock 'n' roller, abundant white hair in a ponytail, face deeply lined. He was a long, lean man, though he had a little round belly over his tight leather jeans. Watts figured late sixties, early seventies: both the musical period and the age of the man.

He was with a woman in her forties who oozed rock chick. She had matching leather jeans tucked into cowboy boots. She was buxom beneath her denim jacket. Leather trousers rarely looked good on anybody, especially an old man with stick-thin legs, but Watts was kind of impressed that these two had the swagger to give it a go.

The man pointed a be-ringed finger at the bright cover of the Crowley novel Watts was holding in his hand. 'Don't see many of those these days.'

Watts glanced down.

'Looks in great nick,' the man continued. 'The colours haven't faded at all.'

The man was familiar and not just because Watts had seen him in here before.

'Worth a bob or two.'

'You know the book?' Watts said.

'Got a copy myself – without the cover, mind.'

'Is it any good?'

'Not that I remember. Not the point though, is it? You must be Don's son.' Watts took a moment, surprised by the statement. 'Don Watts. Also known as Victor Tempest? The late lamented – by me at least.' The man smiled, wrinkles deepening further all across his face. 'And many others, I'm sure.'

'Did I see you at the funeral?' Watts said, though he knew he hadn't. Only three people had attended.

The man shook his head and grinned again. His eyes

glittered with amusement and intelligence and probably the amount of drink he'd consumed.

'Funerals are a bit close to the bone for me.' He sniffed. 'Intimations of immortality and all that.'

Watts didn't correct him. Instead, he nodded and smiled back.

'You want to sell it?' the man said.

Watts lifted the book. 'This? Probably. In due course.'

'Let me know – I'll top anything you get offered.'

'How do I find you?' Watts said.

'Knock on the wall – that should do it.'

Watts looked from the man to the woman, whose laugh turned into a barking cough. 'You live next door?'

'Gustav Holst's old gaff,' the man said. 'Well, his gaff for a bit.' He held out a veined hand. His fingernails were long and almost horny. 'Billy Caspar.' He gestured at the woman. 'And this is Fi, my old lady.'

She gave Watts a shallow nod.

Watts recognized him now. Lead guitarist and vocalist for one of the big rock bands of the late sixties and seventies. Stadium rock.

Caspar was known for dabbling in the occult.

Watts took his hand. 'Bob Watts.'

'The disgraced copper.'

Watts nodded cautiously. 'That would be me.'

'Well, where would rock 'n' roll be without a bit of disgrace, eh?'

Watts smiled.

'I've got a place down Brighton way,' Caspar said. 'The other side of the Downs near Westmeston. Big old Elizabethan job. With a moat yet. Lovely. Bloke who designed Delhi for the old British Raj did a lot of work on it in the twenties. Luytens.'

'Westmeston Manor.'

'You know it?'

'I know of it – I used to live a couple of miles up the road. I thought an American romantic novelist owned it.'

'Michelle Irons? No, she rented it when I was living abroad for health reasons. I bought it from Jimmy Page years ago.'

Fi snorted. 'Health reasons my arse. Tax reasons more like.'

'Doesn't maintaining a healthy bank balance count as a health reason any more?' Caspar said deadpan. He gestured to the book. 'Aleister Crowley. The Great Beast of Revelations, whose number is six-six-six. The mage. The black magician.'

'According to what I've read online, a fraud, a sponger, a sexual pervert and a bully,' Watts said. 'One biographer said he drove more men and women to drink, insanity or death than most incarnate devils.'

'Incarnate devils, eh?' Caspar said. 'Don't see many of them around. Don't forget drug addict. And in later years also guilty as charged of wearing a ridiculous wig.' He took a sip of his drink. 'You're not a devotee then?'

'I admire his chutzpah, I suppose,' Watts said. 'But people who delude and then damage other people . . .' He tailed off.

'He stayed in my house a couple of times before the war,' Caspar said. 'First time, he took a dump on a rare Persian rug in the library. That was his calling card, apparently, wherever he was a guest: crapping on the carpet.'

'Did he get many return invitations?'

Caspar gave a guttural laugh. 'John Dee is supposed to have performed scrying in the original Elizabethan house.'

Watts didn't like to ask what scrying was or who John Dee was.

'Crowley performed black masses. Up on the Downs there's a tumulus where a dozen children's skeletons, bound hand and foot, had been found in the 1880s. Crowley and his gang did sexual magic in an attempt to raise the spirits of those children. There was a black magic chapel just off the library, you know. Jimmy Page had fitted it out with all the clobber. Performed a few ceremonies there back in the day.'

'You were serious about all that stuff?'

Fi coughed a laugh. 'It was just his excuse for a lot of kinky sex with the local gels,' she rasped.

Caspar looked hurt. 'It was a bit more than that.'

'And now?' Watts said.

'Kinky sex?' Fi said, cackling.

Watts felt himself flushing. 'The black magic.'

'Only academic interest, really.' Caspar turned to the woman. 'When was the last time we did a human sacrifice, Fi?'

She shook her head and laughed again. 'Nearest was that goat last summer.'

'Not sure that counts,' Caspar said.

She shrugged. 'Got you in trouble with the law though.'

'True.'

Watts waited for Caspar to say more. The former rock star was holding back a smirk so Watts guessed there was a jokey explanation heading his way.

'That was more because we had a fire than the goat itself.' He grinned at Watts. 'Summer barbecue – whole goat on a spit. Bloody delicious. Smoke-free zone though. Local council played bloody hell.'

Watts smiled again and started to move away. 'I'll let you know if I decide to sell the book.'

'See that you do,' Caspar said.

Watts glanced back as he left the pub and Caspar gave him a little wave before turning to speak to the man with the asthma inhaler who had just come in from the balcony.

FOUR

'Good morning from me, Southern Shores Simon. Lots of theories about that hail of fish yesterday. Even as our fine city's residents are fighting off the seagulls gathering like Hitchcock's hordes from *The Birds* for the spoils of yesterday's fish storm, the experts at our local universities are coming up with theories about what caused the inundation.'

'You're in a lyrical mood, Si,' Kate said from her microphone at her producer's desk next door. 'We have our own expert on the line in the shape of former mayor, Andy Friend, mainly responsible for setting up our magnificent fishing museum down on the Boardwalk.'

'A fish expert on the line?' Simon said. There was a short

delay that he felt obliged to fill, silence being a radio DJ's biggest fear. 'See what I did there? Fish . . . expert on the line?' He gave an exaggerated snort. 'Please yourselves. I'm wasted here, wasted.'

'You usually are, Simon,' Kate said. 'Here's Andy.'

'Morning, Andy the fish expert – tell us your theory about the flying fish. Or rather the falling fish.'

'They're all fish that are local to Brighton. Most of them would usually be arriving in our waters around now. Most of them make the local shipwrecks their habitat.'

'So how did they get out of the shipwrecks and into the air?'

'Water spout.'

'Water spout?'

'A tornado over water,' Friend said. 'We had one in 2006.'

'I don't remember my fish supper dropping on my head in 2006. Although I was clubbing a lot back then so I might not have noticed.'

'It depends if the water spout comes ashore as a tornado. In 2006 it didn't.'

'But this time it did.'

'I believe so. The city got off lightly actually. If the water spout had come ashore near the West Pier, for instance, it could have finished off what remains of the structure.'

'People are saying it's an end-of-the-world scenario – something biblical – but you're giving us a relatively natural explanation.'

'End-of-the-world scenario? Isn't that indicated by a plague of locusts? Aren't frogs involved?'

'Andy, I can see you have the same grasp of the Bible as I do. If anybody does know, please call in. Andy, thank you. What's the catch of the day?'

'Whatever you can scoop up off the street – there's not much left in the sea for the moment.'

'Ha, ha. Indeed. Although, folks, you'll need to fight off the flocks of seagulls roaming the streets of our fair city. Can a seagull roam, Ms Simpson?'

Kate laughed. 'With an ugly disposition and a beak that size it can do whatever the heck it wants.'

*   *   *

Blake Hornby liked his job at the Brighton Museum and Gallery. Providing reception-cum-security wasn't exactly arduous and there were pretty women to chat with who were serving in the shop along from his counter in the foyer. Not that he had any expectations with them. They were all educated and a bit posh and he'd left school at fifteen and couldn't remember the last time he'd read a book. Nor was he a big fan of art, to tell the truth.

There was some stuff in here he liked but most of it went right over his head. A lot of weird furniture. Good for a laugh but you wouldn't want to sit in it or on it. The so-called 'Mae West sofa' made to look like a pair of red lips, for instance. An armchair in the shape of a baseball mitt. A big, solid, marble-topped table with some kind of animal paws for feet.

He looked through the window to his left into the downstairs gallery. Somebody was bent over looking at those weird table legs now. The gallery was quiet but he liked the fact there were no kids rushing around. The mornings could be bedlam when the schools came in and the kids had sheets of paper with lists of things to find in the galleries.

Rachel in the shop had come out from behind the till. She looked very trim in her scoop-top T-shirt, short black skirt and black tights. Facing away from him she bent over to rearrange some cards. Very nice. Very nice indeed. If she'd only turn round and bend over again so he could get the other view. As if there was a God and he had heard Hornby, she started to turn. That's it, Rachel. That's it. Thank you very much.

It's definitely true we have a sixth sense, Hornby reminded himself a moment later. For how many times when you're staring at somebody – all right, ogling somebody – do they sense it and turn to look at you? So now Rachel suddenly raised her head and stared straight at him as he was enjoying the sight of her breasts scarcely constrained by that tiny black bra.

He looked away, flustered, as she straightened. Then there was a crash of breaking glass somewhere in the downstairs gallery and the alarm went off.

Afterwards, he rationalized his slow response by the confusion the unusual conjunction of events caused in him. He was focusing on what Rachel would think of him. He was, after all, some twenty years older than her. So, although he heard the glass shatter it wasn't that loud and it didn't immediately impinge. When the alarm went off at pretty much the same time, it jolted him – it made a horrible racket just above his head – but he didn't associate it with the crash in the gallery.

For one thing, that bloody alarm went off at random about twice a month. Usually it was someone opening the door between the gallery and the corridor separating it from the adjacent Dome concert hall.

Hornby risked a look back at Rachel. She was standing with her hands to her ears, her face pained. 'Probably a false alarm,' he shouted, feeling like a man in command.

'Then can't you shut it off?' she shouted back.

He reached behind him, fiddled with the key in the alarm control panel and reset a switch. The silence was immediate and almost shocking.

Rachel lowered her hands, gave him a look he couldn't read and retreated behind her till.

Blake set his shoulders and hurried into the gallery. As he strode through he saw some people were standing around near the leather chair that was in the shape of a baseball mitt. Others, further down the long gallery, were looking at the exhibits as if nothing had happened.

'No need for alarm,' he said to people as he walked by, brushing off a couple of women who tried to waylay him. At the far end of the gallery he turned left and, sure enough, the fire door was open. Before the Dome had been done up in the late nineties the museum had been linked by this door across a corridor to what was then the central library and was now the concert-hall bar.

He walked into the corridor and through the next doorway into the crowded room. There was some sort of pre-festival event going on. He scanned the room but didn't actually have a clue what he was looking for.

He came back into the museum and closed the fire door by

its bar. On his way back through the gallery some of the
visitors seemed to be giving him odd looks. As he neared
the claw-footed table a prissy-looking woman he'd ignored en
route to dealing with the problem of the door shook her head
and pointed at the large glass case behind the table.

Inside the glass case was a tableau. Another stupid chair
– this one in the shape of a purple flower of some sort – the
Mae West sofa and an odd-shaped coffee table bearing silver
coffee pots and paraphernalia and ceramic stuff.

It all seemed to be there. With something extra, in fact. A
brick lying wedged between Mae's lips. And a big hole in the
centre of the glass with jagged cracks radiating from it.

Jack Lawrence, the public relations director for the Southern
police force, was coming out of the chief constable's office
as Sarah Gilchrist walked into the outer room, her raincoat
folded inside out over her arm. She was feeling self-
conscious in a new trouser suit. Her usual unofficial uniform
was white T-shirt, jeans and leather jacket. She felt horribly
overdressed.

Lawrence looked as neat as ever in his usual uniform of a
lightweight blue suit. He nodded at Gilchrist and smiled tightly.
He glanced at her bandaged hand but didn't comment.

'Sarah.'

'Jack.'

He looked down at the chief constable's secretary. 'I think
DS Gilchrist can go straight in, Tracy.'

Tracy nodded and smiled at Gilchrist. 'Hang your coat up
over there.'

Gilchrist put her coat on a stand and moved towards the
door, nodding her thanks to both of them. She wondered what
Lawrence had to do with her meeting with Chief Constable
Karen Hewitt.

She took a deep breath and knocked. Her future was about
to be decided on the other side of it.

'Come,' Hewitt called.

Karen Hewitt had not been ageing well since she took over
the role of chief constable from the disgraced Bob Watts. The
stresses of the job had clearly worn her down. For months she

had looked exhausted, her long blonde hair framing a lined, thin face. Gilchrist had always thought long hair on a woman in her late forties was taking a risk anyway.

However, it was a month since Gilchrist had last seen Hewitt and she was startled to see a transformation. Hair bobbed, face fresher. Hewitt gave her a brief smile and scarcely a line creased her face. Gilchrist was thinking major makeover, wondering about Botox.

Hewitt turned as stern as her new face perhaps would allow and invited Gilchrist to sit. 'What happened to your hand?'

'Conger eel.'

Hewitt nodded. 'They're saying it was a tornado.'

'Explanations are always good.'

Hewitt clasped her hands. 'Sarah, I'll come directly to the point. You've been on suspension for a month and you've come in here expecting to hear about the disciplinary procedure against you for allegedly importing a volt gun illegally. A stun gun that your friend, Kate Simpson, used to kill a man who was viciously attacking her.'

'Yes, ma'am.'

'I'm aware that in the past couple of days, even whilst on suspension, you've been punctilious in reporting two criminal acts. One, the looting of a jewellery shop in the Laines in that hail of fish; the other the desecration of a church.'

'Yes, ma'am.'

'That punctiliousness would doubtless have been in your favour had there been a disciplinary procedure.'

Gilchrist frowned. 'Ma'am?'

Hewitt seemed to be swallowing something that tasted bad. 'There will be no disciplinary procedure.'

Gilchrist was too surprised to say anything.

'Only because of a technicality,' Hewitt added.

'Ma'am?'

Hewitt unclasped her hands. 'The volt gun has gone missing. It has either been mislaid or mis-registered in the evidence room. It cannot be located.' Hewitt spread her hands. 'No evidence, no disciplinary.'

Gilchrist felt herself flushing. 'I had nothing to do with its disappearance.'

'Did I say you did? Sadly, our evidence room is as porous as every evidence room I've ever known. And it is as chaotic. I wouldn't be surprised if we had the identity of the Brighton Trunk Murderer misfiled in there somewhere.'

'I'm relieved to hear that, ma'am.'

'About the Trunk Murderer's identity?'

'No, ma'am – though I believe that may recently have been established. I mean about my disciplinary.'

Hewitt remained stern. 'I'm sure you are. I hope, however, you have learned your lesson and there will be no repeat of such foolishness.'

'No, ma'am.'

'No?'

Gilchrist lightly touched her bandaged hand. It had started aching. 'I mean: yes, I have learned my lesson and no, there will be no repeat of the foolishness. Ma'am.'

Hewitt's smile was terse. 'With that in mind, I'd like you back on active duty with immediate effect.'

'Of course, ma'am. Thank you. May I ask what the intention is with regard to the charge against Kate Simpson?'

'We'll be recommending that because there is insufficient evidence the Crown Prosecution Service does not proceed.'

'I'm relieved to hear it.'

Hewitt nodded and examined Gilchrist's face. 'I was very sorry Detective Inspector Reg Williamson made the decision that he did. To end his life – well, it is such a sad waste of a good man. Although the official line, as you know, is that his death was a dreadful accident whilst tussling with a known criminal in a police car.'

Gilchrist looked down. She still welled up when she thought of the suffering of her friend and work partner during his life and his decision to drive off Beachy Head after he had lost his wife. When she looked up again Hewitt was still gazing intently at her.

'As you know,' Hewitt continued, 'Reg had been acting DI before his death. I had been intending to formalize that title shortly.'

Hewitt leaned into her desk. Gilchrist got a waft of her sickly sweet perfume. 'His death has left a big hole in our lives but also in my service structure. In consequence, with effect from tomorrow, I'm making you Acting Detective Inspector, rank to be made an official promotion assuming satisfactory service after three months.'

Gilchrist was first startled, then suspicious. 'Ma'am?'

'Don't look so surprised. I don't need false modesty from my officers. If there hadn't been that other mess in Milldean you would have got the chance sooner – and you know it.'

'Gender equality?'

Hewitt looked fierce for a moment, though still without her forehead creasing. Definitely Botox. 'Don't you start, Sarah. I have enough trouble with our male colleagues assuming I'm going to advance women irrespective of their suitability. This is based entirely on merit. You passed your exam an age ago. You have talent. You are a good copper.' Hewitt leaned back and tapped her finger on her desk before she pointed it at Gilchrist. 'Yes, you are an idiot sometimes but I like your grit and tenacity. Plus you're a thinker and thinkers are in short supply around here.'

'Can I ask if Jack Lawrence is involved with the decision?'

Hewitt looked severe again. 'That's none of your business. But, yes, I took advice from him on the possible public relations impact of your promotion. And, frankly, he believed it would play badly and recommended I promote someone else instead.'

'Then . . .?'

'However, the Metropolitan Police special crimes unit, not known for handing out compliments, especially to women, are very grateful for your help with Bernie Grimes. Not that I want to see that kind of vigilantism again from one of my police officers.'

Bernie Grimes was a notorious armed robber who had been tangentially involved with the so-called Milldean Massacre, in which armed police had shot innocent people in a house in the Milldean district of Brighton.

A little while ago, as part of Gilchrist's efforts to bring the crime lord Charlie Laker to book and find out exactly what had happened in Milldean, she had persuaded ex-Chief Constable Bob Watts to go with her to France to confront

Bernie Grimes in his hideaway. Grimes had important information about Laker and the massacre but neither Watts nor Gilchrist, who was on suspension, had the right to confront him, especially in the vigorous manner they decided upon.

Gilchrist shifted uneasily in her seat. 'Yes, ma'am.'

'Plus, I have a special project for you that even Jack agrees is a good fit.'

'Thank you, ma'am,' Gilchrist said, curious but wary.

'Don't thank me yet. I remember you were attacked on the beach by a group of teenage girls whilst trying to rescue Bernie Grimes' daughter from them.'

Gilchrist stiffened. 'What about it?'

'They are the tip of the iceberg in Brighton.'

Gilchrist got a sinking feeling. She thought she knew where this was going. 'Ma'am . . .'

'Because of your first-hand experience I want you to head up a special, multi-agency task force to deal with this problem of violently delinquent young teenagers.'

'Ma'am . . .'

'It's a problem that particularly predominates among teenage girls in the city. And that makes you an ideal head of this task force.'

'Ma'am, I don't know anything about teenage girls.'

Hewitt stood. 'That's agreed then.'

Gilchrist stood. 'I don't have children. I'm no good with youngsters of any age.'

'Tracy is already setting up the first meeting.' Hewitt stuck her hand out across the desk. Gilchrist looked at it for a moment then took it. 'Congratulations on your inevitable promotion, Detective Inspector.'

Gilchrist sighed and shook Hewitt's hand. 'Ma'am.'

FIVE

Bernard Rafferty was not happy, not happy at all. Hornby could see this and quite understood. Bit of a bummer when you spend thousands on security systems and somebody just walks in and chucks a brick at a display case. Then again, such things happened in all the biggest museums, however much they spent on security. No way of defending against the lone nutter.

Besides, nobody was sure if anything had actually been stolen from the glass case. The curator was halfway up the Andes, finding herself on the Inca trail, and Rafferty, whilst he'd been director of the council's museum services for years, was not exactly hands-on. He preferred to swan, with a bit of preening thrown in. When he wasn't doing that, he rarely left his balconied, notoriously well-appointed office on the first floor of the Royal Pavilion. The story went that Rafferty hadn't set foot inside the Booth, the zoological museum up the back end of town, in five years.

In other words, the chances of him knowing what was inside a particular display case in a particular museum was as remote, Hornby wistfully recognized, as the security guard ever getting off with Rachel.

But, frankly, it didn't matter. Hornby had an analytical bent. He'd always reckoned he would have made a good copper with his combination of brains and, in his day, brawn. He'd been astounded when the force rejected him at the get-go for reasons that were, frankly, vague.

He'd figured out that unless the person who'd thrown the brick had very long arms, there was no way he could have stolen anything from the table inside the case.

His theory was that the perpetrator had intended a bit of smash and grab. He had expected the glass to shatter totally so he could grab the silver and make off with it.

'Startled by the alarm,' he was saying now, under Rafferty's purse-lipped, hostile stare, 'he didn't have time to do the job properly and left empty-handed.'

'By the emergency exit at the far end of the gallery,' the policeman said.

'I believe so,' Hornby said.

The policeman – Constable Heap, his name was – looked at Rachel. She and Hornby were sitting in the corner of the shop with Rafferty standing and occasionally pacing. Rachel kept tugging her short skirt down, although Hornby really wasn't looking at her legs.

'Did you see anybody leave by the front exit at the time the alarm went off, who with hindsight might seem suspicious?'

'Nobody left at all,' Rachel said. 'Mr Hornby insisted the doors be locked almost the minute he saw the case had been attacked.'

Hornby sat a little straighter even when he saw Rafferty's scowl. Fuck Rafferty. Most staff in any job wondered what the big nebbies did all day. As far as Hornby could see, museum staff never wondered. They knew Rafferty did bugger all. Too busy writing his boring books about churchyards. Museum staff disregarded or discounted him whenever possible. And when it wasn't possible, he had heard one curator say, they 'managed' him.

'Shouldn't we be looking at the CCTV, Officer?' Rafferty said, trying for resolute and managing peevish. 'The vandalism occurred right underneath a camera.'

'We are focusing on that too,' the constable said mildly.

It was an hour after the incident. Witness statements had been taken from the half a dozen people in the gallery at the time. Nobody had noticed anything, which was quite remarkable since the perpetrator needed to go some fifty yards down the centre of the gallery to get to the fire exit whilst the alarm was blaring out.

Hornby looked across at Rachel's legs then quickly away as her head turned. The woman must have radar.

The policeman was tapping his teeth with his pencil. He was a funny little fellow. Short with pink cheeks and red ears.

He looked like a schoolboy. It peeved Hornby that they'd let somebody that size in when they'd turned him down – what good was a pint-sized policeman?

'Let's go and have a look at the scene, shall we?' the constable said.

He led the way through into the gallery. Another policeman had put tape around the glass case. Heap turned to Rafferty.

'Anything missing?'

'I told you – not that I can see.'

'An attempt that failed,' Hornby said. The policeman gave him a steady look. 'In my opinion.'

'OK,' Heap said. 'Let's take a look at the emergency exit.'

He led the way down the centre aisle, glancing from side to side at the paintings and the glass cases.

He paused at the end of the gallery, just before the emergency exit, and squinted at a small label on the bare wall to his left.

'*The Devil's Altar* by Gluck,' he read out. '1932.'

Hornby's heart sank.

Above the label there was a faint rectangular line on the wall within which the paint was lighter than that on the rest of the wall. Constable Heap pointed to the rectangle. 'How long has this painting been missing?'

'Chief Constable Watts, how flattering.'

Watts turned. A woman in her mid-thirties smiled at him. Trim. Black hair tied back. Navy trouser suit.

'Just plain Mister these days. Flattering?'

'That you should come to search me out. Having scoured Brighton for me, I presume.'

The woman looked familiar but Watts had no real clue who she was. She grinned at his discomfort.

'Nicola Travis. I used to work in the Brighton tourist office and the Royal Pavilion.'

Watts remembered her now. He'd met her just once. She'd been flirting with him at a dinner at the Royal Pavilion, had pushed her card on him with her home number written on the back. Bernard Rafferty had been boring for Britain in a speech. No change there then. Watts' beeper had gone off and he'd excused himself to take the call in the long corridor outside the banqueting hall. The call that told him about the Milldean Massacre, the event that brought his career crashing down around his ears. He had not seen her since.

'You never called, but I guess in the circumstances . . .'

He smiled. 'Exactly. But what are you doing here?'

He'd arrived at the British Museum a little early for his meeting with Daubney so had been looking idly around the room containing the Sutton Hoo Anglo-Saxon treasure. He remembered his father telling him the Sutton Hoo helmet had originally been reconstructed incorrectly. It had looked odd for years before the error had been corrected. He'd told the story as an object lesson in the fallibility of deductive reasoning.

'I work here – on the Friends of the Museum team.'

'A promotion?'

'A step up, certainly.'

'So you live in London now?'

She shook her head. 'I commute. And you?'

'Theoretically living in Brighton but I'm clearing out my father's house in Barnes. He died some weeks ago.'

'I'm sorry.'

Watts shrugged. 'He was a good age. Packed a lot into his life.'

'And why are you here?'

'Picasso prints then lunch with a friend.'

She smiled. 'The Picassos are on the top floor but near the back entrance of the museum – I'll walk you down there if you like.'

She led the way into a long gallery stocked with a mix of objects from different ages and countries. It looked vaguely like the enormous library of a country house, with books stacked high up on a balcony above long wall cases filled with everything from African masks and Etruscan funerary urns to fourteenth-century swords and Egyptian jewellery.

'This is my favourite room,' she said. 'I like the eclecticism of it.'

Two-thirds of the way down she paused at a large case and

leaned in. 'Your ex-colleagues are probably going to be called about this.'

Watts looked into the case. A large card stated that two John Dee artefacts had been removed from display to form part of the Shakespeare and His World exhibition.

'About John Dee's artefacts being moved?'

'About them possibly being stolen. They went missing at the end of the Shakespeare exhibition during the transfer from one display back to this one.'

'What were they?' Watts asked.

'Magic stuff from the Elizabethan age.'

'Magic?'

'Have you heard of John Dee?'

'Just yesterday, actually.'

'One of the most learned men of his day. Expert mathematician and astronomer. Typical for the time, he was also interested in the occult as a means of learning more about the universe. The Shakespeare exhibition borrowed a big wax disc with magic signs and symbols on them and a black obsidian mirror that was originally Aztec.' She pointed at the display. 'You can see the mirror's leather case there. They came to the museum in Sir Robert Cotton's collection – one of the museum's founding collections.'

'You know your stuff.'

She smiled. 'I should but I'm still learning, believe me. We know the disc was his because there's a drawing of it in one of his manuscripts. It was used to support one of his shew-stones.'

'What's a shew-stone?'

'Like the Aztec mirror or some other reflecting object or a crystal ball you can see into. The magician sees things in it.' She pointed to what looked like a small glass ball. 'That's Dee's crystal ball there – at least it probably belonged to him. We know he used one. We're more certain about the mirror. Later, it was owned by Sir Horace Walpole and he put a note inside the leather case stating that it had belonged to Dee and his medium, Edward Kelly.'

'But only two of these objects have gone missing?' Watts said. He pointed at an engraved gold disc. 'I would have thought that would be worth nicking.'

'Beautiful, isn't it? It's the "vision of the four castles" – something Dee experienced in Krakow in 1584. The museum got that during the Second World War – in 1942, I think. There's another of his crystals on a pendant in the Science Museum. Dee used that one to cure diseases and see into the future by looking for the ghosts of people in the stone. Dee's son Arthur gave it to the medical astrologer, Nicholas Culpeper, as thanks for curing his liver complaint.'

'The herbalist with the shops?'

She smiled.

'I think they're just named after him. He was a doctor too but preferred to use herbs as cures. He used the crystal to cure illness but apparently stopped in 1651 when a demon burst out of it.'

'That would make you wonder about the cures you were giving,' Watts said. 'All these crystals – he must have lived in Brighton.'

Travis laughed.

'Has the Science Museum object gone missing too?' Watts said.

She grinned. 'That would be freaky. I don't believe so. We think this was an opportunist theft. That's why these are still here. We have a lot of casual staff working here when we're putting an exhibition together.'

'I would have thought security would be pretty tight.'

She made a face. 'Oh, it is out front but in the back is sometimes another story. We have this dreadful habit of trusting people.'

'And the stuff that was stolen – I presume there's a market for it?'

'For magical apparatus linked to John Dee, the most famous magician in the world? I would say so.'

'I thought Doctor Faust was the most famous magician in the world?'

'He's based on Doctor Dee – certainly in Christopher Marlowe's version.'

They had reached the lift.

'It's funny we should be talking about this,' Watts said. 'I'm meeting my father's agent in a minute to discuss my father's acquaintance with three writers on the occult, including Aleister Crowley.'

Travis stood directly in front of him. Close to him.

'The Great Beast, eh?' she said. 'But it's not so funny. The supernatural is everywhere these days. My colleague's teenage nieces were obsessed with Harry Potter and now *Twilight* and all these vampire things. My colleague calls that chastity porn.'

'Chastity porn?'

'*Twilight* has this vampire. Robert Pattinson in the films. All the girls swoon over him but he's kind of a pervy stalker of this chaste young woman. Kristen Stewart in the films. She's a virgin and if she succumbs to him she'll be damned. So it's a lot of titillation. The books are essentially extended foreplay. Very extended.'

'And you don't like that?' Watts said.

She laughed. 'I like foreplay as much as the next girl . . .'

Watts smiled, suddenly embarrassed by her proximity. He was easily embarrassed by women. He pressed the lift button.

'You want the top floor,' she said.

He nodded and smiled awkwardly. She took out a card and pen and wrote something on the back.

'My old one – which I'm sure you've kept – is out of date now.'

Watts took the card and turned it over.

'My home number,' Travis said. 'Ring me here or there – it doesn't matter which. If you've a mind to.'

She turned and walked away, hips swinging, her hand raised in a little wave goodbye.

'I will,' he called after her. Then he muttered, 'Most certainly.'

SIX

Buggeration. Gilchrist stomped down the stairs of the police station and out into the street. The sky had turned black as night and the first drops of rain were falling. She looked up, wary of falling fish. At least that thought made her smile. She turned into the first café she came to and put the big bundle of files she'd spent the rest of the morning with on the counter.

'Looks like we're in for it,' the barman said, frowning as the rain rattled against the window. 'But at least it is just rain. For the time being anyway.'

Gilchrist nodded curtly, glancing at her watch. She wasn't in here just to get out of the rain. The sun was over the yard-arm somewhere.

'Chardonnay. Big one.'

Talk about giving with one hand and taking away with the other. She was more than relieved that she was not being disciplined or ejected from the police force. She was elated that she had the promotion she always felt should have been hers, though conscious it was in some sense at the cost of her friend's life.

But as a woman who had decided ten years earlier that she never wanted children, as a woman who hadn't liked teenage girls when she was a teenager herself, never mind now, the last thing she wanted to do was have any dealings with them. Especially feral ones.

She glanced at the files with something like loathing. Not that she was allowed to call them 'feral' any more. According to social theorists they were simply 'troubled'. 'Feral' was too judgemental. Yeah, right.

'Oh, Reg,' she sighed. 'I could do with you to laugh at me right now.'

She fished out her phone and called Kate Simpson. She was

put on hold, the current radio programme streaming down the phone line. Kate was mid-show, of course. Gilchrist hadn't got the hang of Kate's new job as producer. She wasn't sure Kate had either.

Kate Simpson's mobile rang. It was Phil, the guy who ran her scuba-diving club.

'A newspaper has asked me to see if there are any fish left in the waters around Brighton. Of course there will be, but I wondered if you fancied coming down with me. I'm putting a little team together.'

Last time she'd been involved in one of Phil's little teams they'd found the remains of a woman killed in the sixties. She recognized that was a one-off. Or so she hoped.

'When?' she said.

'This teatime?'

'I'll see you at the marina.'

The light on her desk phone was flashing. She pressed for the landline.

Kate Simpson's voice broke in on Gilchrist listening to the radio show. She sounded breathless. Gilchrist could hear the hubbub of the radio studio's outer office in the background.

'Sarah – what's up?'

'Thought you'd want to know,' Gilchrist said. 'You're definitely not going to be charged with using an illegal weapon to fight off your attacker.'

Simpson was silent for a moment. 'What's happened?' she said, her voice low.

'The volt gun has gone missing from the evidence room,' Gilchrist said, equally quietly. 'No stun gun, no prosecution.'

Kate cleared her throat, then said, 'Thank God. Oh, Sarah, thank bloody God.' Then, with excitement: 'Does that mean you're off suspension too?'

Gilchrist grinned, even though she knew it was pointless down a phone line. 'And promoted.'

'Wow. Congratulations.'

'Except for what my first job is.'

'What's that?'

'Never mind – I'll tell you later. Are you around tonight? Let's go to Plenty to celebrate.'

Oliver Daubney was on good form. He led Watts at a pretty brisk trot round the Picasso prints. 'Fine work,' Daubney said. 'But, you know, what was once challenging has long been absorbed into the mainstream.'

They moved through a couple of Egyptian galleries to the restaurant underneath the dome of the Great Courtyard. They were seated at a table with a gentle buzz of sound from the courtyard below refracting around them and a soft white light falling from above. And for the next hour, Daubney shared with Watts some of his many stories about writers great and small of the past sixty years.

Even if he didn't represent them, he knew them all. And Watts immediately realized that Daubney wasn't sharing. He was giving a performance. An Audience with Oliver Daubney.

'Agatha Christie?' Daubney said. 'No conversation. None at all. Such a shy creature. Raymond Chandler? A drunk and an egoist – the admiration of T S Eliot went right to his head – but most charming and still talented when I met him. In the late fifties, when I was scarcely an adult, I went on a bender with your father, Ian Fleming and Chandler. I got home some- time in the early sixties.'

Daubney paused for Watts to laugh and the ex-chief constable obliged.

The next time Daubney paused for breath – by which time he'd run through Amis *père* and *fils*, the two Durrells, Willliam Golding, John Fowles, Muriel Spark, Dylan Thomas and Sylvia and Ted – Watts said, 'Did you find out anything about my father and Wheatley, Pearson and Crowley?'

Daubney seemed slightly miffed to be interrupted in mid- flow but he composed himself. 'With Wheatley it was simply a friendship between two fellow writers, I believe. He did a Foyles lunch with Pearson in the sixties but whether the friend- ship went any further I don't know. Crowley – I couldn't find out anything about that connection.'

'I can't imagine my father spending much time with such an obvious charlatan as Crowley.'

'I'm sure you're right,' Daubney said, draining the last of the Burgundy.

They parted shortly after. Watts left feeling he'd been sold short but not knowing exactly how. The cobbled courtyard at the front of the museum was, as usual, thronged with tourists. Small and large groups in lines being photographed from too far away so that people walked between photographer and subjects all the time. Anoraks and umbrellas as far as the eye could see.

The paving stones were slippery with rain and even his rubber-soled shoes didn't help. He made his cautious way out on to Museum Street. The Museum Tavern looked appealing, its Victorian lights glowing through the rainy gloom. Watts liked a Victorian artist called Grimshaw who seemed to specialize in gaslight in foggy, rainy dusks. He might have painted this scene, even though it was only mid-afternoon.

Watts walked past the pub to a bookshop on the left. He remembered his father bringing him to the British Museum and walking down this street when it was all second-hand bookshops and quirky art galleries. Now there was only the one bookshop and a range of cafés and tourist souvenir shops. Plastic police helmets and Union Jacks on mugs, tea towels, beer mats and assorted garments proliferated.

The bookshop was theoretically an occult bookshop but, Watts reflected, commerce gets everywhere. Toy witches on broomsticks hung in the window and inside there was the usual gallimaufry of crystal balls, Tarot cards, angel cards, crystals, Ouija boards and general cheap quasi-spiritual tat.

On the bookshelves Harry Potter predominated along with modern young adult vampire novels. There were New Age novels too: Paulo Coelho featured large.

Over by the sales desk – a bureau complete with ink pot and old-fashioned nib pen – there was a more serious-looking bookcase. Old leather volumes behind glass. A man with long, wet, curly black hair, wearing a shapeless raincoat, was standing in front of it, tilting his head to read the spines of the works there.

In front of him, at the bureau, was a large woman in the kind of kaftan Watts hadn't seen since, as a child, he'd watched some hefty Greek man with a falsetto voice perform on the telly.

She smiled at Watts in an inquiring way. He took the book out of his briefcase.

'I've got this first edition of an Aleister Crowley novel, signed to my father. I wondered if you might be able to value it?'

'I'll buy it,' the man with the wet hair blurted.

Kate had been a bit befuddled for the rest of her shift. After Sarah's call she'd been thinking about her new freedom and flashing back to the awful attack on her in the bedroom of her flat.

A smelly man pawing her, hitting her, tearing her clothes off, falling on her with all his weight. Kate scrabbling under the pillow for the feel of the plastic weapon Gilchrist had left her when they first shared flats. Grabbing it, thrusting it at the man's neck, pressing every button on it she could find. And then she'd been abruptly brought back to the present.

'Kate? Kate?' Simon's voice urgent in her ear. 'Jesus, woman, don't zone out on me again. You gotta start getting a grip. I need the poll results for "George Clooney Gay or Guy?" Kate?'

At the end of her shift she headed down to the marina. She was late getting there but she doubted they were going out. The weather was filthy, the boats in the harbour rolling and rattling.

A regular gang of half a dozen of the keenest divers were below. Phil kissed her on the cheek and looked at her with his startling blue eyes. He shook his head.

'We're going to give it half an hour to see if it blows over then go down the pub.'

Kate looked out of the porthole. 'I'd be as happy skipping straight to the pub option.'

Phil smiled and indicated some packets on a narrow table. 'Scopolamine patches if you want one.'

She shook her head. 'Touch wood, however rough it gets I don't get sick. I might drown but I won't be sick.'

She looked across at the one person in the group she didn't know. He looked like he was about to burst out of his clothes.

His head was tilted back and he had a dropper in his meaty hand poised just above his eye. She watched him do both eyes then blink until he got his vision back. He saw her looking.

'Bit extreme if we don't actually go out, isn't it?' she said.

He grinned but there was a coldness to it.

'Bugger going out – this is to stop the motion of this boat in dock making me heave.'

They all laughed. Phil said, 'Kate, I don't think you and Don have met. Don's with a club over in Worthing.'

The man nodded. 'Call me Don-Don.'

Kate's phone rang. 'Excuse me,' she said, clambering up on deck.

'Kate? It's Sarah. I'm finished earlier than I thought if you can get away.'

Gilchrist was already sitting at the back of Plenty when Kate arrived. Gilchrist got up, towering over her as usual, and gave her a hug.

'Hope I didn't wreck your evening?' Gilchrist said.

'I was going to go to the pub with a bunch of divers but, you know, I like diving with them rather than socializing. Their main topic of conversation is cubic pressure per foot per pound.' She laughed. 'There's a new guy. Bit of a creep but keen – he would dive seven days a week if he could. But he gets serious sea-sickness.'

'A diver with sea-sickness?'

'Some do. They slap on a travel sickness patch and that's fine. This guy uses a dropper in his eyes to dose himself up with liquid scopolamine.'

'Scopolamine?' Gilchrist said. 'Isn't that the truth drug?'

'Don't know about the truth thing,' Kate said. 'I think it's the basis of the travel patches but you can get it more concentrated in liquid form.'

'You use it?' Gilchrist said.

'Never had a need. Plus I'm a drug novice. I'm reluctant to take even aspirin. It's the same with alcohol. You know me: if you have a drink I get a hangover.'

'Have you been diving since the fish thing?'

'We were supposed to but I'm glad we haven't. That water

spout churned things up so much I wouldn't be surprised if we bumped into the Loch Ness Monster or a great white down there.'

When their drinks arrived they chinked their glasses.

'Onward and upward,' Gilchrist said.

'God, I hope so,' Kate said.

Plenty had been voted the best vegetarian restaurant in Britain about six times in a row. As usual, the description of the meal was like a work of art in itself. Then the food came. For the next half hour different tastes zinged across Kate's palate.

'What did we just eat?' she asked Sarah at the end of the final course, as the bottle of organic wine took hold.

'Fuck if I know,' Sarah said. 'Great though, yeah?'

What they then talked about became a bit of a blur. Sarah talked about a church being desecrated but what Sarah was doing in a church Kate couldn't imagine. Kate blethered on about the guy with the eye dropper.

Getting home was more of a blur, although Kate remembered the two of them tumbling into a taxi together. Then she remembered the two of them staggering into Sarah's flat.

What she didn't remember was what happened between then and the moment she woke up the next morning in bed with her friend.

SEVEN

'Those of you who are early risers – and include me out of that category except when I'm dragged, kicking and screaming, from my bed to do this show – may have seen a Wicker Man go up in flames on Brighton beach this morning. Love that film. The original, British classic obviously, not the mad Nicolas Cage remake.

'That's right. No sooner are we shot of falling fish and aggressive seagulls than we've got a Wicker Man on our beach. And the Brighton Festival hasn't even started yet. What do you say, Kate? Oh, I forgot, Kate isn't in yet. Who knows what my producer was up to last night?

'Anyway, you'll recall from the original film of *The Wicker Man* that Christopher Lee, the Lord of Summerisle, believed that the failure of his island's crops could be reversed by the sacrifice of a virgin policeman in a pagan ceremony. So he lured to his island a poor virgin copper, Edward Woodward, who ended up burned alive inside a Wicker Man. Gruesome.

'I'm not sure if any crops have failed here in Brighton, though my window box is looking a bit sad. And, so far as we're aware, unlike the film, no virgin policeman went up in flames this morning – no offence to the Brighton police but they might be hard to find in our fair city.

'But, anyway, this morning's burning coincided with the sunrise so it may have been part of a pagan ceremony. No one has yet come forward to claim responsibility or provide an explanation.

'If you know anything about the Wicker Man's construction and the reason for it please get in touch with us here at Southern Shores Radio. We await your call. And if you witnessed it going up in flames, phone in too and tell us what you saw.

'The fire service was summoned but decided against dampening down the fire as it was on the water's edge and did not constitute a hazard. Having said that, we have Johnny Clarke from the council's seafront team on the line to warn against any copycat activity. Johnny, good morning to you.'

'Morning, Simon.'

'You're not expecting anyone else to plonk a Wicker Man on the beach, I assume. But, in general terms: a fire on the beach – what's wrong with that?'

'I know it sounds a bit odd and we're certainly not trying to discourage people from making the most of the beach. However, a fire – especially a big one like this – even on a beach is potentially dangerous both to humans and to physical structures. It only needs a few sparks to carry on the wind and we might end up with the rest of the West Pier burning down – or some even more solid structure catching fire.'

'And yet the fire brigade deemed it wasn't a hazard.'

'I can't speak for them but I believe they made that decision because it was a very still morning, with only the slightest of breezes. Having said that, once the flames had damped down a bit, they killed the fire with foam and have put a cordon round the remains of the structure.'

'Right. Just hang on a minute, Johnny, my producer has finally arrived and is talking in my ear but not about why she's so late. As you know, when she speaks, I listen. OK, boss, will do. Johnny, we're told the police, who have been on the scene a little while talking to witnesses, have now thrown their own cordon round the remains of the Wicker Man. What's that about?'

'I can see them doing that but I don't know why. The main thing I want to say is that the council is relieved nobody was hurt but that we strongly discourage this sort of activity.'

'Thanks, Johnny. There you are, folks – you heard it here first on Southern Shores Radio, your local look at the world. Hello, my producer, Kate, has now entered my inner sanctum. Oooh, missus. That usually means Simon is in bother. What have I done now, Kate? You're looking great, by the way – especially your face. The white tinged with green look is very fetching. Though maybe change out of your pyjamas when you've a moment?

'Hang on – she wants to address you directly. Hope that doesn't mean I'm out of a job. I was only kidding wid ya, Kate. Ladies and gentlemen, I give you the beautiful and talented – and probably hung-over – Kate Simpson. Not that she's mine to give.'

'Morning, everyone,' Kate Simpson said. 'Just an update on that police activity on the beach before I hand you back to Simon. We're hoping to have a police spokesperson on the show later but for now police are asking those of you who took any photographs or video footage of this morning's Wicker Man ceremony – if ceremony is what it was – to get in touch with your local police station, or even just your community copper, if you have such a thing.

'They would also like whoever was behind this morning's burning Wicker Man to come forward. Any problems with these instructions just phone us here at Southern Shores Radio and we'll put you in touch with the right people. OK? Now back to you, Simon. Oh, and your job is safe – for the time being.'

'Thanks, Kate. Now back in your coffin.'

Bob Watts was wondering what to do about the Aleister Crowley novel. He had intended to sell it – and he had two offers – but the inscription intrigued him.

He was tucking into his breakfast at the French café across from Ye Olde White Hart. He could cook. He had indeed a half-dozen pretty impressive signature dishes. But breakfast was too much of a faff. Especially when he'd just done his run.

So he usually came in here after his run, dripping with sweat, to replace the calories he'd just burned up. The café people were tolerant of him stinking up the place.

Today his run had followed a dawn conversation with his wife, Molly, calling from Canada. 'How are my children?' Watts said. Although his wife now lived three thousand miles away, their two children had more contact with her than him.

'Your daughter is going to be in Brighton this week.'

'I saw it on her Facebook page.'

'When was the last time you actually got in touch with her?'

'I leave phone messages. She doesn't reply.'

His wife didn't comment.

'How are things with you?' Watts said to change the subject.

'I'm doing a writing course. An MA.'

'Great. That's not quite what I meant.'

'I know that's not what you meant. I'm going to write about us.'

Watts said nothing.

'What am I, after all? I have no definition except in terms of others. Mother. Wife. Negatives.'

Watts sighed. 'What's negative about that?'

'What does it say about my life up to now?'

'Mine was the same – I was a father and husband.'

'You were lousy at both because you were forging your

fucking career. And once you were Chief Constable of Toytown you might as well have been a single man.'

'The kids had left home by then.'

'I hadn't. What did I have?'

Watts didn't know what to say. He hadn't asked her to give up work. She had been eager to do so when the first baby and the post-natal depression came along.

He looked down at his hand resting on his knee. It was fisted.

When the call ended Watts paced the room. He'd always regarded himself as a man of action but of late he'd felt paralysed, unsure what to do with his ruptured life.

He changed into his tracksuit and running shoes and crossed over to the towpath beside the river. He headed towards Chiswick. The river made a slow curve. There was the old Fullers Brewery on the left.

The towpath was boggy and treacherous and frequently flooded, especially at the slipway into the river beside the brewery. Watts tiptoed through the water and mud then continued down towards Chiswick Bridge. He increased his pace as he neared the steps up on to the bridge then took them two at a time.

It took him the length of the bridge to regulate his breathing again. He dropped back down on to the opposite bank and started to run towards Barnes Bridge. He'd had the sense there was someone running some thirty yards behind him, keeping pace, but when he glanced back there was no one.

It was drier here as it was higher up. He increased his pace now, lengthening his stride. He loved the rhythm of breath and stride and arms pumping. Occasionally he glanced down at the river. The early-morning rowers were out in force by now.

The route veered away from the river, across an abandoned park with a sad-looking bandstand and allotments off to the left. He glanced back. Still no one. The route re-joined the riverbank at Chiswick.

The rain held off for the entire hour that Watts ran. When he got back to the White Hart he stopped beneath the balcony of the pub to cool down. It was muddy and Watts inhaled the strong tang of the river. He looked out at the individual rowers sculling by. He took deep breaths, resting a hand on his chest. His chest was his breastplate to keep people out. That's what Molly used to say.

He cleaned the muck off his trainers and put his tracksuit trousers on over his muddy legs and walked up the passage beside the pub and across to the café.

When he left the café he bought a pint of juice and the newspaper from the supermarket across the road. He checked his father's car, an old Saab convertible, hadn't been stolen in the night from its on-street parking space. It hadn't but someone had parked a battered old *deux chevaux* bumper to bumper with it. Watts decided against driving today.

Traffic was already building along the road by the Thames as he walked beneath Barnes Bridge. Early-morning commuters were filling the pavement on their hurried way to the station.

He glanced at Caspar's house as he walked by. He stopped when he saw the door. He stepped into the porch.

The door was black with a gold-coloured mailbox and a door-knocker in the shape of a lion's head. Above the knocker, a bloody heart had been nailed to the door. Thorns were sticking from it.

Watts looked up and down the street. A steady flow of people were passing beneath the bridge on their way to work. Something made him look up at the parapet of the bridge. Was it his imagination or did someone duck back out of sight?

He looked back at the door and at the blood pooling on the doorstep.

Gilchrist's head emerged from the toilet bowl for the third time.

What the fuck happened last night?

Whatever they'd eaten in the restaurant had not gone down well. That had happened before in some mild form and she only blamed herself. Eating such pure food after a week of her usual rubbish always discombobulated her system. Always. But this seemed more. She almost felt like she'd been hallu-cinating at one point. She'd certainly had some weird dreams.

Maybe it was the wine. Who knew organic wine had such a kick?

Great. Her first day back at work and she was wrecked. And nagging at her was the thought that something definitely out of the ordinary had happened with her friend Kate Simpson. But what it was she wasn't entirely sure. How had they ended up in the same bed?

She was getting ready to go into work when Kate rang. She realized within a moment that Kate was as befuddled (and embarrassed?) as she was.

'Main reason I'm ringing is to see if you know the police position on this Wicker Man thing.'

Gilchrist heard the slight tremble in Kate's voice. 'Wicker Man thing? Don't know what you're talking about.'

'Sarah, I think you're about to. It's going to be big.'

'I'll get back to you. How are you feeling?'

'Aside from running off to the loo to be sick as a dog every ten minutes, you mean?'

'You too?'

Simpson was between calls so Gilchrist let her go, then, her own interest piqued, called the desk sergeant at the station. 'It's DS Gilchrist . . .'

'You can't fool me, ma'am,' the sergeant said. George Appleby. Nice man. Old school. Which meant he'd cracked a few skulls in his time.

'George, I know I've not been around for a few weeks but it is DS Gilchrist. Sarah.'

'No such person. We do have a Detective Inspector Gilchrist though.'

'Yeah, yeah.'

'Congratulations, Sarah. Well deserved.'

'Thanks – but it's only acting.'

'It'll be yours as long as you don't mess up.'

'My point exactly, George.'

He chuckled. 'So how can I help you today, Detective Inspector?'

'What's going on with this Wicker Man?'

'Nasty. Very nasty.'

'Nasty how?'

'There was somebody inside when it went up.'

'Alive?'

'Not now but possibly then, yes.'

'Jesus.'

'That's what he is alleged to have said. Or words to that effect. A couple of people heard him call out before the flames or the smoke got to him.'

'Poor sod. OK. Thanks, George. Who's in charge of it?'

'Don't think it's been assigned yet.'

'Can you put me through to the chief constable?'

Hewitt's assistant, Tracy, put Gilchrist on hold for five minutes. During that time, Gilchrist tried not to think about the acrobatics going on in her stomach.

There was a click on the line and then Hewitt's voice: 'DI Gilchrist – first day in and already you have something to tell me about our troubled teenagers? Even though you're not, I understand, actually in?'

'Only just started on the teenagers, ma'am.'

'But not from your office, evidently. Why are you calling?'

'I wondered if you had something else for me to investigate.'

'I beg your pardon?'

'Ritual murder. This person burned to death in a Wicker Man?'

Hewitt paused. 'Why should I give that to you?'

Why indeed?

'I thought it may tie in with the church desecration,' Gilchrist stammered. 'Plus there may be a link to the satanic abuse of children – if you believe those satanic abuse nutters who still lurk in the dark corners of conventional psychiatry.'

'If, as you say, Sarah, those psychologists are – to use your technical term – nutters, there is no connection.'

'Best to be sure, don't you think, ma'am?'

Hewitt was quiet for a moment. Then: 'You've seen the film, I suppose?'

'Films, I believe,' Gilchrist said. 'One a terrible remake of a terrible sixties hippy thing.'

'But you know about them both.'

'I do. And about Wicker Men. Against my better judgement I once went to a wedding reception just outside Hebden Bridge in Yorkshire where, as the climax of the party, they set fire to one of these Wicker Men.'

'With the happy couple inside it?'

'No, ma'am.'

'I always think going north of Watford is unwise. And that was a wedding you say?'

'It didn't last.'

Hewitt barked a laugh then became more solemn. 'Unfortunately, this one did have someone inside. Burned to a cinder.' Hewitt sighed. 'God, what a city.'

'I'm guessing that God had nothing to do with it – rather the reverse.'

'These were pagan worshippers in the films?'

'They were. Not to be confused with black magicians. Modern pagans are all supposedly benign – hugging trees and worshipping the moon and all that. Not generally known for human sacrifices. Or, indeed, animal ones, as I think they are all veggies.'

'Hmm. All right, Sarah, I'll put you on the investigation as well as that of troubled teenagers.'

'As well as?'

'You drew the connection, not me.'

'Yes, but I was thinking of the Wicker Man investigation as a potential way into a future troubled teenager investigation . . .'

'In tandem, Sarah. Unless you don't want the Wicker Man investigation? Because this is the only way I can justify giving it to you. There's copper theft from railways to fall back on, too. That's a more pressing problem.'

Gilchrist ground her teeth.

'I'll be delighted to do the investigation in parallel with my work with the task force,' she ground out.

Hewitt was brisk. 'Get on with it, then.'

EIGHT

'There's a heart nailed to your front door,' Bob Watts said. 'I'm hoping it's animal not human.'

'Yeah, we found it,' Fi said, her voice sounding even throatier down the phone line. 'It's a sheep's heart.'

'Someone has killed a sheep and torn its heart out?'

Fi rasped a laugh. 'You're not a cook, are you, Bob? This is Barnes – it's from the local butcher.'

'They sell sheep's hearts?'

'They do. Getting the ventricles out is a bit of a bugger but they're very nice stuffed. Tender. I think Jamie has a recipe.'

'What's the significance of it?'

'It's a warning.'

'Warning about what?'

'Somebody is threatening us with doom – or worse.'

'Who?'

'Some devil-worshipping nutter, no doubt.'

'You're not worried?'

'Happens every couple of months. Have you decided about the Crowley book yet?'

'I wanted to talk to you about that. I've had another offer.'

'Come round for lunch. Caspar's will be mostly liquid but I'll rustle something up for you, me and our lodger.'

Watts put down the phone and picked up the card of the man who'd made the offer on *Moonchild* in the occult bookshop. Vincent Slattery, an antiquarian bookseller from Lewes.

He phoned but the call went straight to voicemail.

With nothing else to do and his curiosity piqued by the odd inscription in Pearson's book, he'd been in touch with Colin Pearson's publisher to try to arrange a meeting with the author. Pearson's publisher, after a bit of to-ing and fro-ing, had given him a number with a Brighton code. Watts dialled it now.

Someone picked up the phone and immediately replaced it. When he tried again the phone was engaged. He gave up after ten attempts over the next hour.

The rain had relented although the sky remained angry. Gilchrist didn't feel sick any more but she had sudden moments of dizziness and twice she thought someone had called her name. When she turned to respond, however, there was nobody there.

She went down to the beach to look at the remains of the Wicker Man. The entire structure had collapsed into a black, smoking mound only partly covered in grey foam. The policeman keeping guard by the tape was young, short and pink-faced. She showed him her warrant card, conscious she was towering over him.

'I've been put in charge of this investigation. Detective Inspector Gilchrist.'

He looked at her warrant card and frowned.

'All right,' she said. 'Acting DI. And you are?'

'Constable Heap, ma'am.'

'First name?'

'Bellamy, ma'am.'

'Bellamy?'

'Ma'am.'

'That's quite unusual?'

'Actually quite common, ma'am.'

'As a first name?'

'Not quite so common.'

'So how come?'

He shrugged. 'I wish I knew. I never thought to ask my parents when I was young and when I thought of it they weren't around to ask.'

'I'm sorry.'

He gestured to the smoking debris behind him. 'There are worse things in life.'

Gilchrist grimaced. 'I understand there are human remains.'

'Remains, certainly, ma'am. What exactly they are I don't believe we know yet. Scenes of crime and Mr Bilson from forensics are here.'

Gilchrist nodded and walked over to a familiar figure. 'Frank Bilson.'

'Sarah Gilchrist,' the forensic analyst said. He was a tall, lean man, some ten years her senior, with a sharp face and intelligent eyes.

'Human remains?'

'Possibly. Badly burned. The fire was particularly intense around the body. Probably an accelerant. It's slow work separating it out from the other remains. Should have it back in the lab by late afternoon. I'll start on it first thing in the morning.'

Gilchrist nodded and looked at the crowd of the curious gathered in small groups along the ridge of shingle some ten yards away. She walked back over to Constable Heap.

'You were first on the scene?'

He nodded.

'Statements?'

'Not written up yet.'

'Anything of particular note?'

'Some clubbers claim to have heard someone inside the Wicker Man screaming, then yell, "Why hast thou forsaken me?"'

'Biblical.'

'King James' Bible, ma'am. *Eli, Eli, lama sabachthani?* Jesus said it on the cross, according to Matthew's Gospel. "My God, my God, why hast thou forsaken me?"'

Gilchrist examined Heap's pink face. 'You a churchgoer, Bellamy?'

'Sometimes, ma'am.'

'Sounds like our victim was a churchgoer. Did they say whether it was a male or a female voice?'

'They couldn't tell, ma'am. The poor soul would have been in agony.'

She nodded.

'I should point out, ma'am, that only two people heard the voice calling out. Nobody else around them heard anything but screams.'

Gilchrist was trying to remember what the martyred policeman in the film called out. As if he'd read her mind,

Heap said: 'He sang, ma'am. In *The Wicker Man*. Called out a few "Oh Gods" and "Oh Lords".' He blushed at her surprised look. 'I thought that might be your train of thought.'

'Did you indeed?' Gilchrist said. 'Have you got much on at the moment?'

'Someone stole something from the council's museum and art gallery. I'm trying to find the thief on CCTV.'

She nodded. 'Put that to one side for the moment. Call the station and say I want a replacement for you down here then get off and write up those statements. I want them on my desk by teatime.'

'Where is your desk, ma'am?'

Gilchrist laughed. 'Good point.'

She walked away a few yards and phoned Hewitt. When she got through she said: 'This Wicker Man thing, ma'am – I'm going to need an incident room and a team.'

'I'll assign you Sergeant Donaldson,' Hewitt said. 'It'll take him a day or so to tie up his other cases but then he's yours. Have you worked with Donaldson before?'

'No, ma'am, but I know him.'

'A capable man,' Hewitt said.

'Yes, capable,' Gilchrist said. But a tosser.

'Sort out three constables and three support staff for yourself. Make your old office the incident room for the time being.'

'Yes, ma'am.' She glanced back at Bellamy Heap. 'I've already got the second member of my team.'

Kate Simpson was feeling pretty spacey. She'd stopped being ill but she was definitely not with it. She kept zoning out, going into weird little daydreams. Simon blathered on regardless.

She was nervous about what might have happened with Sarah Gilchrist the previous night. She knew what she'd always wanted to happen with her friend but now that it might have she was a bit freaked. Especially as she couldn't remember a thing about it.

So she'd decided to focus on something else. She realized that until she'd heard her fate over the volt gun thing she'd been unable to concentrate on anything. Now she was keen

to get on with her research into the wacky churches of
Brighton.

Fi Caspar led Bob Watts down a long hallway from the front
door to a conservatory at the back of Caspar's house. Watts
had been expecting rock star gaudiness but the dark blue walls
of the corridor were hung with expensive prints of the Thames
in Georgian and Victorian times.

The conservatory was warm and comfortable, despite the
rain rattling on its roof and pelting the windows. It was bright
too, with one brick wall hung with big prints of Georgia
O'Keeffe's highly sexualized flower paintings.

Caspar got up from a deep sofa and came over to give Watts
a hug. He smelt of patchouli and alcohol.

'Great to see you, man.'

Watts proffered the Crowley book. 'Thought you might want
a closer look.'

'We've got a nice Riesling on the go,' Fi said.

'Bone dry,' Caspar said, taking the book. 'Bloody delicious.
Pete Townshend turned me on to wine years ago. Not that he
had much of a palate back then. Keith Moon, that madman,
used to piss in his bottle when Pete wasn't looking.' Caspar
guffawed. 'Pete never noticed the bloody difference.'

'He must have had a tiny willy to piss down the neck of a
wine bottle,' Fi said, pouring Watts a glass.

'Now, now, darling,' Caspar said, waving Bob to a big
wicker chair piled with cushions. 'Size isn't everything.'

Fi passed Watts his wine. 'He's only saying that because
he's got a huge todger,' she said out of the corner of her
mouth.

'Don't be giving away all my secrets,' Caspar said absently.
He'd removed the dust jacket of the Crowley novel and was
turning the pages with surprising delicacy. He sighted along
the spine and opened it, flexing the binding carefully.

Fi saw Watts looking at the O'Keeffe prints.

'Sexy, aren't they? Freud said they were particularly sexual
because they looked like both male and female genitalia.'

'Genitalia?' Caspar said, not looking up from the Crowley
book. 'Isn't that a town in Italy?'

Fi croaked a laugh. Watts was remembering the tiny bits of gardening knowledge he'd got from his wife.

'Is a lily a hermaphrodite plant then?'

'I'm not sure they're self-seeding,' Fi said.

Caspar handed Watts the book back. 'Who was that fifties film director who made films about sexual repression? He had women's bedrooms full of these sheaves of sexy flowers in the foreground of shots.'

'Douglas Sirk,' Fi said. 'Love those films. Red anthorium in Dorothy Malone's bedroom in *Written on the Wind*. Gay director, Rock Hudson, heterosexual love story – hilarious.'

She gestured at the prints.

'These are the calla lily. Exported from South Africa in the mid-eighteenth century. Californians really took to them. Diego Rivera used them a lot too, especially in his murals.'

'They're beautiful,' Watts said.

'They are,' Fi said. 'But the calla lily isn't a true lily. Nor is the arum lily. They are *zantedeschia*.'

'See what you've started now?' Caspar said. 'I was always trying to get Fi to try for *Gardeners World* back in the days when that Charlie Whatsername was jiggling her boobs. Good-looking bird but her tits weren't a patch on Fi's.'

Watts smiled. 'I believe you.' He put the Crowley book on the table beside his chair.

Caspar gestured at it with his chin. 'Binding is in bloody good nick. I reckon it hasn't been off your dad's bookshelf almost since he got it. Sometimes that means the pages get stuck together but Crowley used expensive paper for his press.'

He looked at Watts.

'You know the Mandrake Press was Crowley's? The UK version of the press published quite a lot of other stuff – some interesting poetry by avant-garde poets of the time – but essentially it was a vanity publishing outfit. Over the years, he paid for the publication of pretty much every one of his hundred books. Began life a wealthy man but blew through it all.'

Watts nodded at the book. 'So what do you think?'

'This is the original short run US version, that's what makes it so valuable. When war broke out he buggered off to America to get out of it. He set up the Mandrake Press again in London when he came back and reissued this some years later.'

'A bloke made me an offer in that funny occult bookshop in Great Museum Street.'

'I know the one. They get interesting stuff in there occasionally among all the tat.'

'They have to stock the tat,' Fi said from a table where she was laying out bowls of food. 'They're just trying to make a living, like everybody. Everybody who isn't living off their ill-gotten gains like you, that is.'

'It's true enough,' Caspar said. 'But I worked bloody hard to get my money.' He leered at Watts. 'With a lot of fun on the way.'

Watts smiled.

'This bloke – called Vincent Slattery – offered me ten thousand pounds for it.'

Caspar whistled.

'Good money – but Vincent has always been over the top.'

'You know him?'

'Sure. I've done a lot of business with him down the years. When I bought Westmeston House I bought its library too. Being local he'd done the valuation and I went through the library with him when I took possession.'

'I didn't know if you'd want to go that high?'

'As I said: I'll match any offer you get. The money's not a problem but I'm intrigued by Vincent. He usually only buys stuff when he's got a purchaser in mind.'

'I don't want to part with it quite yet anyway. I'm intrigued by the inscription.'

'Crowley calling your dad *magister*?'

Watts nodded. 'That, but more the *mon semblable, mon frère*. He's got some signed Dennis Wheatley and Colin Pearson books with the same phrase in the inscription. I don't suppose you know what it means?'

'It rings a bell,' Caspar said after a moment. 'But by my time of life, after all the drugs and the booze, my brain has more holes in it than a Swiss cheese.' Caspar sipped his wine. 'So you want to find out if your dad was secretly the Wizard of Oz?'

'Something like that.'

'Family secrets, Bob. Those skeletons in the closet are usually kept in there for a bloody good reason.'

'I've already rattled a few.'

'Have you?' Caspar said, giving him an intrigued look. 'And your father knew Colin Pearson?'

'Yes. Do you?'

'A bit. Know his wife better. They live in a big cottage at the Devil's Dyke.'

'Appropriate.'

'It fits, doesn't it, for the author of *Magic*? His cottage is part of a big farming spread. Bits of the main farmhouse go back to the Middle Ages; most of it is around four hundred years old. The Templars owned it for a century or so. The National Trust have it now.'

'Lots of legends surrounding it, I suppose,' Watts said.

'Got it in one. But about your dad. If he had been any kind of heavyweight on that occult scene I would have known about it. And he would probably have mentioned it to me on the odd occasions we talked about my well-known past proclivities.'

'Unless he was part of AA,' Fi said, dropping into the chair beside Watts.

Caspar gave her a nod. 'True.'

'My dad liked a drink but—'

'Not that AA,' Caspar said, tilting his glass at Watts and taking another sip of his wine. 'This is something else.' He looked into the garden. 'And here's the very man to tell you about it.'

Watts turned round in his chair. The man in the paint-splattered pullover was walking through the garden, ignoring the rain, cigarette clamped between his teeth, asthma inhaler in his hand.

'Our lodger, Nick,' Fi said. 'Lunch can now be served.'

NINE

In the incident room Gilchrist stood by the window looking up at the gloomy sky. Her hastily assembled team clacked on computer keyboards and worked the phones behind her. There were three constables and three civilian support workers in an office that used to seat two. She'd never run a team before and would have been panicking if she hadn't felt so bloody weird.

She'd read the statements of the four clubbers to see if there was anything there. All heard screams, two claimed to have heard the victim shout out.

Bilson's office had been in touch to say the remains of whoever had burned to death in the Wicker Man were too badly damaged for any normal kind of recognition but the pelvic saddle was more or less intact and from that Bilson was concluding the victim was male. DNA samples had been extracted from the bones and the results were being hurried through.

DS Donald Donaldson came into the room, glad-handing the constables and civilian staff sitting there. He had a cocky, shoulder-rolling walk. Gilchrist nodded and smiled and he joined her at the window. They shook hands.

He was shorter than her but a bear of a man who seemed too big for any space he occupied. He was a fanatical body-builder so always looked as if he was bursting out of his clothes. Gilchrist suspected steroid use but if he wanted to wreck himself, that was his choice.

'What is it, Don-Don?'

'Well, first off: what do I call you? I've been calling you Sarah for the past five years. Do I start calling you ma'am now?'

'Sarah's fine,' she said.

'OK. So what do you want me to be doing?'

She turned to face him. 'I'd like you to check the witness

statements Constable Heap took on the beach. See if anything stands out.'

'Heap, eh?'

She caught his tone. 'What's wrong with Constable Heap?'

'The pocket policeman? Nothing. A bit too arty-farty for my taste. These university types usually are.'

'Nevertheless, he's a member of this team.'

'As you say,' Donaldson said, turning away. Gilchrist craned her neck back out of the window. From here she could just see the smouldering pile of wood and wicker on the beach. The tide was coming in. Within half an hour it would be dispersed. She hoped scenes of crime and forensics hadn't missed anything.

There were still people loitering near the remains. She recalled the wedding she'd been to on the moors above Hebden Bridge. The burning Wicker Man had been quite a sight.

She pondered for a moment. Such a sight that if you were the person who set the Brighton one alight you'd want to stay and watch it go up, surely? Especially if you'd dumped a body inside it.

'Who's collating the video footage?' she called out to the room.

A young female officer stuck her hand in the air. Sylvia somebody. Gilchrist's mother had been called Sylvia but it wasn't a name you came across much in younger generations. Sylvia Wade.

'Sylvia, aside from looking to see if there's evidence of who set the Wicker Man alight, we need to try to match everybody watching on the beach with the witness statements Bellamy took. It's possible whoever put the body in there stayed around to watch it burn but not to give a statement.'

'Ma'am,' Sylvia said to her.

'Someone else double check the witnesses' addresses – see if we've a wrong one.'

A young, eager-faced constable volunteered for that with a wave of his hand. Gilchrist nodded.

'Right,' she said. 'I'm off to see the chief constable.'

Caspar made a phone call to Colin Pearson's wife to arrange a meeting for Watts. When Caspar made the call, Watts was standing with Fi and the artist, whose name was Nick Brunswick. He lived in the basement and used a shed at the bottom of their garden as his studio.

'You know Pearson too?' Watts said.

Brunswick nodded. 'Back in the day.'

'Can you get down there tomorrow?' Caspar said over his shoulder to Watts.

'The Devil's Dyke?' Bob Watts said. 'Sure. What time?'

'He'll be expecting you late afternoon.'

Watts nodded.

'That's cool, Avril, thanks,' Caspar said, putting the phone down. 'Avril. Very cute cookie in her day.'

'I suppose you had a thing with her,' Fi said.

Caspar shrugged.

'*Everyone* had a thing with her. It was the sixties and seventies and rock 'n' roll.' He winked at Watts. 'And no HIV plague to worry about.'

'What's this about AA?' Watts said to Nick Brunswick. 'Do they call each other *mon semblable, mon frère*?'

Brunswick looked at Caspar and Fi.

'We told him you're the expert,' Fi said.

'It's a super secret cult set up by Crowley linked to but separate from his Temples of Thelema, which are the churches he founded,' Brunswick said.

'It's so secret that even its members don't know if it exists,' Fi said.

Watts frowned. 'I don't get that.'

'It's more that they don't know how many members there are,' Caspar said.

'You only know the person above you – your mentor – and the person below you – your mentee,' Brunswick said. 'So you don't know how high you are in the hierarchy or who the top person is. Every so often someone has proclaimed that they are now in charge but others have contested that so now there could be as many as six AA organizations running side by side.'

'Essentially, if your mentor dies or leaves you're fucked in terms of your own progress but you control the one below you,' Caspar said.

'You're all members?' Watts said.

'Not me,' Fi said with her throaty chuckle. 'A mere woman.'

'I was,' Caspar said. 'Nick here was my mentor.'

'And your mentor?' he said to Brunswick.

'Disappeared.'

Watts thought for a moment. 'That sheep's heart anything to do with this AA?'

Caspar bared his teeth. 'In a moment of drug-induced madness I declared myself the big cheese a few years ago. It was total bollocks, of course – as Nick was the first to point out. It pissed off more than a few people.'

'So you have enemies.'

'Lots. But as long as they keep their violence on the astral plane with a few bloody hearts thrown in I can cope.'

'The shit through the post isn't so good,' Fi said.

Caspar patted her shoulder. 'That's what PO boxes were created for.'

Watts looked at Brunswick. 'Do you know where *mon semblable, mon frère* comes from?'

'Sure.' Brunswick shrugged. 'It's from T S Eliot's *The Wasteland*.'

Hewitt's face remained immobile. Gilchrist wondered what she would do if ever she reached Hewitt's career heights. She'd want to be accepted for her achievements but she knew she'd also be judged for her looks – if only as a sign of how she was dealing with the stress.

Tony Blair's haggard face, photographed during the Iraq War, was still being used in the windows of Brighton's many alternative therapy and massage centres to represent the 'Before' of the treatments they were giving. And there had been no 'After' for Blair. So Gilchrist didn't judge Hewitt. Well, she tried not to.

'Pleased you made it in, Sarah,' Hewitt said coldly.

'Sorry, ma'am. Something I ate last night.'

'Suppose you were in Plenty too.'

Gilchrist frowned. 'Too? Have other people eating there been sick?'

'Six or seven – one man is on life-support. Public Health

has been called in.' Hewitt's tone softened. 'So you really were ill? I must say, you're still looking peaky.'

'My friend has been ill too.'

'I've warned you before about all this health food stuff. You know where you are with steak and chips.'

'Yes, ma'am.'

'So: the Wicker Man?'

'We're collating,' Gilchrist said, giving a brief run-down on the investigation.

'No one has come forward saying they built it or think they know who the victim might be?'

Gilchrist shook her head. 'But it is early days.'

Hewitt tilted her chair back. 'This film – the person inside the Wicker Man was a sacrifice, wasn't he?'

'Yes – because the crops had failed.'

'Have the crops failed around here?'

Gilchrist paused, then risked it: 'With respect, ma'am, do I look like Alan Titchmarsh?'

Hewitt laughed. 'He's gardening, Sarah.'

'Who's the agriculture man then?' Gilchrist said.

'With respect right back at you, Detective Inspector, why would I know that? I'm a town girl. However, I've always taken you for a striding-across-the-Downs woman. There's agriculture up there, surely?'

'The last time I was on the Downs was for an Anish Kapoor thing up at the Indian memorial.'

'I think it was an installation rather than a thing. I didn't realize you were into art, DI Gilchrist.'

'I was arresting some scumbags up there – it was my wilderness period, ma'am.'

When Gilchrist had been returned to duty after her first suspension over the infamous Milldean Massacre she had been given all the shitty jobs that were around. That would have been on Hewitt's instructions. The chief constable chose not to comment now. Instead: 'Did you like the installation? It was a big mirror wasn't it?'

'A big curved mirror that made you and the landscape look weird. Before Arts Council grants came along the Hall of Mirrors on the seafront did pretty much the same job.'

*   *   *

Watts met Nicola Travis for a drink after work. He hadn't expected it to be so soon after they'd bumped into each other but it was her proposal. She suggested the bar on the top floor of the National Portrait Gallery.

He went up on the Piccadilly line from Hammersmith to Leicester Square and got there far too early. He walked down Charing Cross Road in yet another deluge and on a whim ducked on to Cecil Court. He loved the feel of the Victorian thoroughfare with its antique bookshops and poster and print shops. He'd read somewhere that the aristocratic freeholders kept the rents affordable to allow for the shops that gave it a unique character.

He'd visited the second-hand crime fiction bookshop a couple of weeks earlier to discuss selling his father's crime fiction collection. Next door there was an esoteric bookshop. Now he spent ten minutes browsing the shelves. There was a lot of Colin Pearson, including several of his notoriously unreadable didactic novels. There was a whole section devoted to Aleister Crowley, of course.

Watts picked up a second-hand biography of Crowley by John Symonds. The cover was a different image from the fat, bullet-headed Crowley that Watts was used to. This was a portrait of a younger man, looking vaguely Roman in profile and wearing what looked at first like a scarlet toga.

Watts looked at the picture credit on the dust jacket. It was a painting by Leon Engers Kennedy in the National Portrait Gallery. Painted in 1917 in New York. The year *Moonchild* was first published in a limited edition.

Watts stepped back out into the rain and made his way past the Garrick Theatre. A new production of *The Devil Rides Out* was on. In the Portrait Gallery he went into the shop and bought a postcard of the portrait of Crowley. At the till he asked where the painting itself was.

A long escalator in a kind of middle foyer took him up to the first floor. The room where Crowley's portrait hung was deserted.

He couldn't explain why he was so curious about Crowley and his father's relationship with him. Then again, he couldn't really say why he'd invited Nicola Travis out for a drink. He didn't feel a need for any kind of commitment to a woman and, a single occasion with Sarah Gilchrist notwithstanding, he'd never been interested in one-night stands. Maybe it was all part of the feeling he had of being in limbo.

He looked back at the picture and the blurb alongside it. The artist Engers Kennedy had joined Crowley's cult in 1912. Crowley moved in with him in New York in 1917 and they both tried painting. According to the blurb this painting showed Crowley's mystical and transcendental aspects. Watts just saw a ridiculous poser. He glanced at his watch.

He was sitting at the corner of the bar in the top floor restaurant when Nicola Travis came in. He'd been admiring the view across rooftops past the National Gallery and down Whitehall.

Travis was dressed demurely in trousers and jacket but her smile was mischievous. She took her jacket off and draped it over one stool before sliding on to the next one and leaning over to kiss him on the cheek. As she settled herself on the stool she glanced down at his glass of wine.

'You want the same?' he said, gesturing the barman over.

'Actually,' she said, addressing both Watts and the barman, 'I'd like a negroni.'

Watts didn't know what that was but the barman smiled at her choice.

Travis pointed at the postcard beside the wine glass. 'I was looking at that, not your drink, by the way.'

'I bought it in the shop,' he said, then felt foolish for stating the obvious.

'Aleister Crowley, eh? You're really getting into researching your father's books.'

'Just curious,' he said. 'I'm impressed you know who he is.'

'I know the portraits in the gallery pretty well. I was here before I came down to Brighton. You should take a look at the half-dozen images of Elias Ashmole if you really want to pursue all this magic stuff.'

'Who's he?'

'His private collection was the foundation of the Ashmolean Museum in Oxford. A lawyer by training but when the civil war broke out in the mid-seventeenth century he moved to Oxford and got interested in astrology, then anatomy, medicine and alchemy. Collected ancient manuscripts on the subjects then donated them to Oxford University as long as they built something to put them in. At least three of the copies of the *Key of Solomon* in the Ashmolean came from him.'

Watts nodded sagely then felt he should fess up.

'What's the *Key of Solomon*?'

She laughed.

'A *grimoire*: a book of spells and magic. This one was attributed to King Solomon. The Solomon and Sheba bloke? Wisdom of Solomon?'

'The one in the Bible who sorted out the real mother from the false by suggesting they cut the baby in two and have half each?'

'The very one. But I only know about the *Key* because I know one of the people who run the Rare Books Collection at the Jubilee Library in Brighton.'

'Aren't all books rare in libraries these days?'

She acknowledged his pathetic joke with a little smile. 'It's really a fabulous collection. Fifty thousand books.'

'And they've got a copy of this book of magic?'

'Had – it was stolen a couple of weeks ago.' She put her hand to her mouth. 'Oops – not sure anyone is supposed to know that.'

He leaned in and lowered his voice. 'I assume the police know so as I'm ex-police it's kind of all right.'

'I'm not sure the police do know,' she whispered.

'It's still safe with me,' he said, leaning back. 'But are you certain all this magic stuff isn't a hobby of yours – you being a resident of the city of all things wacky.'

She laughed. The barman put her drink down before her.

'I'm a witch really – especially after a couple of these.'

Watts looked at her drink.

'Campari and brandy and gin and vermouth,' she said. 'I think.'

They chinked glasses and Watts noticed the patch on her arm. She caught him looking.

'How's it going?' Watts said. 'Nicotine's a tough drug to quit.'

'Oh, it's not for smoking; it's for travel. Did I tell you I get terrible motion sickness?'

'A commuter who gets sick travelling. I didn't know you could get patches for that.'

'You can probably get patches for anything these days. I've got whatever is on the patch in more concentrated form if I need it.'

'But why don't you move back to London?'

'And abandon my allotment? I could never do that. Besides, I'm only up here three days a week at the most.'

'You grow your own veg?'

'A lot of flowers too. Gardening is my passion. I even did a part-time gardening course at the Royal Horticultural College. It took me so long to qualify that by the end of the course I'd forgotten all I'd learned at the start.'

He laughed.

· 'You like gardening?' she said.

'I like gardens. I like lying in a garden in a hammock with a glass of wine and the newspapers.' He looked away. 'My wife was the gardener.'

'I bet you did the lawn and the heavy digging. Men always do that.'

He looked back. 'I paid for someone else to do that.' He gave an embarrassed shrug. 'I wasn't around very much.'

'Damn, I was hoping to get you to help me move an oak tree.'

She saw his startled look.

'Joke! God, you really don't know much about gardening, do you?'

'Guilty.'

'In more ways than that, I can see,' she said.

He dropped his eyes. 'As charged,' he said.

'And there I was flirting with you shamelessly that night and you a married man. What a scarlet woman you must think me.'

'Not at all,' he mumbled.

'Although in my own defence you were far more interesting

than Bernard Rafferty banging on about the beauty of the churchyards of Sussex.'

Watts laughed and looked up. Travis was staring at him and the pressure around them changed in that indefinable but instantly recognizable way. She had certainly recognized it, judging by what she said next.

'Get your coat, ex-Chief Constable. You've pulled.'

TEN

Sarah Gilchrist was thinking about sending everyone home for what remained of the day when Bellamy Heap came over.

'Ma'am, the case I was on when you brought me into this investigation . . .'

'Somebody stole a painting from the Brighton Museum and Art Gallery, didn't they?' she said. 'What about it?'

'I wonder if it might somehow be linked.'

'Because?'

Donaldson was listening in from the next desk. He leaned forward, his meaty shoulders bulging against his tight shirt. Gilchrist thought a big breath from Donaldson would blow Heap over.

'I've always thought security was a bit loose there,' Donaldson said. 'There's a lot of silver in those cabinets. Did they not get the person?'

Heap looked down at him. 'No, sir.'

'But what's it got to do with our case?' Donaldson said.

'Sorry, sir. It's the name of the painting.'

'Which is?' Gilchrist said.

'*The Devil's Altar*. By an artist called Gluck.'

'Gluck?' Donaldson barked a laugh and Gilchrist thought the buttons of his shirt might pop. 'Sounds like someone with catarrh.'

Gilchrist looked around the room. '*The Devil's Altar*. Is it just me or is something spooky going on in Brighton?'

There was a ripple of laughter from the others.

'So what happened?' she said to Heap.

Heap filled her in.

'What?' she said. 'The security man didn't notice the picture had been stolen?'

'Not until I pointed it out to him and Mr Rafferty, the museum director.'

'That weirdo,' Donaldson muttered.

Gilchrist ignored him. 'Go on, Bellamy.'

'The glass was possibly broken to get at the silver but more likely as a diversion – a diversion that worked. Anyway, we interviewed some people who were there but others had gone by the time we arrived. The security guard has no powers to detain people *en masse* and, in any case, assumed the people had gone out of an emergency exit.'

'People?'

'I think there were two, ma'am. The picture is pretty big and I see one person throwing the brick into the glass case whilst the other takes the picture off the wall.'

'CCTV?'

'I'd started on it but I handed it over to someone else to analyse when I was transferred here.'

'*The Devil's Altar* title fits with the desecration in the church,' Gilchrist mused. 'What does the painting look like?'

Heap frowned. 'That's the odd thing. It's two flowers in a vase.'

'Called *The Devil's Altar*? Are they some horribly poisonous flower?'

Sylvia Wade had been tapping at her keyboard. She peered at her computer screen and called out. 'Look like lilies.' She angled her screen to the eager young constable next to her. He nodded.

'So why the title?' Gilchrist looked around the room. 'Anyone know what lilies represent in the occult?'

Blank faces. Sylvia was tapping away again but frowning.

'OK. Somebody figure out why the artist, whoever this Gluck is, called a bunch of flowers something spooky and what wider significance that might have for the loopy occult brigade.'

Donaldson leaned forward, muscles bunched. 'Know the artist, know the painting,' he said, all but cracking his knuckles. 'Let's find out about her.'

Gilchrist gave him a sideward glance. 'Thanks, Detective Sergeant.'

'I'll do it, ma'am,' Sylvia Ward said.

Gilchrist nodded.

'If I may suggest, ma'am . . .' Heap said.

'Suggest away, Heap.'

'We must keep clear in our minds that the paganism the Wicker Man represents and the occult are miles apart.'

'Thanks for the reminder. OK, gang, it might seem unlikely that this is not somehow linked to the Wicker Man but Bellamy is right – let's not get too carried away.'

'Although, ma'am . . .' Heap continued.

Donaldson gave an exaggerated sigh.

'Lilies are used in Catholic iconography – paintings and such – to represent Mary and purity. But at Easter they represent Christ's death and rebirth. May Day is about rebirth – spring and everything. So there is a kind of link to neo-pagan beliefs.'

Gilchrist stood. She looked down on Heap. He really wasn't very tall.

'Thanks for muddying the waters again, Bellamy.'

'My pleasure, ma'am.'

His face was deadpan as she gave him a second look. She looked across at Sylvia Wade. 'Sylvia, you chase up the CCTV. See if we're lucky enough to find someone who was in the gallery *and* on the beach. To use DS Donaldson's technical term: some weirdo.'

The others smiled at that but smirked at Sylvia, knowing what a tedious job was before her.

'Will do, ma'am,' she said flatly.

Kate Simpson was a good researcher – one of the few things she recognized she was good at. Perhaps the *only* thing she accepted she was good at. She'd been researching extreme churches on and off for weeks. At eight in the evening she put her phone down, rubbed her eyes and logged off her computer.

She gathered up her papers and her laptop and left the office. It was raining again; stinging rain. She walked down the busy street from the station and turned left to splosh through puddles down the back end of the North Laines. She cut along the narrow alley that had the sorting office's wall on one side and a terrace of old flint and cob cottages behind shallow gardens on the other.

She glanced in Bob Watts' front window but there was no sign of his presence. She didn't understand why he wanted to live here. The cottages were tiny and he was a big man. Orderly and organized but sprawling too.

And looking out on to a blank wall was just weird. Especially as she knew he used to have a fabulous view of the Downs when he lived on the other side of them. Then again, she wasn't even sure he still did live here. She hadn't seen him for weeks.

She cut diagonally across Church Street and through a little dog-leg path next to the multi-storey car park into Bond Street, almost opposite the Theatre Royal's narrow stage door. The theatre was showing a touring stage adaptation of the sixties horror film *Rosemary's Baby*. She'd seen the original on late-night telly once and it had been kind of creepy.

A wet, simpering actress called Mia Farrow had almost wrecked it though. Kate, perhaps because she had always needed to work at keeping her weight down, had no patience with grown women who flirted with anorexia as this actress with the whiny voice clearly had. She'd known too many lovely teenage girls when she was growing up who'd suffered terribly and genuinely from the illness.

Kate was vaguely aware of the actress and associated her with nepotism. She'd read somewhere she was the daughter of Hollywood royalty, had been the wife of decades-older Frank Sinatra (what was that about?) then partner of Woody Allen who, later in her life, gave her the only acting gigs she got. How easy do you want it?

Kate knew that her visceral dislike of such nepotism was because that was entirely the world in which her parents operated and she had rejected it. Hence Southern Shores Radio and not Broadcasting House.

She cut across North Street and up into the Laines. The fish were pretty much gone now but she could see the occasional tail or fish head sticking out of guttering. Seagulls were still strutting along the alleys looking for fishy remains. She had to walk round them to pass through the tiny square that was leading her to the Druid's Head pub.

Her parents. She had to deal with them sometime but maybe that was why she was throwing herself into work. Specifically, she was avoiding dealing with the fact that her father, the government adviser William Simpson, had been implicated in the Milldean Massacre and involved with the gangster Charlie Laker. The gangster who had tried to have Kate raped and beaten as a warning to her father.

She wondered what Laker had threatened her mother with. She was guessing that something like that – or perhaps the fact that her father seemed to be getting drawn deeper and deeper into a criminal morass – had prompted her mother to leave her father after so many years.

Her mother was now ensconced in the flat in Kemp Town for which Kate had been paying her parents a peppercorn rent. It was one of the reasons Kate was still living with Sarah Gilchrist. Live with her mother? No, thanks very much.

Kate came out on Brighton Place, opposite Brighton's old jail house, and turned into the Druid's Head.

As usual it was full of Goths: black-garbed, white-faced, tattooed, pierced men and women in clumpy boots. Given how she felt, she would fit right in. She ordered a cranberry juice and took it over to an empty sofa just inside the door.

She liked this pub. Its name was cheesy – invented sometime in the past few decades – but a pub had been on this site for centuries. It had thick flint walls and a high ceiling. Angst was the music of choice but sometimes that was OK.

She opened her laptop and looked at her notes.

She'd found an odd link between a black magician called Aleister Crowley and the Church of Scientology, whose UK headquarters were just up the road in East Grinstead.

She didn't intend to go into them for her programme – her bosses would have a fit if she tried investigating such a wealthy, powerful and touchy organization. Even the threat of a massive lawsuit would probably close the station down.

Nevertheless, Aleister Crowley had been an influence on L. Ron Hubbard, the science-fiction writer who had founded Scientology. In a lecture in 1952 Hubbard had called Crowley 'my very good friend'. There were similarities between their teachings. Crowley had said that the sole object of all 'true' magical training was to become 'free of all limitations'. Hubbard, in a clip from a 1952 lecture she'd listened to online, said: 'Our whole activity tends to make an individual completely independent of any limitation.'

In 1945, before he founded Scientology, Hubbard had been involved with Crowley's Church of Thelema, although how he'd been involved was debatable. A man called Wilfred Smith had founded a lodge of Crowley's church – the Ordo Templi Orientis – in Pasadena.

Another man called Jack Parsons had taken over as boss of that lodge at the start of the 1940s. He was a rocket engineer – he'd founded Cal Tech so was a man of some stature. But he was a believer in Crowley's mystical mumbo-jumbo.

At the time Hubbard was a Captain in the US Navy stationed nearby. He moved in with Parsons in Pasadena. There was a letter still in existence from Parsons to Crowley saying something about Hubbard being quite knowledgeable about esoteric matters and in perfect accord with their own principles. Through a magic ceremony Parsons aimed to create a moonchild – mightier than all the kings of the earth – whose birth Crowley had prophesied in *The Book of The Law* and in a novel of the same name.

To create this child Parsons and Hubbard did eleven days of rituals and early in 1946 found a girl prepared to become the mother of this moonchild. The three days of rituals at the start of March involved Parsons as High Priest having sex with the girl whilst Hubbard looked on and acted as scryer, describing what was happening on the astral plane.

Hubbard told a different story and Kate had no means of knowing whether to believe or disbelieve him. He agreed that he did move in to Parsons' house, that Parsons was leader of a black magic group and that a girl was used in a sex ritual.

But he insisted he was sent in by Naval Intelligence to make friends with Parsons then break up this evil black magic group and rescue the girl. All of which he said he did.

Kate didn't know why Naval Intelligence would be bothered. She also noted that Hubbard stole Parsons' mistress, Sara Northrup – or perhaps he would have said that he rescued her. They married, but bigamously as Hubbard already had a wife.

Crowley ended up living in Hastings, a tired and drug-addicted old man. He died there two years later. Until his death this Pasadena sect paid his rent.

Sarah Gilchrist plumped down beside Kate with a bottle of lager at around nine.

'How's it going?' Kate said.

'Not great,' Gilchrist said. 'Bad things coming up.'

Sarah was really stressed, that was obvious. The police-woman jiggled her foot and ran her hand continually through her hair.

'I've found out something you might not know about,' Kate said. 'In passing, when talking to church authorities and vicars, I've discovered that in recent months there have been a dozen cases of sacrilegious behaviour in churches around Brighton.'

'I saw an example of it.'

Gilchrist described what she'd seen at St Michael's.

'I've just heard the heart is that of a pig. It looks almost identical to that of a human.' She grimaced. 'I don't mind telling you I'm starting to get seriously freaked.'

Gilchrist looked at her bottle of beer, seemingly surprised she had already finished it.

'You don't believe in magic though?' Kate said.

'Everything can be explained, I know that,' Gilchrist said. 'It isn't the thing, it's the bloody people. Who knew there were so many nutters around? Is this what the world is turning into – a bunch of loony people believing in absolute garbage?'

'You're describing Brighton then.'

Gilchrist gave Kate a look.

'When has it ever been different?' Kate laughed. 'Wait until you meet the man with the hole in his head.'

Gilchrist sighed. 'You think he'll be the first man I've met with a hole in his head? Remind me to give you the history of my love life.'

Kate laughed again. 'No, really. He's been trepanned – a hole drilled into his head to release, well, something or other in his mind. There's a church for it. There's a church for everything in Brighton.'

'A church of – what did you call it – trepanning? Not Christian, I assume.'

'Not so you'd notice. There are some fundamentalist, happy-clappy Christian churches where they exorcize demons and fall into ecstatic fits and sometimes just sing really bad Christian pop songs. The most extreme – which I'm visiting on Saturday – is supposed to be the Church of Holy Blood.'

'How come you're doing that? You're planning a programme?'

'Yes. I was partway through when the fish fell out of the sky – do you think I should have taken that as a sign?'

Gilchrist smiled, her face relaxing for the first time since she'd joined Kate. 'You going to drink something stronger than cranberry juice?'

When she came back with two beers, Kate said: 'We need to talk.'

'About what?'

Kate lowered her voice. 'About what happened last night.'

Gilchrist paused for a moment. 'I don't know what happened last night,' she said, 'except that Plenty poisoned us. Whatever happened, happened because of that.'

A man came in with a girl of about sixteen. A father getting his access, Simpson guessed. They sat down a couple of tables away.

Gilchrist looked down, then at Kate. 'I'm not really sure how that happened,' she said. 'I woke up this morning and there we were.'

'And there we were,' Kate murmured.

'I'm not . . . you know . . . that way,' Gilchrist said.

Kate took a breath and leaned forward. 'I am.'

Gilchrist tilted her head. 'I didn't know.'

'Sort of. Brad Pitt comes along, it's "*sayonara* missy".'

Gilchrist laughed. 'I'm a Clooney gal myself.'

Kate nodded. 'That's a generation thing. If you were for Robert Pattinson I'd be worried.'

'Who he?'

'Vampire guy. *Twilight*?'

Gilchrist did a mock groan. 'Don't go back to that.'

Kate laughed.

While this conversation had been going on both of them had been aware of the loud voice of the man with the young girl a couple of tables away. Now they both tuned in, Gilchrist absently gnawing at a fingernail.

'I tell you what,' the man said. 'You're heavier than you used to be. Too much lasagne.'

Gilchrist glanced at Kate.

A couple of minutes later the girl got up to go to the bathroom.

'Hang on a minute,' Gilchrist said.

Kate watched her walk across to the man. He was wearing a neat grey suit but terrible pointed black shoes with purple soles. Yuck.

'Excuse me,' Gilchrist said, flashing her warrant card.

The man looked bemused.

'Nothing heavy – just a moment.'

The man stood and they moved away a couple of yards, the man giving an expressive shrug to nobody in particular.

Gilchrist tried to get the guy to focus on her eyes. His eyes were looking from side to side. She jabbed him in the chest.

'Hey . . .' She eyeballed him. 'Never, *ever*, tell a young girl she's overweight.'

He was befuddled but he tried for indignant. 'I didn't – I said . . .'

'You said she was heavy and it was too much lasagne. *Big* mistake.'

'I'm not getting you,' he said, temper showing. 'And what's it got to do with you anyway?'

'What you said to her is going to resonate for the rest of her life.'

'Whoa,' he said, rearing back from her vehemence.

Gilchrist, head down, took a moment. She leaned in next to his ear. 'Reassure her. She's a beautiful kid. Tell her that. Again and again. Never *ever* tell her she is overweight.' She pushed him in the chest again. 'Got it?'

He nodded, mumbling.

Gilchrist turned, picked up her bag and left the pub. Kate grabbed her own bag and followed.

ELEVEN

'There's a flaw in *The Wicker Man.*'

'I'm sure there are many flaws,' Southern Shores Simon said. 'That's part of its charm. As it is of mine.'

Kate snorted a laugh.

'Ignore Miss Piggy and carry on, sir,' Simon said.

The caller had a nasal voice.

'Do you remember the scene where Britt Ekland, the publican's daughter, is offering herself to the copper – Edward Woodward – by dancing naked in the room next door to him and driving him mad with lust?'

'Who could forget? She's tempting him for sure – although I believe they used a body double for some of that dance.'

'But why?'

'Maybe Britt was shy about showing her bum.'

'I mean why was she trying to seduce him? Christopher Lee had gone to a lot of trouble to get a virgin copper to the island. They'd built this Wicker Man to burn a virgin copper. For the plan to work the copper *had* to be a virgin. What if Woodward had opened his door and spent the night with Britt – the film would have ended right there. No virgin, no Wicker Man sacrifice, no crops.'

Kate Simpson laughed. She'd seen the film a couple of times at the Duke of York's and on telly. The caller was right.

Sarah Gilchrist was kicking herself for losing her rag the night before. A private person, even with a friend such as Kate, she also felt she had revealed herself and that annoyed her even more.

Kate had followed her out of the pub and they'd walked back to the flat in near silence. Neither of them mentioned the waking up in bed together incident and Kate had resumed the sofa bed in the corner of the lounge.

Gilchrist had slept like a log and Kate had already left for work when she got up. After a hasty shower she hurried in to the office, her head buzzing with the things she needed to achieve today.

The others dribbled in over the next hour and settled in front of their computers and phones with mugs of lousy office coffee.

Gilchrist telephoned David Rutherford, the vicar at St Michael's.

'I was checking nothing else had happened to your church,' she said. 'That heart was animal, not human, by the way.'

'I'm relieved to hear it,' he said. 'I believe your policemen are driving by quite regularly during the night and we ensure we keep our eyes peeled during the day. It's timely that you should call, however, as I was toying with the idea of calling the station myself.'

'Why?'

'First, though, I owe you an apology. In all the kerfuffle the other day I omitted to ask how I might help you. You never told me why you came to my church.'

Gilchrist gave a quick look round the incident room. 'Something and nothing,' she said. 'But why were you going to call us?'

She guessed Rutherford took the hint because he moved on. 'My fellow vicar has gone missing. We share our mission at the church.'

'How long missing?'

'Hard to say. He took a leave of absence three weeks ago but was due back three days ago. He has not been in contact and does not return our calls. I have visited his flat but if he is there he does not answer the door. His upstairs neighbour can't even remember the last time he saw him.'

'Three days isn't very long, Vicar.'

'Call me David, please. You mean old ladies have been stuck in lavatories longer?'

She smiled. 'Something like that.'

'You're right but Andrew has been very troubled lately. The

Reverend Andrew Callaghan, I should say. He's young and quite narrow in his views. He's had a bit of a bee in his bonnet about the rise in interest in the supernatural and what he regards as Devil worship. So you can see how I'm wondering if his disappearance might somehow link to what happened in our church.'

'You said leave of absence, not holiday. What was that for?'

'He was quite worked up. He needed a break. There had been threats against him. He believed he was in a battle with the forces of evil.'

'And do you believe the same?'

'Whilst not being a proponent of Satanism I am perhaps more ecumenical in my approach.'

'Have you been in touch with his family?'

'He has no family that I'm aware of. He was an orphan.'

'Friends?'

'He was what is often called a loner, although he was a full member of our church community.'

'Do you know where he took his leave of absence?'

'He was unsure of his destination.'

Gilchrist looked at her watch. 'Give me his address and I'll have someone call round.'

'And if he isn't there?'

'We'll have to see,' she said. 'We try to avoid breaking into citizens' houses without due cause.'

There was a silence on the other end of the phone and she wondered if he was thinking Milldean Massacre, the occasion when the police had not only broken into the wrong house but had also shot everybody inside it.

'And you don't think there is due cause,' Rutherford finally said.

'I'm not sure,' Gilchrist answered honestly.

Bob Watts looked again at the inscription in Colin Pearson's book that called his father *mon semblable, mon frère*. *Frère* he knew was brother. He looked up *semblable* in an online French dictionary. It meant 'likeness', possibly 'double'. He didn't have a hard copy of Eliot's *The Waste Land* but he found the text online. Watts had done it in the sixth form and vaguely remembered the poem was based on two books: one about the search for the Holy Grail and the other a multi-volume Victorian tome about ancient fertility rituals and religions.

The French phrase concluded the poem's first section. The lines before 'my double, my brother' were about someone called Stetson planting a corpse in his garden and the poet asking whether it would bloom that year. Rebirth then, but Watts couldn't see what the French phrase had to do with that.

He read on. He came to another French phrase – *Et O ces voix d'enfants, chantant dans la coupole*. An online translation was: 'And O those children's voices, singing in the cupola'. He knew a 'cupola' was a dome, usually of a church. The line was from Symbolist Paul Verlaine's poem *Parsifal*. It occurred when the knight, Parsifal, found the Grail and became its guardian.

Almost at the end of Eliot's poem Watts found another French quote: *Le Prince d'Aquitaine à la tour abolie*. The Prince of Aquitaine in the ruined tower. Wasn't there a ruined tower in the Tarot pack? The line was from a poem by a near-symbolist French poet, Gerard de Nerval.

Watts read to the end of *The Waste Land* and started on Eliot's lengthy notes. He remembered how pretentious he had found these as a teenager. Eliot used quotes in their original languages but without any translations. If you weren't conversant with Italian, French or German you were lost. Watts distinctly remembered wondering if the Notes were Eliot's po-faced joke as they read like parodies – and probably had been much parodied since.

He remembered his mates double-checking the Latin name for a hermit-thrush Eliot quoted in one daft line reference because the Latin name – *Turdus* something – was just too funny to be true for any schoolboy. But it was true.

Now he found that Eliot took 'my double, my brother' from Charles Baudelaire, perhaps the first Symbolist poet. The line was from a poem, *To the Reader*, which acted as the foreword to Baudelaire's controversial 1857 collection: six poems from the collection had been banned in France until 1949.

According to Baudelaire, Satan controlled people's every move.

Baudelaire identified boredom as the worst misery in the world and said that extreme acts he called 'pleasant designs' – 'rape and poison, dagger and burning' – might take a reader who was bold enough out of 'the banal canvas of our pitiable destinies'. Watts wasn't sure if Baudelaire was being serious or tongue in cheek to make a point.

'*Mon semblable, mon frère*' appeared in the final two lines. The bored man was having a drugged dream of going to the gallows for those crimes mentioned earlier and Baudelaire was suggesting he was only thinking what the reader – 'my double, my brother' – was thinking.

On Wikipedia someone had called Baudelaire's attempt to implicate the reader in his own dark imaginings a malediction. Watts had to look the word up. It was a curse, a magical word or phrase uttered with the intention of bringing about evil or destruction.

Watts Googled Baudelaire. He had translated Gothic horror writer Edgar Allan Poe into French. That figured. Fellow drug addict. He had influenced a generation of poets including Arthur Rimbaud, whose first collection of poetry was called *Season in Hell*.

Watts read the translation of the whole poem again. He thought it infantile, written by someone out to shock. He couldn't imagine his father, who had seen death more than once in wartime, would value this kind of poser.

Baudelaire had given the collection the title *Les Fleurs du Mal*. The Flowers of Evil.

'Anything yet on the flower painting?' Gilchrist asked Sylvia Wade.

Wade grinned. 'Just this second, ma'am. We've located the part of the CCTV footage from the museum showing the theft.'

'And?'

'The footage isn't too clear – you can't see features,' Wade said.

Gilchrist peered at the screen. 'Isn't there something we can do with pixels?'

'Not if the picture isn't clear in the first place,' Wade said.

They were looking at a person swathed in waterproofs hurl a brick through the glass case. This person made no attempt to take anything from inside the case. Another camera further up the gallery caught another swaddled figure, taller, take the painting off the wall and walk calmly round the corner. Just before the CCTV lost them, the two of them hoiked the picture out through the emergency exit.

'Show it again,' Gilchrist said to Wade. Then, to no one in particular, 'Can we even determine the gender of these two?'

'I can't,' Wade said.

'Bloody great,' Donaldson said, scowling. 'So what can we analyse?'

Wade clenched her jaw. 'We have pictures of two people, gender indeterminate, faces obscured by rain hoods, stepping close, stepping away. Unhurried.'

'Height?'

'The person who throws the brick appears to be medium height, gender non-specific. The other is taller. That's about it.'

'Aside from the gait,' Heap said.

'Gate?' Donaldson said. 'Is this the one there's no point closing because the horse has already bolted?'

Heap flushed again. 'The way the taller one walked, sir.'

'Gait,' Donaldson said.

'Tell me,' Gilchrist said.

'I believe this person is a woman.'

Donaldson snorted. Gilchrist recognized that Heap's hesitant delivery and his flushed face did not necessarily inspire confidence.

'Why would you think so?' she said, managing to combine an encouraging look at Heap with a fierce stare at Donaldson. She hoped. 'About the woman, I mean.'

'I'm hesitant to be s-sexist,' Heap said, flushing more deeply. 'But it's the way that person walks. It's a woman's ambulation.'

Donaldson gave him a look.

'I've seen you walk that way, Belly,' somebody muttered, loud enough to be heard.

Gilchrist stared into the room. Sylvia Wade was the only other woman. Gilchrist was out of her depth dealing with a bunch of men like this. Nevertheless she gave each person in turn the hard stare. Perhaps her height helped or they were cutting her slack because she was newly promoted. Whatever the reason, they calmed down.

'Or rather,' Heap persevered, 'it's the way a woman walks when trying to walk like a man.'

Gilchrist was trying to be patient. 'In what way?'

How red can a person go? Bellamy Heap looked round the room, his ears pulsating. Gilchrist wanted to give him a hug.

'It's a hip swivel thing, ma'am. Men and women have a different way of walking because of the hip structure. Gay men sometimes imitate women but there's a natural difference. I think this is a woman trying to walk like a man.'

Gilchrist knew what Heap meant. In Brighton that thrust of the hip, that deliberate parody of a man's walk was common among lesbians who wanted to play tough but, for better or worse, weren't the real thing. A bit like Donaldson with his Jack-the-Lad shoulder roll. All for show.

Gilchrist stood. She looked from one to the other of them. 'Thanks Bellamy and Sylvia. So: what were these people up to? Let's tentatively assume, based on her *gait*, that one of them is a woman. Why did she steal the picture?'

'We'll find out when we find her,' Donaldson said.

Gilchrist ignored these words of wisdom. 'Sylvia, you've got even more boring hours ahead of you because I want these people tracked on CCTV from the moment they stepped on to Church Street from the Dome café to wherever home is.'

Sylvia didn't even nod her perfectly coiffed head.

Bob Watts pulled into the narrow car park at the side of the road opposite Saddlescombe Farm just as another car pulled out. He'd driven his father's from London, with the roof up since he'd come through yet another thunderstorm.

For the moment the rain had stopped. He looked across the road at a ram with enormous curled horns rubbing itself against a wooden fence. Beyond it was a wide dewpond stacked with rushes.

To his immediate right there was a steep track leading, he assumed, to the Devil's Dyke. Watts crossed the road. There was a sign for Saddlescombe Organics on the wall. He started walking up a wide, dirt pathway, the overgrown dewpond on his right.

Saddlescombe Farm was more of a hamlet. He could see on a ridge above him a row of eight or nine farm cottages. There was a big house in front of the dewpond at the edge of the farm property and beyond he could see a range of outbuildings. The farmhouse itself was in the middle of the outbuildings.

The National Trust owned the farm and he knew the main farmhouse was tenanted. As far as Watts understood it from the Trust's website, it rented out a working farm here which visitors could access only a couple of times a year although an ancient donkey wheel and a café could be visited at any time.

He wasn't exactly sure where Colin Pearson's home was. He walked slowly up the dirt road between two large barns. The yard for the one on the left had been converted into the café. The barn on the right had information placards from the National Trust about the farm's history.

An old man in a bright yellow sou'wester and hat was sitting at a table outside the café. Watts nodded at him.

'You here for the organic farm or to visit the Witchfinder General?' the man said.

Watts smiled. 'You live here?' he said.

The old man nodded. 'Man and boy,' he said. 'Two houses along from the Witchfinder. You here to talk about the goats?'

'Goats?' Watts said. 'No. Yours?'

The old man shook his head. He indicated a sign pointing towards Newtimber Hill.

'I saw them fall off the hill yesterday. Arse over tit. Up by the giant.'

'Really?'

'Aye – six of them. Probably broke their bloody necks. All had to be put down, I wouldn't be surprised.'

'Aren't goats supposed to be sure-footed?'

The man laughed, scratching under his hat. 'Drunk as buggery they were.'

Watts knew there was a pub on the top of the dyke. He pointed in that direction.

'Regulars?'

The man laughed again. 'They looked possessed to me. Up on their hind legs prancing about like they wanted to be human. I was on the opposite ridge. I watched them get to the edge and just drop off.'

'What's this giant? Another chalk man?'

'Them hippies running the organic farm. Commune, they call themselves. Made it out of wicker. They stuck it up there to burn come Mayday then for some reason didn't.'

'Do you think it frightened the goats?'

The old man leaned forward. 'Bugger that. If you ask me Old Scratch did it.'

'Who's he?'

The man laughed. 'You know him,' he said.

Watts frowned, out of his depth. Again. 'Give me his real name,' he said.

'He has many names. Mr Grimm for one. I'm partial to the Goat of Mendes—'

'Hang on. You're not talking about a person.'

'That's a matter of opinion.'

'You mean the Devil.'

The man gave him an odd look. 'Who did you think I was talking about?'

'You think those goats were possessed by the Devil?'

'This is the Devil's Dyke. You have a better idea?'

Watts smiled. 'Which one is Colin Pearson's house?'

The old man ignored the question. He took off his hat, revealing flattened-down lengths of white hair scraped across his pate.

'You know the history of Devil's Dyke?' he said. 'The Devil dug it as a trench to the sea to drown all the churches in these parts. But he was making such a racket he woke an old woman who lit a candle which woke up a rooster which began to crow, thinking it was dawn. The rooster crowing made the Devil think it was dawn too so he fled, leaving his trench unfinished.'

'Why didn't he finish it the next night?'

The old man cackled. 'Bloody good point,' he said. 'Before he went he threw the last shovelful of earth over his shoulder and it landed in the sea and created the Isle of Wight.'

'That so?' Watts said.

'The Devil is buried at the bottom of the dyke with his wife.'

'His wife?'

'Absolutely. There are barrows there. If you run seven times around them – backwards, whilst holding your breath – the Devil pops up.'

'The wife too?'

'Not that I'm aware of.' The old man pointed up towards a little gathering of outbuildings. 'The Witchfinder's house is up there.'

TWELVE

'A word,' Gilchrist mouthed to Heap. She crooked her finger and Heap followed her into the corridor. He looked wary.

'Ma'am?'

'Actually, two words,' she said. 'Gait and ambulation.'

Heap frowned. 'Ma'am?'

'Bellamy, this bunch will continue to take the piss out of you as long as you talk like that.'

Heap confirmed her worry. He shrugged and said, 'If they're ill-educated ignoramuses, that's not my lookout.'

Gilchrist laughed. 'Do you actually know any small words?'

Heap nodded. 'With respect, ma'am, I know two.' He gave her a surprisingly impish grin. 'Fuck them.'

As Watts opened the garden gate of Colin Pearson's house a striking woman came round the side of the cottage. She was probably in her early sixties, with a trim figure, long, grey/blonde hair tied back and a slash of bright red lipstick on her full lips.

'You must be Mrs Pearson,' Watts said. 'I'm Bob.'

She was carrying a bunch of flowers with their bulbs dangling down. She transferred them to one hand and pulled the gardening glove from the other with her teeth. She had long, strong incisors.

'I'm Avril, Mr Watts. Colin isn't expecting you but I am.'

'Bob, please. But I thought we'd confirmed?'

'No, no – you and I have. What I mean is that for something as mundane as a meeting or an appointment Colin has a memory like a sieve. I've come to accept that he lives in his own intellectual world and day-to-day matters pass him by.'

'But I won't be interrupting . . .?'

'You would be interrupting whenever you came and whatever arrangements had been made – for Colin the world is an interruption.'

Watts smiled. 'Has he always been the same?'

'The only interruptions he ever tolerated were when he wanted to fuck me.' She gave him an intent look. 'And that hasn't changed.'

Watts nodded, avoiding her candid eyes. He gestured at the flowers. 'You grow lilies.'

She frowned at the clumsy change of subject then looked at the flowers in her hand.

'I grow all kinds of things. For the kitchen usually.' She pointed at the bulbs. 'Very good substitute for potato. Good for thickening soups.'

'This weather must have put a damper on your summer crop.'

'I grow most of it in poly-tunnels and my greenhouse. But, yes, perhaps rice would have been a better proposition this year as much of my garden is like a paddy field.'

She half-turned towards the cottage. 'Let me take you to Colin,' she said.

She led the way into a rickety-looking porch, navigating a narrow path between a deep freeze and a teetering pile of abandoned chairs. It led into a room that was equally jumbled. There were old-fashioned records and videos, CDs and DVDs piled floor to ceiling on every wall. In the centre of the room more chairs and three sofas and a big old TV were crammed together. A parrot eyed him from a perch in an ancient birdcage on a stand by the window. The cage door was open. Bird shit was piled on newspaper laid out on the carpet beneath the cage.

Watts followed Avril into the kitchen. The clutter was absolute. Piles of washed-up pots on the drying board. Crockery and cans and bottles and cutlery piled on the one narrow work surface. There were no cupboards so every available surface was being used for storage. On a table in the middle of the room, more flowers and bulbs and vegetables from her garden. Watts assumed they were vegetables: he didn't recognize any of the gnarled and twisted roots.

She looked back and seemed surprised he was following her. 'I must get on. He's in the other room.'

Feeling dismissed, Watts walked back through the crowded room and poked his head into the next one. More of the same clutter and in the middle of it, lying legs apart and scratching his balls in a reclining armchair, was Colin Pearson, seventy-year-old intellectual.

He was swigging a large glass of red wine. The bottle was on a table beside his chair next to a remote for a giant TV that was on but with the sound off. He was listening to music from an ancient record player. Watts thought he recognized Miles Davis – *Miles Ahead*? Pearson probably couldn't hear it because he was wearing on his head, covering his ears, what at first sight looked like a giant cotton tea cosy with a tube coming out of the side. It was plugged into the mains and the contraption was making a racket like a vacuum cleaner.

Pearson looked across at the doorway and bellowed: 'If you're from that fucking cock next door tell him it's not my wife's fault if his goats strayed into her vegetable patch. Frankly, if they eat stuff that doesn't belong to them without first checking out what it is, that's their fucking lookout.'

Sarah Gilchrist was looking up at a four-storey Georgian house. It was on a corner just off Seven Dials. She'd decided to visit vicar Andrew Callaghan's home herself as she felt the need to get out of the office.

There was an old-fashioned bell pull inside the tiled porch with a neatly typed note behind cellophane saying: 'Not working but antique – Please Do Not Pull'. Instead she used the knocker in the shape of a lion's head on the old green door. She heard it echo down the corridor beyond but no sign of movement in the house. She rapped again. Still nothing. To her right, beyond a short railing, there was a narrow basement yard. On the railing was a hand-painted wooden sign saying Basement Flat with an arrow pointing down.

She went back out into the street and down a steep, worn set of steps. The door to the basement was underneath the steps into the house above. She rang the bell. Whilst waiting for an answer she peered in through the window but dark drapes blocked her view. No answer to the bell. There was a small nameplate beside the bell with 'Andrew Callaghan' printed in neat script.

As she turned away from the door something dropped in front of her from the street above. Involuntarily, she reared back. The object hit the floor and exploded.

Watts sorted out with Pearson who he was. Pearson accepted his presence without question. He turned back to the TV screen. Watts recognized images from *The Wicker Man* flickering across it.

'Turn that music down, will you?' Pearson said. 'You'll have to put up with the hairdryer for another ten minutes.'

'A hairdryer?' Watts said, indicating the tea cosy on Pearson's head.

'Of course. Portable. Had it forty years and it's never needed repairing.' He lowered his voice as Watts lowered the volume on the music. 'What – did you think I was some mad scientist trying to enhance his brain power or send telepathic messages? You wouldn't be the first fuck to think that about me. Or write it either.'

Watts grinned sheepishly. That's exactly what he'd been thinking, although Pearson also looked like some peculiar pasha lying there so indolently.

'Want a glass of Beaujolais?' Pearson said. He waved at a table covered in piles of papers. 'Should be a glass over there.'

There were three or four. Watts chose the least dirty, gave

it a surreptitious wipe with a tissue from his pocket and took it over to Pearson.

'Help yourself,' Pearson said, his eyes glued to the screen. 'Great tits, that Ingrid Pitt.'

Watts glanced up at the screen to see the actress sitting naked in a bathtub when Edward Woodward as the policeman burst in on her.

'She does indeed,' he said, taking his glass over to the least lopsided-looking armchair and sitting carefully down in it. 'Funny you should be watching this . . .'

'No, it's not,' Pearson broke in. 'I know what you're going to say but the Wicker Man on the beach in Brighton *is* the reason I'm watching it. That and the one up the hill here. Always got to be sure you get your reasoning the right way round. That's the trouble with half those fucking plonks these days. Can't reason their way out of a paper bag.'

'Which particular fucking plonks?'

'Philosophers. So-called. Thinkers? I've shat 'em.'

Watts could think of nothing to say to that. 'I'm here because you knew my father, Donald Watts.'

'I knew him as Victor Tempest, yes.'

'How did you know him?'

'It must be twenty years since I last saw him. I remember your father had a great intellectual curiosity . . .'

'He did,' Watts said. 'What did you talk about?'

Pearson gave him a look. '. . . However, if I may be blunt, he lacked the intellect required to make anything of what he learned. But at least he was open-minded about things. He was interested in peak experiences.'

'What are they?'

'The crux of my endeavours. Maslow came up with the term. You know his work?'

'His hierarchy of needs. That's about it.'

Pearson nodded. 'This is something else. Maslow didn't believe his peak experiences could be recreated at will. I do. Those moments when you reach a completeness. Athletes operating in what is known as The Zone experience it. Sex addicts go in frustrated search of it through orgasm.'

'That sounds like my father.'

Pearson gave him an odd look. 'Is that so? I mostly recall he quoted Camus at me constantly.'

Me too when I was young, Watts thought. His father's favourite paraphrase of Camus – which Watts was surprised he hadn't used when his son had lost his job – was 'freedom is what you do with the hand you've been dealt'.

'I'm assuming he knew Camus,' Watts said now. 'There are signed copies of his books, as there are of yours.'

'He met Camus several times. But, I believe, conversation never went much beyond football. I'm too young to have met Albert, alas. Your father's fondness for Camus' philosophy came down to the fact that the goalkeeper was trying to provide something that worked for the common man in the modern world. I've always been trying to give wider significance to experiences that, in his view, would always be abnormal – never the norm for the common man. Well, of course, I don't give a fig for the common man. My interest is in the uncommon one.'

Avril walked into the room balancing trays of open smoked salmon sandwiches in each hand. She handed one to Pearson and the other to Watts. She returned a moment later with her own tray and sat down in the chair beside Pearson. The parrot was perched on her shoulder.

Gilchrist looked down at her trousers covered in shit from the exploding bag. She cursed, partly because she'd only just bought her trouser suit, partly because the mess was disgusting and partly because her disgust had slowed her responses. By the time she had got back up on to the street whoever had tossed it down at her had disappeared.

Holding down bile, she returned to the front door of the basement flat. She rang the bell again. No answer. She looked at the shit-smeared trousers of her new outfit. She'd be binning them.

She examined the locks: a Yale and a Chubb. She pushed against the top and then the bottom of the door. Bolted. She went back up on to the street and round the corner to the side of the house. There was a low wall and, about three feet below it, a garden. The garden stopped a few yards before the house and dropped away to a basement yard.

Gilchrist lowered herself into the garden and sank into mud. She squelched over to the fence that separated it from the yard and climbed over it, lowering herself into the yard. The drapes were closed on the rear windows and a blind was down over the glass of the back door. This door had only a Yale lock. Gilchrist rooted in her purse for her gym's plastic membership card. She slid it between door and its frame beside the lock then rammed her shoulder against the door. It popped open, momentarily unbalancing her.

Regaining her balance, she grinned. She'd always known about the plastic card trick but had never actually tried it before. She pushed the door fully open and stepped inside.

Pearson took a big bite of a sandwich and a glug of his wine and said, his mouth full: 'What I'm interested in, Watts, are those glimpses of the bigger reality. We get it sometimes and it makes life worth living. But how do we prolong that?'

Pearson took another glug.

'Human consciousness operates at too low a pressure. If consciousness could be made to work properly man would learn to use various powers and faculties that are perfectly natural to us but are at present "occult". Remember that "occult" doesn't mean anything magical, it simply means latent or hidden.'

'And how do you make consciousness work properly?' Watts said.

'That's what magi down the centuries have tried to discover. It has already happened naturally two or three times in our history. Do you know Julian Jayne's book *The Origin of Consciousness in the Breakdown of the Bicameral Mind*?'

'I missed that one,' Watts said through his own mouthful of smoked salmon.

'I've used it as the basis for a couple of my novels. It posits, among other things, that there was a time when we had two brains operating independently – you're aware of discussion of left brain and right brain?'

'I've heard something about it.'

'In biblical times, when prophets or warriors heard the voice of God commanding them it was actually their left brain talking to them, although they didn't realize that. They thought these voices were from outside them. As the brains fused these left brain commands became our consciences. By then the damage had been done in terms of establishing a belief in the existence of God or gods.'

'You don't believe in a God?'

'I believe in the perfectibility of man.'

'All men?'

'Don't be stupid. Which is why communism failed – and why, incidentally, everything else that ignores the existence of greed will fail.'

At that point the parrot raised its tail and shat down Avril's blouse. She ignored it and carried on eating.

'But everyone would be uncommon if they could access this full consciousness,' Watts said.

Pearson was gulping down his food like a starving man. His mouth full again he said: 'Could be, but won't be because not everybody will be capable of accessing it – or have the inclination to do so.'

Pearson emptied the last of the wine into his glass. He waggled the bottle at his wife.

'We're going to need another.'

The flat stank. If Gilchrist didn't throw up by the end of the evening she'd be impressed with herself. The flat also seemed to have been turned into a fortress. The front door was barricaded with furniture. A bar to fit across the inside of the back door was leaning against a wall in the kitchen. The walls were covered with blue-tacked pieces of paper with quotes from the Bible.

The bedroom was bare of any furniture. On the exposed wooden floor a pentacle had been drawn in chalk. At the tip of each point there was a glass bowl containing some blobby silver material and some kind of white crystals. There was a jug of water and a mat in the middle of the pentacle.

The Lord's Prayer and the psalm about walking through the valley of the shadow of death but fearing no evil were handwritten on opposite walls.

Someone had spray-painted across them in red: Lucifer Has Risen. The walls in the sitting room were smeared with shit.

Gilchrist looked into the bathroom last, nervously because she was convinced she'd find the vicar dead in a bath of his own blood. She pushed the door open, took a deep breath and walked in. It was empty.

There was no sign of Andrew Callaghan anywhere in the flat.

She pondered what to do. She didn't know for sure that a crime had been committed. However, the state of the flat certainly suggested something was amiss. She called for scenes of crime, then Bilson. She mentioned the shit on the walls. She started to tell Bilson about the shit that had been dropped on her when he interrupted.

'Does the faeces on the wall look like it has been smeared pretty recently?'

'Well, I'm not looking too closely but I don't think so.' She looked down at her leg. 'I do have some on my leg that fits that bill, however.'

'I'm sorry to hear that. Stress can exhibit in unpleasant ways. But you can get good pads these days, you know.'

'Fuck off, you patronizing bastard.'

He chuckled. 'If you believe it's from the same person get a sample from the wall and another from your leg into plastic bags straight away.'

'Why?'

'That's beyond your pay grade, Sarah, but it's amazing where you can get DNA from these days.'

Feeling a bit of a wuss Gilchrist put a wodge of tissues over her nose and mouth and peered closely at the shit on the wall. It didn't look particularly fresh. She went into the kitchen and got a couple of spoons from the cutlery drawer. Five minutes later she had the faeces in two separate evidence bags and the spoons in two others.

Pearson gazed fondly – lasciviously – at his wife. 'First time I saw Avril was at a party for the launch of *Sergeant Pepper*. All the life-size cardboard cut-outs Peter Blake had done for the cover were around the room. I was arguing with that cunt

Ronnie Laing about something or other. Ronnie was always an argumentative bugger but when he'd got a few Scotches inside him – which was most of the time – he'd argue about the colour of shite.

'We both had bestselling books out that year. We were the two big-name thinkers in the room – except he didn't know how to think. All that anti-psychiatry garbage. Therapy was just an excuse for him to shag all his patients.

'Anyway, we were arguing, standing on either side of the cardboard cut-out of Aleister Crowley. And it was turning into a Morecambe and Wise sketch because we kept turning to Aleister to ask his opinion. We thought we were hilarious and we both knew this beautiful dolly bird, sitting on a white sofa nearby, her short dress virtually up to her waist, was watching and laughing.

'She had great tits and these great legs and we had a bet on what colour her knickers were but we couldn't quite see them. Then, as if guessing what we were up to she stood up and bent across the table for a cigarette lighter, showing us her lovely arse under the dress. And she wasn't wearing any.'

Avril's unwavering gaze was on Watts as Pearson told his story. 'They were flesh-coloured,' she said quietly.

Pearson didn't hear. 'I said to Ronnie: "I've got to fuck that." "Me first," he said, but I pushed him into Aleister Crowley. The two of them fell over and one of the security blokes came over, most concerned that Mr Blake's artwork might be damaged. By then I was leading Avril into the cloakroom.'

He threw her what was intended to be a loving look but was definitely lascivious. Her eyes didn't leave Watts as she said: 'That's right, Colin. You got to fuck *that* and you've been fucking it ever since.'

Watts looked down at his salmon. Way too much information.

THIRTEEN

I t was dark by the time the scenes of crime officers arrived. Bilson arrived moments after. Gilchrist dangled the plastic bags at arm's length. Bilson took them in passing as he headed into the flat.

'And?' Gilchrist said.

'Valuable evidence in a piece of shit. The fresher the better, but it all tells a story. The perpetrator has virtually signed his or her name. One test I can do right now. Total long shot but we've got nothing to lose.'

He went off into the kitchen. Gilchrist followed. Bilson took a card from his bag and a couple of phials.

'What was all that black magic stuff on the walls?' he said.

'I dread to think,' Gilchrist said. 'Especially as the tenant of the flat is a vicar.'

'Where is he?'

'Missing.'

'So what crime is this the scene of?'

'Maybe abduction. How are you getting on with DNA on the Wicker Man remains?'

Bilson gave her a look. 'You think it's this vicar?'

'It's crossed my mind. The victim cried out to God asking why he'd been forsaken.' Gilchrist gestured round the flat. 'Looks like this vicar felt pretty forsaken.'

'Two sides of the same coin,' Bilson said. He saw Gilchrist frown and gestured towards Lucifer Has Risen.

'God and the Devil. If you believe in one, you've got to believe in the other.'

'So I understand,' Gilchrist murmured.

Bilson took a wooden spatula and spread some of the faecal matter on the card. Using a dropper he applied two drops of clear liquid to the sample.

'This is going to freak you,' Bilson said.

Gilchrist took a step back. 'Is it going to explode or something? I've already had shit on my legs once today.'

'Ha,' Bilson said as the liquid around the sample changed colour. 'I meant the name of this test will freak you.'

'Because?'

'Because it's called the faecal occult blood test.' He glanced over and grinned. 'Spooky, eh?'

'Spooky.'

'But occult just means hidden or concealed.'

Gilchrist nodded, looking down at the colour change on the sample. 'What's going on here?'

'What's going on here is that I'm virtually doing your job for you.'

'Thanks. Which sample is this?'

'The one that was dropped on you.' He looked at her again. 'Thanks? That's it? Your acting status is about to become permanent and I get a throwaway thanks.'

'What do you want?'

She saw his leer.

'In your dreams.'

He leaned towards her and lowered his voice. 'You already are.'

'*Doctor* Bilson – tell me more about this test.'

'Well, well,' he said. 'There is a God.'

'Don't you start. This test.'

'It's looking for hidden blood. Indicates colorectal cancer. And we have a hit. Your perpetrator may have cancer. Or not.'

'What do you mean "or not"? You're giving with one hand and taking away with the other.'

'What better definition of life could you ask for?'

'I'm not asking for any definition of life – that is definitely above my pay grade. I'm asking for help solving a possible crime.'

'Colorectal cancer can definitively be indicated by blood in the stool – but not all blood in the stool is there because of colorectal cancer.' Bilson ticked off his fingers as he spoke. 'Anal fissures, colon polyps, peptic ulcers, ulcerative colitis, Crohn's disease . . .' He waggled the little finger of his other hand. 'Or aspirin causing a stomach haemorrhage. All these cause blood in the stool. I'll know more when I get back to the lab.'

'Well, we're in Brighton. Couldn't it just be haemorrhoids from anal sex?'

'No, this is hidden blood – haemorrhoidal blood stays on the outside. This is blood you can't find with the naked eye. Hence occult.'

'You can get DNA from this too?'

'Sure. Bog-standard stool test – so to speak. And if there's abnormal DNA from cancer or polyp cells we'll know it.'

He opened the second bag of excrement. Gilchrist looked at Lucifer Has Risen scrawled across the wall.

'Let's see if we get the same result from this,' Bilson said.

Gilchrist was trying not to breathe.

'Bingo,' Bilson said, waving the spatula in front of her. 'Same result so the two samples probably came from the same intestine.'

'Thanks, Bilson. And we need DNA from the flat to see if it matches the DNA from the burn victim.'

He nodded.

'Have you seen those little bowls in the other room?' Gilchrist said. 'You wouldn't happen to know what's in them?'

'No, but I can find out. This guy was seriously scared if he was doing the whole pentacle thing.'

'You know what it means?'

'It means he was bonkers.'

'But you know about a pentacle like that?'

'It's a refuge. If he stays inside it, the Devil or his minions can't get at him – they can't cross the threshold of it.'

Gilchrist frowned. 'You're into this stuff?'

Bilson shook his head. 'I'm into the theatre. I saw the pre-West End touring production of Dennis Wheatley's *The Devil Rides Out* when it came through town last month. The big set piece is when the heroes take refuge inside a pentacle whilst the Aleister Crowley figure sends all kinds of horrors at them. The lighting effects were first rate.'

'You constantly surprise me, Bilson,' Gilchrist said.

He leered again. 'Just give me half a chance.'

That night, the Goat of Mendes crept up on Brighton. Yard by yard, its shadow made slow, deliberate progress across the town. It stood on the rim of the Devil's Dyke, arms outstretched, the sinking sun behind it, a low bank of clouds lying before it. It had the body of a man and the head and horns of a gigantic goat. It cast its shadow over Brighton and the sea beyond. Those who saw it fall upon them feared it. Those who didn't see it would learn to fear it.

As the second bottle was drained, words tumbled out of Colin Pearson. He paused only for Avril to wheel the hairdryer away into a corner.

'I'm very angry about Schopenhauer and Sartre because they so nearly got it but they stopped short. I am an existentialist. I do believe – as Sartre believed – that the world is a meaningless place. But for me that means we have to navigate it with our perceptions focused. And that is quite possible. Husserl taught us perception is intentional. You can hurl it like a javelin.'

His wife sat placidly looking at the television screen. Edward Woodward's painful demise was growing ever closer, though in mime as the volume was still turned down.

At around eight thirty, Watts gave up on the idea of asking the questions he had come for answers to. He decided to leave and hope to come back another day. Woodward had long ago been burned to a cinder.

Pearson got up and excused himself to go to the toilet. As he left the room he called back: 'I could have been a guru but it would have taken time away from what I want to do.'

Watts looked over at Avril, who was reading a gardening magazine, the parrot still on her shoulder.

'I'd better make a move,' he said.

'He'll expect you to stay,' she said without looking up.

'What time does he normally go to bed?' Watts said.

'He's gone,' she said. She glanced up and saw Watts' look of surprise. 'We're not big on social niceties. He'll want to talk to you in the morning.'

'You mean *stay* stay?'

'There's a guest chalet in the back garden. It's got everything you'll need. We're early risers in the summer and he'll be impatient to start work so if you could aim to come in for breakfast by seven he'd appreciate it. He'll want to show you around. And talk, of course.'

Watts didn't want to stay but nor could he think of an immediate excuse. He stood.

'Well, you probably want to get to bed too.'

She put her magazine down. 'I'll take you to the chalet.'

The parrot hopped off her shoulder when she stood. It perched on the back of her chair, its baleful eye on Watts as she led him into the kitchen. She picked up a screw-topped bottle of red and handed it to him with a glass.

'In case you need a nightcap.'

'I'll be fine, I'm sure.'

She shrugged. 'Then bring it back in the morning.'

They went out into the back garden. At intervals there were half-a-dozen garden sheds and a couple of bigger chalet-style sheds each with a small veranda.

'He keeps books in the sheds,' she said, stopping at the nearest chalet. It started to rain as she opened the door and stood aside to let him step in. She followed him inside and turned on a garish fluorescent light. She looked up at him. 'Would you like me to suck your cock?'

He thought at first he'd misheard. Her face was still wearing that same placid expression. He glanced at the long dribble of yellow bird shit encrusted on her blouse.

'That's kind of you,' he finally said, conscious of the ludicrousness of his remark.

'I'm very good,' she said matter-of-factly.

'I'm sure . . .'

She scrutinized his face then turned and opened the door. 'Breakfast at seven,' she said without turning, closing the door behind her. Watts stared at it. He was bewildered by the oddness of the whole evening but Avril's offer had capped it. There had been no coyness or seductive tone in her voice. No lust. It had been as matter-of-fact as if she'd been asking if he needed a towel. She had seemed indifferent to his response.

He turned and examined the chalet. Aside from a vase of lilies by the bed, the cloying scent of the flowers filling the room, it was a mess. Watts wasn't particularly house-proud but even he recognized filth when he saw it. The floor was covered in crumbs. He opened a cupboard. It was full of filthy crockery. The reading lamp was a small strip of fluorescent tubing above the bed. Garden chairs and a barbecue had been haphazardly tossed into a corner.

Everything looked bodged. He pulled the duvet off the bed. There were crumbs and other unidentifiable things down the bottom. He touched the mattress. It was cold and damp.

He'd been in the army and was used to roughing it but even so he contemplated sneaking to his car, driving to the nearest hotel and coming back at the crack of dawn.

He went to the door and looked out at the hard rain now falling through the blackness. He went back inside the chalet.

FOURTEEN

'Another day, another spooky happening in Brighton. Simon here. Last night, as many of you will have seen, the Devil cast his giant shadow over the city and far out to sea. I know, I know, but Simon is just paid to read this stuff. Blame my producer Kate – she wrote it. Actually, Simon didn't see the shadow and he's truly cheesed off – it's not as if he was doing anything more interesting. No offence, Phil, if you're tuned in. And if you're not – why not?

'Anyways, a giant man with the head of a goat cast a shadow some ten miles long – that's my kind of guy – from somewhere on the Devil's Dyke – naturally – over the city and out to sea. Kate, I have to say I'm finding this hard to comprehend but I know we've had lots of calls from people who saw it. People who are freaking out, quite frankly. Calm down, madam. Oh, except I'm freaking out too so carry on.'

'Let me help you here, Simon,' Kate said. 'In certain atmospheric conditions this phenomenon is quite common.'

'A man with the head of a goat casting an enormous shadow over the city is common? We have *got* to do something about the licensing hours here.'

Kate laughed. 'The phenomenon is common. If someone is standing at a high point with a low sun behind them and clouds below them they cast an exaggerated shadow in front of them. The original is the Brocken Spectre. Those who know what that is perhaps weren't too alarmed. Those who don't were probably pretty spooked.'

'That figures. Men are always bragging they're ten miles long but rarely are. But, producer-mine, gotta ask: what's the Brocken Spectre?'

'It occurs in the high mountain areas of Brocken, Germany. Oddly enough where witches in the Middle Ages used to hold their sabbats on Walpurgis Night – coming up any night now at a spooky place near you.'

'But here it was the shadow of a giant man with the head of a horned goat thrown on to a bank of clouds over the city.'

'That's right. One legend about the creation of the dyke is that the Devil was in the form of a giant goat when he made it. He was intending to crush the surrounding area. He smelled the tang of salt water in the wind and worried his coat would get damp and spoiled so he ran off, leaving nothing but the hoof-print we now call Devil's Dyke.'

'Or Big Wuss's Dyke as I now call it. Running off because of a bit of damp.'

'Last night's goat was making a hieratic gesture.'

'Filthy beast. What's one of those when it's at home? As I boringly was.'

'Arms outstretched.'

'You could have just said that, Kate. No need to rub my nose in your university education.'

'You need to be kept in constant check, Simon.'

'Probably right. Was it some kind of video installation?'

'I don't think there's the technology to do that.'

Simon laughed. 'These days there's the technology to do anything.'

Bob Watts had a restless night. There were no curtains in the chalet and lightning flashed, thunder rolled. Rain hammered on the roof and against the windows and the wind gusted so strongly the hut trembled on its foundations.

When he did sleep he had vivid, lascivious dreams. They muddled Pearson's wife with the mystery woman who had come to his parents' house to see his father so many years before.

At one point in the night, when he didn't know for certain whether he was asleep or awake, a lurid flash of lightning lit up Avril, kneeling between his legs, head bobbing. Then she threw back her head, baring those long, vulpine incisors. He struggled to come to consciousness and at the next flash of lightning she was gone.

When he woke in the morning he still remembered the dream vividly. So vividly, he wondered if it had been a dream at all. He thought to check himself but felt ridiculous.

The scent of the lilies was even more cloying than the night before.

'Avril's working on her vegetables,' Pearson said when Watts walked into the sitting room. Pearson was eating toast and jam on a tray. He waved a buttery knife at the big pot of coffee on the table.

'Coffee there, muesli and fruit on your tray. If you want toast you'll have to make it yourself.'

Pearson was listening to the *Today* programme on a modern-looking radio. When Watts tried to ask a question, Pearson shushed him. 'Not over breakfast, old man. After.'

But after breakfast Pearson wanted to show Watts round what he called 'the estate'.

'Must be pretty unique,' Watts said.

'There's no such thing as pretty unique. Unique or not unique.'

They walked out of the cottage garden past a duck pond and between old buildings. There was a blacksmith's forge, pens for pigs, a dairy.

They stopped in front of a tall, relatively narrow wooden structure housing the famous, 400-year-old donkey wheel. There was an ancient bucket on the ground in front of it. Behind the wheel was the well. The donkey used to draw water from it in the bucket by using the wheel as a treadmill. Now the well had a padlocked wooden cover on it.

'Still used?' Watts said.

'We're on the mains,' Pearson said absently, looking up at the Wicker Man planted on the horizon.

'Lovely spot,' Watts said.

'I'm indifferent to nature,' Pearson said. 'I walk along the dyke and never see where I am. There are traces of Roman and Saxon habitation around here apparently. Doesn't interest me.'

'And the Templars?'

Pearson gave him an odd look.

'You know about them? The National Trust owns the farm and the land around it. They mention the Templars because they figure after Dan Brown it has a magical effect on people. If they could somehow attach Harry Potter too, they'd be even happier.'

He gestured with his thumb at the wheel.

'This is the only bit of the Templar tenure that has survived.'

'The donkey wheel?'

'Not this one, though they would have used something similar. But, no, I mean the well itself. They cut a shaft through flint and chalk for a hundred and fifty feet to get to the water table. Now that shows something about strength of character.'

'Although I doubt they did it themselves. Some poor peasants would have done the hard graft.'

Pearson grinned. 'I'm sure you're right.' He looked back up at the Wicker Man. 'When we lived at Burling Gap that Harry Potter writer used to come down, you know. Descend from the sky right on the cliff top.'

Watts suspected a gag. 'On a broomstick, you mean?'

Pearson looked at him oddly. 'Of course not. She's an author, not a witch. In a bloody helicopter.'

Watts was no wiser. 'Why?'

'Speed? Privacy? Because the publisher could afford it?'

'I mean: why was she coming there?'

'Her publisher's summer party. The main man had a cottage over there. Big summer parties. She came with that English Patient fellow.'

'You were there as an author?'

'My stuff is a bit below the salt for that sort of gathering.

Plus I avoid publishers like the plague. Cheapskate profiteering bastards.'

'Your books sell well though.'

'I have a small, dedicated following. Some readers really get me. Most are cranks, frankly. You should witness one of my book signings, Watts, if you want to see all the world's eccentricities gathered in one place.'

When Sarah Gilchrist arrived at the office, Donaldson, Heap and Sylvia Wade were already there.

Bellamy Heap came over to her and shifted his feet.

'Are you going to swear at me again, Constable?' Gilchrist said.

'With respect, ma'am, I wasn't swearing at you.'

'Call me Sarah, Constable.'

'Yes, ma'am.'

Gilchrist looked at him. 'What is it?'

'We've tracked the picture thieves through the streets on CCTV. We can follow them up past the clock tower but then we lose them. They go into the Imperial Arcade and don't come out.'

The Imperial Arcade was a once-glamorous Art Deco arcade with flats above it on the seaward side. The Churchill Square shopping centre had been built opposite, presumably totally blocking what in the twenties would have been a privileged view down to and over the sea.

'Don't ever come out?'

'Not in the next six hours.'

Gilchrist thought for a moment. 'Then maybe we haven't lost them; maybe we've found them. They live in one of those apartments in the front or maybe work in one of the shops. Do we now have a clearer image of them?'

Heap shook his head. 'They were savvy about the cameras. They kept their heads down.'

'No face shots at all?'

'I'm afraid not. S-Sarah.'

Gilchrist looked at him for a moment. 'No, you're right.'

'About what, Sarah?'

'About calling me ma'am. Stay with that.'

'Yes, Sarah. Ma'am.'

Donaldson and Sylvia Wade joined them.

'Knowing how busy Constable Heap here was,' Donaldson said, 'Sylvia and I have been finding out about Duck or Fuck or whatever she's called.'

'Gluck, Detective Sergeant,' Gilchrist said, unamused.

'Yes,' Wade said. 'Or rather Gluckstein – her real name.'

'And?'

'Lesbo artist,' Donaldson said. 'Usual fuck-up. Big exhibitionist.'

'DS Donaldson,' Gilchrist said, giving him her hardest stare. She knew it didn't count for much but she was trying. He played along.

'Sorry. Forgot we were in Lesbo-land.'

'Meaning?'

'We're in an equal opportunities country. Ma'am.'

'That we are and that we should be,' Gilchrist said. 'And just as well you remember it.'

'Ma'am,' Donaldson said. 'Gluckstein was a spoiled little rich girl with a private income. Her uncle set up the Lyons teashop chain. Didn't have to work. Called herself a painter but in any other field of endeavour would be – what are they called, Belly?'

'Dilettantes?' Heap said.

'That'll do. She faffed around on her paintings for ages, doing little bits when she felt like it, lazing around when she didn't.'

'Insisted on just being called Gluck,' Sylvia said. 'I mean just the one name. Once resigned from some art committee which had called her Miss Gluck on a letterhead. Loved to startle people by dressing as a man. She went to the best fashion designers to have her clothes tailored but had a tin ear as far as that awful name was concerned.'

'A poser in Brighton, eh?' Gilchrist said.

Cheap shot. She knew when she said it she'd get the laughter that followed.

'She was into Devil worship?' Gilchrist continued.

'Not that we know of,' Wade said. 'She lived in Steyning for the second half of her life with her lover and her lover's sister.'

'Yeah, Devil worship and Steyning don't quite go together, I agree.'

'I didn't mean that, ma'am.'

'What's the meaning of *The Devil's Altar*?'

'We're still trying to determine what it means,' Wade said. 'She painted lots of flowers in the thirties under the influence of another lover, a woman called Constance Spry.'

'Constance Spry?' Gilchrist said.

'You knew her?' Donaldson said.

'I'm not that old. But she's one of those names like Elizabeth David or Cecil Beaton—'

Heap coughed. Gilchrist glanced at him.

'I think you might mean Mrs Beeton.'

'Right,' Gilchrist said. 'Thank you, Bellamy.'

'Fanny Craddock?' Donaldson said.

'No, not her,' Gilchrist said. 'Too vulgar. But, you know, my grandmother's generation – these people were who they referenced.'

'Middle-class grand-mums,' Heap said, but not critically. Even so, Gilchrist flushed.

'Constance Spry was a *flower arranger*,' Donaldson said, in the bewildered voice of someone who'd only ever bought flowers on garage forecourts. 'Cook. Married twice.'

Heap looked up at that. Gilchrist caught the look.

'Means nothing,' she said. 'Most husbands didn't know how to satisfy their wives back then. Certainly wouldn't think of doing some of the stuff women do with each other.'

'Women do with each other?' Donaldson said. 'That might need some clarification.'

Everyone but Donaldson flushed. He clearly relished the moment. 'Anyway,' he continued. 'According to Wikipedia, Gluck had a thing with her close friend Constance Spry in the thirties.'

'There's a biography of Gluck,' Heap said. 'I've ordered it online. Maybe that will explain *The Devil's Altar* title.'

Gilchrist shook her head. 'Let's save time and just ask the biographer.'

FIFTEEN

Pearson showed Watts around his cottage. Everything about it was chaotic. Pearson just wasn't interested in his surroundings. It was clear he actually wanted to show Watts not the house but the books, music and films in it.

Watts wondered if it was so that he could say: *how can people ridicule me when I know so much?* For being ridiculed was his main topic of conversation.

'Those fucking reviewers. I used to be able to quote them off by heart but then I thought: what's the point?' He wagged a finger. 'I've been hurt. Those things get seared into your mind. But now? Fuck them. They don't affect me.'

He was saying this as they were standing in one of the two tiny bedrooms.

'These are the kids' bedrooms. All flown the coop now, of course.' He indicated the books. 'So I use them as library space.'

Watts looked at the unmade bed in the corner but said nothing. It had probably been like that for a couple of years. There were books everywhere, as there had been in each of the rooms. Books on shelves, books in piles.

'How many children have you got?' Watts said.

Pearson seemed to hesitate for a moment before he said: 'Two.'

Watts didn't imagine such a solipsistic man would be a very good father. But who was he to talk?

Pearson led the way down into the basement. 'My work room,' he said.

More chaos. Books on every wall, a table inside the door piled with books, then a chaise longue covered with layers of open books.

His computer, an antique by modern standards, was on a stand next to a giant printer behind which, very low, was a reclining chair with a loose cover and cushions on it.

'That's where I do my thinking,' he said.

Watts clasped his hands. 'Could we talk about my father?'

'Come and look at the sheds first.'

Pearson led the way out into the back garden. 'Sleep well?' he called back over his shoulder.

'Fine, despite the storm.'

'No bad dreams, I hope.'

Watts looked at Pearson's back. What was that question about?

'I never remember dreams,' he said.

Pearson stopped and turned, a big smile on his face. He had strong teeth, like his wife. 'Dreams are the Royal Road to the unconscious, according to Freud. One of the few intelligent things he wrote.'

He pulled open the door of a shed the size of a small branch library.

'Keep all my magazines in here. I never throw anything away. Books or magazines.'

He led the way from one shed to the next, flinging open each door to reveal shelf after shelf of books. Watts was getting increasingly impatient but even so was intrigued when Pearson headed towards the second chalet then suddenly veered away.

'Let's go back to the house,' Pearson said.

'What about that chalet?'

'Just more books. We used to store a boat in there but we got rid of it.'

'You are a bit landlocked,' Watts said with a smile.

Pearson pointed at the track leading to Newtimber Hill and the Wicker Man.

'You can see the sea and the tall buildings of Brighton from there.' Pearson turned. 'Anyway, Watts, time to look at your father's books.'

Back in Pearson's living room Watts passed him the copy of *Magic*.

'I earned a hundred thousand pounds for this,' Pearson said. 'Bloody good money in those days. I spent it all on books and vintage wines. And countless CDs to add to my already vast vinyl collection.'

'You know it's still in print,' Watts said.

'I know I still get royalties.'

'I wondered if you could explain the inscription to my father.'

Pearson turned to the title page. Frowned at his own handwriting. He rested the book on his knee and looked up at the ceiling. 'From *The Waste Land*,' Pearson said.

'And Baudelaire.'

Pearson gave him a quick look and nodded. '*Les Fleurs du Mal*.'

'I can't imagine my father reading Baudelaire. There was no poetry at all on his shelves.'

'Baudelaire was one of us, in his chaotic way.'

'One of us?'

Pearson spread his hands in front of him and examined them. 'A man who wanted to escape from the banality of life through more vivid experiences. Your father was like that too.' He pointed at the inscription. 'That's all I meant by it.'

'Were you and my father close?'

Pearson thought for a moment. Watts was expecting some profound answer. Instead, Pearson seemed to change the subject totally.

'You know my first book – *Outsider Looking Out* – was assured of success when it got two cracking reviews on the same Sunday by two leading reviewers. Well, the two cunts who praised me to the skies then spent the next ten years trying to bury me. Until this came along.'

He looked down and tapped the book. 'Long, thoughtful reviews from the pair of them.'

'Great you got intelligent analysis.'

'Fuck that. Praise that could be used in newspaper adverts and on the back of the paperback editions.' He shook his head. 'They were still a pair of cunts. Next time I saw them they cut me dead.'

'Were you and my father close?'

Pearson pulled on his lower lip. 'In a manner of speaking.'

'What manner? Were you engaged in some esoteric exploration together?'

Pearson bared his strong teeth again. 'In a manner of speaking.'

Watts was clearly not going to get any more out of him.

'Aleister Crowley called my father *magister* in his inscription to *Moonchild*.'

Pearson cocked his head. 'You've got a copy of *Moonchild*?'

Watts nodded. 'In good nick too, I'm told. Perfect dust jacket.'

'Crowley was here at Saddlescombe in the twenties and again in the forties. In the main farmhouse. In 1942, the Germans tried to kill him by bombing the farm.'

Watts frowned. 'Why would they do that?'

'They were frightened of his power. He was fighting them on the astral plane. Casting spells on their leaders.'

'Do you believe in his power?'

Pearson shrugged. 'Germany lost the war, didn't it?' He handed the open book back to Watts. 'This inscription: it's the kind of thing we used to say. It doesn't mean anything.'

'Was my father into magic and the occult?'

'I told you. He was a man of wide intellectual curiosity.'

'Did he take part in rituals and such?'

'Not when I knew him.'

'Earlier?'

'That I wouldn't know.'

'Did you?'

Pearson glanced to the side and looked down. 'As part of my research I felt it was important to know how these things worked. To see if there was anything to it.'

'And was there?'

Pearson kept his head down but Watts saw his eyes dart to the side again. He glanced the same way. Avril was looking in on them through the window, her face still without expression.

Watts unaccountably blushed and looked back at Pearson. Pearson was watching his face. 'There were hints,' Pearson said quietly. 'Possibilities.' He looked down again. 'But certainties?' He looked almost wistful. 'Not for me.' He spread his hands. 'I've taken enough of your time. I'm sure you're eager to get on your way.'

Watts and Pearson stood. Both men glanced at the window at the same time. Avril had gone.

Pearson escorted Watts to the front door. 'You know,' he said, 'I really do believe I'm a genius. But I told that to a friend of mine in the French House and he used it in an article. That did for me. An Englishman who was unwilling to be self-deprecating? One who was also known to call himself an intellectual? Just not done, old boy, just not done.'

Watts smiled and nodded. 'The French House in Soho? I think my father used to go there.'

'Everybody did – especially all those poof artists – not all of whom recognized they were queer. "Hey, I paint bare-chested and hold my trousers up with my old school-tie but that doesn't mean I want to take it up the arse." Of course it does, you public school tit, however many women you fuck. The giveaway is that you fuck your women so badly they go elsewhere.'

'Say goodbye to Avril,' Watts said, shaking Pearson's hand. 'Thank her for the hospitality.'

'Oh, I will, Watts, I will. I'm sure she got as much pleasure from your stay as you did.'

Pearson gave that strange smile again and went back into the house. Watts got into his car with his books and briefcase and drove slowly away.

Karen Hewitt was wearing a tight two-piece that made the rest of her as immobile as her face.

'What is happening, Sarah? Apparently there was some Devil Goat casting its shadow over the town yesterday evening.'

Gilchrist had heard. 'Turns out there's a whole lot of sick black magic stuff that's been happening across the region before this. It's just that nobody had put it together before.'

'Tell me,' Hewitt said.

'At the moment, as you say, we have these reports of this goat-headed man casting a shadow over the city. We have the Wicker Man and the missing vicar—'

'Is he the victim inside the Wicker Man?'

'It's a possibility, of course. I'm waiting for confirmation from forensics. Then we have the stolen painting. The desecrated church. But it's not the first church to suffer in the region – there have been almost a dozen. Plus a few graves despoiled.'

'When you say despoiled . . .'

'Broken into. Bones scattered.'

'Not the recently buried, I hope?'

'No, ma'am, all very old.'

'Do we know what this means?'

'Not yet, ma'am.'

Hewitt nodded and made a note on her pad. 'These churches broken into – not just for copper?'

'Copper and lead long gone, I think, along with the gold and silver. No: altars trashed, crosses turned upside down, symbols sprayed on walls. Faeces left on the altar.'

'Anything significant about the symbols?'

'Too early to say.'

Hewitt made another note. Nodded. 'That's it?'

'Pets have gone missing.'

'Nothing new there. We had that spate of petnapping a couple of years ago.'

'A couple of them found nailed to church doors. Crows too.'

'Hope the animal rights folk don't find the perpetrators before we do.' Hewitt sighed. 'There's a lot going on that we have to deal with. We're stretched. What I'm saying, Sarah, is that I need results from you, fast.'

'I'm aware of that, ma'am. All the members of my team are working long hours.'

'Do you think there's a coordinated attack from black magicians going on? People who believe they are black magicians, I mean.'

Gilchrist shook her head. 'It's my understanding that black magic appeals mostly to mixed-up teenage boys who feel powerless.'

'In my day, they'd just listen to The Smiths and have done with it.'

'But this is something else.'

'What?' Hewitt said.

Gilchrist threw up her arms. 'I have no idea.'

Hewitt grunted. 'A religious nut – that's all we need,' she muttered. 'Pray it ain't so.'

'Ma'am?' Gilchrist said.

'Religious nutcases feel they have to explain everything with reference to the scriptures on single-spaced paper in very small handwriting. You've seen *Seven* – thousands of pages of madness – with diagrams. You've read the serial killer novels. Reams and reams of justification in italic writing.'

'Oh, I get you,' Gilchrist said. 'An unhealthy interest in the poetry of William Blake or the rantings of some medieval self-flagellant.'

Hewitt looked sharply at her. 'Self-flagellant?'

Gilchrist felt awkward. 'Although in Brighton there's probably a club for them.'

Kate Simpson phoned Plenty. A recorded message stated that the restaurant was closed for a week but then she was given options. She got through to administration and introduced herself.

'I wondered what the news was on the food poisoning?' she said.

'We still don't know what caused it. Our produce is being tested.'

'Where do you source your ingredients?'

'Local organic farms, usually. As you know we look always for the unusual ingredient.'

Kate told her what she had chosen from the menu. 'Anything unusual in there?'

'Lily bulbs, maybe, although they're not that unusual.'

Kate remembered each table in the restaurant had a lily on it. 'Eating dandelions I know about – but lilies?'

'The bulbs are essentially a root vegetable. Some can be bitter but the non-bitter ones – especially *lilium pumilum* – are used in cooking. They're like potatoes – equally starchy, although much smaller. If you're in China you can't get away from them. Often sold in a dry form. You reconstitute for stir fry or to thicken soup.'

'Are they poisonous if cooked badly?'

There was a pause on the other end of the phone. 'They're like potatoes – eat them raw and they can upset your stomach. But otherwise they're fine. Unless you're a cat.'

'What have lilies got against cats?'

'Lilies are toxic to them – especially the Easter lily. Causes acute renal failure.'

'But cats know this, right?'

Another pause. 'I would know that how?'

Kate laughed. 'Where do you get the bulbs from?'

'An organic farm near Poynings. Saddlescombe Organics. You can buy them yourself at the Brighton Farm Market up on North Road. On Wednesdays and Saturdays Saddlescombe Farm has a stall there.'

SIXTEEN

Bob Watts was drinking coffee in the café on the balcony at the rear of the Brighton Gallery and Museum. He liked to drop in from time to time. There was something peaceful about the place, notwithstanding the racket of school-children rising from below to the iron rafters as they clattered around the ground-floor gallery in search of the objects listed on their teaching sheets.

He could see, just below him, Bernard Rafferty in conversa-tion with a much younger, androgynously good-looking man. God, Rafferty irritated him. So self-regarding. In Watts' past life as a high-flying chief constable they had shared many a television and radio studio. Somewhere, Watts had a signed copy of one of Rafferty's books that the pompous man had pressed upon him. He was some sort of expert on Sussex churches, which interested Watts not in the least. He couldn't remember even opening the book.

Rafferty was standing beside yellow and black police tape that protected a small area at the edge of the gallery. He was pointing at the wall and speaking earnestly. The androgynous man was nodding slowly. Watts didn't know what that was about.

He called Sarah Gilchrist. He knew she was back on duty. He had read about the Wicker Man on the beach and seen her name as officer in charge. He thought she'd be interested to know about the other construction on the Devil's Dyke.

He and Sarah had briefly been an item – the cause of his break-up with his wife – and he felt their story wasn't yet over. But he was drawn to Nicola Travis, no doubt about it.

Travis had invited him down to Glyndebourne opera house this coming weekend. She said she had a spare ticket as a friend had bailed. He was excited at the prospect of seeing her again.

Gilchrist's mobile rang when she was standing with Donaldson and Heap. Bob Watts. She excused herself and took the call. He wanted to meet.

'I thought you were pretty much in Barnes these days until your father's house sells.'

He explained he was trying to find out more about some books on the occult his father owned.

'Especially one by Aleister Crowley. The Great Beast?'

'I've heard of him vaguely,' Gilchrist said. 'But the occult – not you as well.'

Watts laughed and picked up the leaflet from his table. 'There's definitely something in the air,' Watts said. 'I'm looking at a flyer for a vampire club in the Laines. They were advertising a screening of a film about Abraham Lincoln as a vampire killer on telly the other day.'

Gilchrist laughed too. 'I think Jane Austen characters now hunt zombies.'

'You know there's a Wicker Man up on Newtimber Hill near Devil's Dyke?' Watts said.

'I didn't.'

'Local hippy commune put it there.'

'How local?'

'Saddlescombe – they run the organic farm there.'

'Thanks for that, Bob.'

Donaldson had gone when Gilchrist put the phone down. She glanced at her watch. Probably gone for his lunchtime workout. She was restless. There would be little progress until the forensics results came in and the beach footage was fully examined. She called Heap over.

'Any joy with the Imperial Arcade trace?'

'I was going up there in a minute.'

'I'll come with you. Then we need to arrange a visit to Saddlescombe Organics out on the Devil's Dyke.'

Bob Watts walked through the North Laines to the station and took a ten-minute train journey to Lewes through flooded fields. It hadn't rained all morning but black clouds tumbled together in the sky and the light was leaden.

The antiquarian bookseller, Vincent Slattery, had his shop just beside the Archaeological Museum in a cobbled courtyard opposite the old castle keep.

It was like something out of Dickens. Sagging shelves packed with large books. Creaking floorboards pitched at all kinds of odd angles because of dips and declivities. Soft light coming through small, square-paned Georgian windows, augmented by lamps in the corners and on the long, heavily varnished desk at which Slattery sat. And the smell – that musty, leathery smell of old books.

'You're here to sell the Crowley?' Slattery said without looking up.

'I'm afraid not but I hoped you might be able to give me some information.'

'About Crowley? What would you want to know?'

'Just about the book really. Is it for you or one of your customers?'

Slattery looked surprised. 'That's actually none of your business but it's for an American client.'

Watts nodded. 'It was the price offered made me ask. Sorry. What do you know about Crowley?'

Slattery laughed. 'How long have you got? He was the son of a rich Midlands brewer. He went to Cambridge in the 1880s. He had a reputation as a mountaineer. Climbed in the Alps. Walked across the Sahara, he claimed. He paid to have his never-ending poetry published. Probably paid to get into Cambridge.'

'You don't sound too much of an admirer.'

Slattery tugged at his ear absently. 'When Crowley got interested in magic that's when I get interested in him.'

'You're interested in the occult?'

'An academic interest only. Crowley's own interest led him to the Golden Dawn, the quasi-spiritual, quasi-occult society of which W B Yeats was a member. The members were trying to access the power of the Other Side. Crowley tried to take it over so they threw him out. He developed his own magic centred round *Thelema* – his posh word for willpower. If you willed it, it would happen. Another credo of his was: "Do what you want is the whole of the Law", which essentially means do whatever you want.'

'I read that. So it was a philosophy of absolute self-indulgence?'

'In some ways. But his magical practices were designed to raise demons and spirits. His usual practice was sex magic with a succession of Scarlet Women – usually drug addicts or prostitutes or the mentally unbalanced. At the same time – and sometimes literally at the same time – he liked being sodomized. In Cefalu in Sicily he started a community in 1920 where he had sex with men and women and tried to force his then Scarlet Woman to have sex with a goat.'

'All in the name of revealing hidden knowledge?' Watts said.

Slattery nodded. 'And he must have been on to something because the Germans tried to kill him in 1942.'

Watts spread his hands. 'I've heard that mentioned but it makes no sense to me.'

Slattery smiled. 'In the early part of the Second World War Crowley performed secret rituals in Sussex to cast spells on the leaders of Nazi Germany. The same magic John Dee used to raise the storm that blew the Spanish Armada off course.'

Watts laughed. 'You're going to have to run that last bit by me again.'

'John Dee – the Elizabethan magus? Damon Albarn did an opera about him not so long ago?'

'I know who he is,' Watts said. 'He seems to be cropping up in every conversation I have lately. But Dee did *what* at the time of the Spanish Armada?'

'You know there was nothing to stop Philip of Spain conquering England in 1588? Our nobles were resigned to it even if Queen Elizabeth wasn't. The rest of us knew bugger all outside of our own villages – probably didn't even know what year it was. The Spanish Armada dwarfed our puny navy. Spain was the greatest sea power in the world. Our ships were out-gunned and out-classed.

'And then a storm blew up in the Channel. Sent most of the Spanish fleet to the bottom of the sea or wrecked it on the British coast.' Slattery raised an eyebrow. 'What were the chances of a storm starting up at just that moment of England's greatest need? That's the kind of coincidence you pray for – or conjure up demons for.'

Watts was sceptical but nodded politely. 'And that's what John Dee did?'

'So they say.'

'And here they were doing something similar in World War Two to defend our shores.'

'It would appear so. But not Crowley's usual sex magic, as far as we know. Crowley did battle on the astral plane. The details of the rituals are sketchy but the occasion we know about seems to have involved dressing up a dummy as a Nazi sitting on a throne. Among the people attending this particular ritual were Ian Fleming, Dennis Wheatley and Victor Tempest.'

Watts looked sharply at Slattery, whose grin had turned to a sly smile.

'You didn't know your father was there?' Slattery said.

Watts didn't know. For a moment he couldn't think what to say because he was thinking through the idea his father had been part of this. It just didn't compute. He didn't think Victor Tempest had known Fleming and Wheatley until later in the war. And his father had been fighting in Europe and then been a prisoner of war – in 1942 was he even in the country?

'They tried to blow Crowley up at Saddlescombe Farm, didn't they?' Watts finally said.

'That's right.'

'Where did they get a throne?' he said. 'Not that easy to come by, I would have thought.'

Slattery laughed. 'Exactly. These things are a lot of speculation. But it's certain there were bombs dropped on Saddlescombe when Crowley was staying there. The official line was that this was a German plane returning from a bombing raid on

London with a few bombs left that the pilot decided to jettison over the South Downs.'

'Was Crowley hurt?'

'Apparently not. Nobody was. Some windows of one of the farm cottages were blown out. The farm worker who lived in it was cheesed off because he'd only just cleaned them. He said if he'd left them another day he needn't have bothered.'

'The ritual was at Saddlescombe Farm?' Watts said.

Slattery nodded. 'Where else?' He glanced at his watch. 'Listen – there's an archaeologist I'd like you to meet. Expert on Saddlescombe and a lot more round here.'

Gilchrist had always had her feet on the ground. When she was a teenager most of her friends went to fortune-tellers and read their stars and went in for all of that but she just thought it was rubbish. As far as she was concerned, what happens, happens – and what happened to her was pretty shitty when she was a kid.

She walked with Heap up to the clock tower in the centre of town. 'So how religious are you?' she said to Heap.

'It soothes the soul,' Heap said.

'What soul?' she said. 'Who can genuinely believe we have a soul?'

Heap glanced at her. 'Well, religion soothes something in us,' he said.

'Listen,' Gilchrist said. 'God is absence. Either that or he's deaf.'

'But even if God doesn't exist I really want him to,' Heap said. 'And so do most people.'

Their way was blocked on the pavement outside the chain bookstore by a group of some twenty young men and women in white sweatshirts. Written on front and back of each sweat-shirt was the slogan 'For Christ's sake – give God a chance'. One of them had a guitar and they were singing, though what they were singing wasn't exactly clear.

A pretty, long-haired blonde girl gave Gilchrist a flyer. Gilchrist glanced at it. 'What's going on?' she said to the girl.

The girl looked at her and said earnestly: 'We're against Satan and all his works.'

Gilchrist tried not to smile. 'Good for you.' She gestured at the shop. 'Why are you congregating here to tell people that?'

Heap pointed at the window display. 'Ma'am.'

It was a display for Young Adult fiction. She looked more closely. Young Adult vampire fiction to be precise. Stephanie Meyer's *Twilight* series. A pile of books from a series called *The Vampire Diaries* by L J Smith. Stills from the TV show. And from the TV series *True Blood*.

Vampire Kisses was propped next to *Vampire Cheerleaders*. There was a series called *Vampire Princess of St Paul*, another called *Confessions of a Teenage Vampire* and a collection of short stories called *Sexy Teenage Vampires*.

Gilchrist was bemused. The teenage girls who read these and swooned over all the vampire TV shows and films – were they the same ones mugging each other and creating chaos on the buses? Presumably not.

She looked at the tall, blonde girl who was watching her response to the display. As far as Gilchrist was concerned these young Christians were just as bonkers as the girls obsessed with vampires. She nodded at Heap. 'You move them; I'll go ahead to the arcade.'

She crossed the road and walked up to the Imperial Arcade. She rarely went into it. In its time it must have been quite something. What remained now in these lovely old shops were hairdressers and cafés and pop-up shops.

Gilchrist went into each outlet, showing the picture of the people captured on CCTV. A New Age shop called Crystal had a sign on the door saying 'back in ten minutes'. It didn't say when the ten minutes had started.

Gilchrist stood in the exit to the arcade looking across at the people going in and out of Churchill Square shopping centre. The day looked so ordinary, so banal. She checked the sky. No flying kippers today. Actually, the sun had come out for the first time in what seemed an age.

The Christian group had gone. Heap was crossing the road. She looked back into the arcade, the sun slanting down through the glass canopy. A slender young woman with tumbling red hair was unlocking Crystal's door, a beaker of coffee in her other hand.

Gilchrist gave her a moment then followed her in. The shop was heavy on incense. Some music that seemed primarily to involve chimes tinkled in the air. Angel cards and crystals and New Age mumbo-jumbo was scattered around. She'd concluded some time ago that all the New Age shops in Brighton were just selling another sort of tourist tat and she wished them good luck if they could find people dumb enough to buy it.

Gilchrist flashed the photo. The girl didn't seem surprised. She waited for Gilchrist to speak. 'Do you recognize these people from around the arcade?'

'Are they men or women?'

'I was hoping you might tell me that. We think probably at least one is a woman. Do you recognize the clothes?'

The girl scrutinized the picture.

'Did you see them yesterday, for instance?' Gilchrist went on. 'CCTV footage shows them crossing the road from the clock tower and heading into this arcade.'

'To shop?'

'Or perhaps they live here. In one of the flats upstairs?'

The girl shrugged, still examining the photograph. 'People come and go in those flats all the time.' She looked at Gilchrist and handed the photograph back. 'I don't recall seeing these people before.'

Gilchrist started to leave.

'You've got a good aura,' the girl said.

Gilchrist half-turned. 'What?'

'Bright. Clear. You're a good person.'

Gilchrist couldn't think what to say. 'Thanks very much.' She waved her arm around the shop. 'All this stuff – you believe in it?'

The girl looked puzzled. 'Don't you?'

'Sorry,' Gilchrist said. 'That came out wrong. I didn't mean to be rude.' She turned back to the door. 'Thanks for your help.'

The girl called after her. 'Do you believe in all this *stuff*?'

Gilchrist didn't turn this time. Or speak. She wasn't even sure, as she left the shop, whether she shook her head.

SEVENTEEN

When Watts left Slattery he walked up the cobbled lane past the bowling green on his right. A former jousting field, according to the sign on the flint wall that edged it.

Slattery had arranged for him to talk further in twenty minutes about the magical importance of Saddlescombe Farm to an archaeologist at the Archaeology Museum next to his shop.

Watts walked on to a viewing deck. The folds of the Downs were spread before him, an unearthly green beneath the lowering clouds.

A stainless steel plaque noted that the Battle of Lewes had been fought on the portion of the Downs laid out before him in 1264. Simon de Montfort, the creator of the modern parliament, had defeated King Henry III and taken him captive.

Looking out over the Downs, Watts phoned his father's agent, Oliver Daubney. 'I'm not sure you were entirely straight with me over lunch at the British Museum.'

'My dear fellow, I'm shocked you would think that,' Daubney said, chuckling. 'I'm an agent. I'm always straight – albeit in a devious sort of way.'

'What's this about my father with Crowley, Wheatley and Ian Fleming at Saddlescombe Farm, during the war?'

A momentary silence, then: 'Bit before my time, old man.'

'Come on, Oliver, you know where all the bodies are buried going back to the Year Dot.'

'Robert, in a discussion linked to the occult the fact they are buried means nothing.'

'Saddlescombe Farm?'

'I'm sorry. Where you are standing is a little windy. I'm not hearing you clearly.'

'Saddlescombe?' Watts bellowed. A man nearby glanced over.

'Your father might have mentioned something about it,' Daubney said after another moment's hesitation. 'Fleming was always coming up with off-the-wall ideas in his role in military intelligence. He proposed that idea to drop a dead pilot into occupied territory with fake dispatches in his pocket to mislead the enemy. That worked rather well, I believe.'

All Watts really knew about Fleming was that he was the author of the James Bond novels.

'So this Saddlescombe Farm jaunt might have been his idea. But did my father know Fleming so early in the war? I didn't think they'd met until near the end.'

'I can confirm that your father knew Fleming from around 1942.'

Watts laughed. 'I'm not sure I wanted to hear that. How do you know?'

The steel plaque had a map etched on it that showed the disposal of the opposing forces across the Downs at the battle of Lewes. Watts looked from hillock to slope as Daubney spoke. A streak of lightning zipped behind the clouds.

'Fleming, in his role in naval intelligence, formed a unit of commandos,' Daubney said. 'Thirty Assault Unit or ThirtyAU? He got the men from other commando units. Fleming, in his proprietorial way, called these men his Red Indians. Apparently they hated that – most of them weren't that fond of his arrogance.'

'And my father was in this ThirtyAU?' Watts said.

'He was indeed.'

Watts thought he knew all about his father's commando experience but this was news.

'What was ThirtyAU exactly?'

'It was an intelligence-gathering troop. Aside from the usual unarmed combat and weapons expertise these men were taught safe-cracking and lock-picking. I believe it came in very useful for a couple of them who turned bad after the war. They were usually ahead of the front line. Their job was to seize enemy documents from German HQs.'

'Fleming actually fought alongside my father?'

'I don't think Fleming fought,' Daubney said. 'He selected

the targets and directed operations from the rear. Before the Normandy landing they were operating mostly in Sicily and Italy. Your father did a big job in a place called Chiusi.'

Watts knew about his father in Chiusi but not about intelligence gathering there. 'I thought he was in Chiusi to protect an Italian count from the partisans when the Germans withdrew,' he said.

'That was part of it,' Daubney said. 'But there were other things going on. You know Hitler got increasingly preoccupied with the occult and secret powers?'

'Here we go again. I've read about it.'

'The count had an ancient library and there were, apparently, some valuable manuscripts. I think one of your father's jobs was to secure them.'

As usual with any new disclosure about his father, Watts was both despairing and astonished. 'Did he succeed?' he said.

'That I don't know,' Daubney said.

'Were these manuscripts to do with the occult?'

'I believe so.'

None of the residents of the flats above the Imperial Arcade answered their bells.

'So what are your thoughts on this?' Gilchrist said as she and Heap walked back into town.

She was aware she was turning increasingly to Heap. He might only be a constable but underneath his blushing nervousness there was an acute brain. He was brighter than she was – though she knew that wasn't saying much. He was also a good lateral thinker, coming up with things that wouldn't have occurred to her.

'You're asking me, ma'am?' he said.

'Unless the Invisible Man is walking with us and I'm asking him.'

'In that case I think everything is connected. The missing vicar, the Wicker Man, the desecration in Saint Michael's and the theft of *The Devil's Altar*.'

'All done by the same person?'

'Not necessarily but all linked.'

'A painting of lilies though . . .'

'In Victorian times lilies were linked with death. They were scattered over Queen Victoria's coffin.'

'But lilies and the Devil?'

'That's a bit more abstruse.'

'Abstruse?'

'Sorry, ma'am. It means—'

'I know what it means. Once you joined my squad I bought a dictionary specially.'

Heap ducked his head, a smile at the corner of his mouth, cheeks red.

'You were going to explain the abstruse link between the Devil and lilies.'

Heap paused to let Gilchrist go ahead of him down a narrow alley into the Laines.

'Not quite the Devil. Lilies are a symbol of chastity and piety in Christianity. In early Christian art the white lily symbolizes the Madonna as the flower is associated with the Virgin Mary. The angel Gabriel is often holding it. Then they are used at Easter to symbolize the death and the resurrection of Christ. But Jesus wasn't the first god to die and be reborn – it's a constant in ancient myths. And lilies have always been associated with those dead and then reborn gods.'

'Go on.'

'But you also get lilies on Tarot cards: on the Magician, Temperance and the Ace of Pentacles.'

'Pentacles? The vicar had chalked a pentacle on the floor of his flat. No lilies though. So what do they mean?'

'There are different interpretations, no single one – you know, it's the sequence in which the cards appear that gives the meaning. If you believe there is a meaning.'

'The usual bollocks, I suppose,' Gilchrist said sourly.

Heap glanced at her. 'As best I can understand it each of those cards represents, in some way, making the most of your inner power. The Ace of Pentacles stands for new beginnings so the lilies fit in with the idea of rebirth. The Magician is about making use of all the powers you have. Beginnings are involved again.'

'And the other one: Temperance, was it? Some non-drinking thing?'

'Not exactly. It stands for harmonizing opposites. It's about balance. The androgynous figure, neither one nor the other, is weighing up what's in her left and right hands. The main thing is where it's situated in the pack – you know each card is numbered? Temperance has Death on one side and The Devil on the other.'

'So whoever stole *The Devil's Altar* is into some kind of power thing. Do you think that could be the case with the Wicker Man?'

Heap shook his head. 'That's a different order of things.'

They paused at traffic lights.

'I don't understand why all this is happening here,' Gilchrist said.

'Ma'am, historically Sussex was cut off from the rest of the country for centuries by poor roads. It was a lawless place and that made it a superstitious place. Way after, in the 1960s, you had an influx of hippies at the university and in nearby villages. The occult was fashionable in the counter culture. Aleister Crowley – the Great Beast – was one of the icons The Beatles put on the cover of *Sergeant Pepper* in 1967. And then when New Age spirituality came in the occult came in with it through the back door.'

'And Brighton is the California of England. No trend too weird.'

On the other side of the road they passed a flower shop. Heap pointed at the lilies in a metal vase.

'Lilies are hermaphrodites, you know. They've got staminates – those are the male, pollen-producing things there – and carpellates – those female, ovule-producing things.'

'You are indeed a fount of knowledge.'

'Font, ma'am. My preference is for "font of knowledge".'

Gilchrist flashed him a look. 'That's because you're a churchgoer. Either way you're full of it.'

Heap faced straight ahead, the smallest of smiles returning to the edges of his mouth.

Watts came back down the cobbled slope to the Archaeological Museum beside Slattery's bookshop. Slattery was waiting for him inside a small, flagged foyer. He was with a tall, grey-bearded, bald-headed man with rheumy eyes. The man's name was Philip Perkins.

'You want to know about Saddlescombe Farm,' he said.

'What was special about it? Why was Aleister Crowley doing rituals there in the Second World War? Because of the Devil's Dyke – the association with the Devil?'

Perkins waved at the display cabinets on the wall behind him.

'Which particular pack of lies do you want? About the Devil? About the ley lines conjoining there? About the Druid stone circles and the Druids worshipping there centuries ago? About the Templar treasure buried there?'

'Just the truth,' Watts said.

'Just the truth,' Perkins repeated, rubbing his beard. 'Whose truth?'

Watts waited.

'Archaeologists are not unlike police detectives,' Perkins continued. 'They make deductions from evidence. They also use inductive logic, which is to say that if a thing has been proven in one place that conclusion may be applied in another place. But that doesn't mean we get it right. Our conclusions are provisional and affected by what is fashionable at any particular time.'

Watts nodded. 'The Sutton Hoo helmet,' he said.

Perkins looked pleased. 'Precisely. Well, there was a period in history when our ancestors built megaliths across Britain – stone circles. They occur on Downland all over the country, particularly in Wiltshire. Stonehenge and Avebury, of course. No reason they shouldn't have existed on the South Downs, therefore. But no one has ever found evidence of a stone circle here.

'Does that mean they didn't exist or just that we haven't found the evidence? Did they exist but there are simply no traces left because farmers cleared their fields for ploughing or – good building material being hard to come by round here – took the stones for building?'

'I get that there are limits to knowledge,' Watts said. 'But what do or don't we know about Saddlescombe Manor?'

'What we know is mostly speculation before the Domesday

book. There is no evidence the Druids were ever there –
or anywhere on the South Downs – the Goldstone
notwithstanding.'

The only Goldstone Watts knew about was the former
Brighton and Hove football ground.

'Not one single artefact or image has been unearthed
anywhere in Europe that can definitely be connected to the
Druids, even though much archaeological evidence for the
religious practices of Iron Age people has been uncovered.'

Watts looked from one man to the other. 'The Druids made
human sacrifices, didn't they?'

'Only according to their conqueror, Julius Caesar,' Perkins
said. 'And you know victors write history?' Perkins smiled.
'Though in light of recent events in Brighton you might be
interested to know that, according to Caesar, the Druids made
these sacrifices by burning people alive in giant men made of
wicker.'

Watts frowned. 'So what about Saddlescombe and the
Knights Templar?'

'Ah, our most famous medieval searchers for the Holy Grail
of secret wisdom,' Perkins said. He saw the look on Watts'
face. 'You're sceptical,' he said. 'What do you know about
the Knights Templar?'

'Grown men who should know better are fascinated by
them,' Watts said.

'Women too,' Slattery said mildly.

'All that Dan Brown secret Templar stuff is nonsense,' Watts
said. 'No offence.'

'Maybe,' Slattery said. 'But just because it's not true doesn't
mean people don't believe it.'

Watts looked at Perkins. 'Do you believe it?'

'There are some curious features of the Templar story in
England. You know they were Monks of War – a fighting
religious order?'

'I do,' Watts said. 'The Order started out with nine men
defending pilgrims on their way to the Holy Land during the
Crusades. They ended up as international financiers, bank-
rolling kings and merchants.'

'That's right,' Perkins said. 'They were powerful – they

even had their own fleet. But things began to go wrong for them at the end of the thirteenth century when they lost their power base in the Holy Land. Then, in 1307, King Philip the Fair of France concocted a scheme to take advantage of the Order's weakened state and get at its wealth.'

Slattery interrupted. 'He was into them for so much money and he needed so much more money that he decided to destroy them. Not just to cancel his debt but to steal their wealth.'

'So far, so Dan Brown,' Watts said.

'So far, so historical fact,' Perkins said. 'On one famous Friday the thirteenth in 1307, King Philip the Fair ordered all the Templars in France to be arrested on the grounds of heresy. This heresy was supposed to have begun in Agen, in Provence. The main charges against the Templars were that during their admission ceremonies they denied that Jesus was divine, spat on the cross, demanded sinful kisses from the initiates – kissing people's arses, basically – and that they committed sodomy.'

'And they worshipped a head called Baphomet,' Slattery said. 'That was either a bearded or a three-faced man. Crowley used that as one of many names for himself.'

'But these charges were all trumped-up, weren't they?' Watts said.

'Probably. Philip had used similar accusations against a hostile pope earlier. It was a smear campaign.' Perkins tilted his head. 'But these accusations against the Templars led to all sorts of wild imaginings. Most of them rubbish.'

'Most of them?'

Perkins grinned. 'There are no absolutes.'

'How did this affect the Templars in Saddlescombe?' Watts said.

'The Templars were granted Saddlescombe sometime in the mid-twelfth century. They made it a receptory – a main head-quarters – and from it they ran a pretty big estate stretching from Hurstpierpoint and Hassocks to Newtimber and the sea at Shoreham, where they had a farmhouse, chapel and saltpan.'

Watts pictured Shoreham, with its big muddy river estuary exposed at low tide.

'A saltpan?'

'Collecting salt from the sea was crucial for preserving fish and meat. The Shoreham property was intriguing.'

'How so?'

'It keeps popping back up in the Templars-in-Sussex story.'

Watts caught the gleam in Perkins' eye.

'What is the Templars-in-Sussex story?'

Perkins looked at Slattery and both men burst out laughing.

EIGHTEEN

'You find the Templars amusing?' Watts said to Slattery and Perkins.

Perkins raised his hand in apology. 'There are opportunities for much speculation about what went on with them in England and specifically in Saddlescombe,' he said. 'From the scant records we have, Saddlescombe had some unusually important visitors during the one hundred or so years the Templars owned it: Grand Masters of the Temple in England, kings and princes. We need to ask why they came.'

'Is it so surprising Grand Masters visited?' Watts said.

'No, except that it seems they came to deal with what at first sight appears to be quite a trivial matter: the transfer of the tenancy of that farm and saltpan in Shoreham.

'At Easter in 1253 Grand Master Roncelin de Fosse assigned them to a William Bishop and his wife from nearby Steyning, for the duration of their lives. Almost forty years later, in 1292, Grand Master Guido de Foresta came to Saddlescombe to grant that same property to a John and Matilda Lot. A year later Jacques de Molay, Grand Master of the entire European Templar Order, came from France to England in a Templar ship. He docked at Shoreham and came up to Saddlescombe from there.'

'So you're saying the farm in Shoreham is important, not Saddlescombe itself,' Watts said.

'I'm saying it's possible. But, again, there's no archaeology. There's nothing of the Shoreham property left – we don't even know precisely where it was. But there was clearly something important about the place for it to attract the attention of such powerful men.'

Watts nodded, looking absently at a display cabinet behind Perkins' head. 'You mentioned kings and princes coming to Saddlescombe as well.'

'Henry III, you probably know, had to deal with a baron's revolt, led by Simon de Montfort, his former friend and godfather of his son, Prince Edward. In 1264 they fought a battle outside Lewes.'

'I've seen the plaque up by the bowling green here about the battle,' Watts said. 'Simon de Montfort won.'

'He did. For a few months he ruled England. But Prince Edward defeated him at the battle of Evesham and ordered de Montfort's body to be hacked to pieces.'

Perkins tugged on his beard again. 'What the plaque doesn't say is that the night before the battle of Lewes the king and his son stayed at Saddlescombe.'

'Why?'

'How can we know?' Perkins said. 'Prince Edward became King Edward I, also known as Edward Longshanks. He fought beside the Templars on two brief crusades in the Holy Land. One of the Templars he went into battle with was Jacques de Molay. They corresponded through the English Grand Master William de la More as late as 1304. Longshanks came again to Saddlescombe in 1305, two years before his death.'

'He's the king in *Braveheart* who threw his gay son's lover out of the window?' Watts said. 'I thought he was busy hammering Mel Gibson and the Scots. Why did he come to Sussex?'

Perkins shrugged. 'We don't know. That gay son in the movie was actually bisexual in reality. He became King Edward II in July 1307 on the death of his father.'

'The year the Templars in France were accused of heresy,' Slattery reminded Watts.

'And here's the strangest thing,' Perkins said, tugging on his beard. 'Edward II did everything he could to protect the English Templars even though it made no political or financial sense. He was expected to follow the French example, if not for religious reasons then for political. He was in negotiations to marry Isabelle, the daughter of the king of France, so wasn't supposed to piss the king of France off. Plus, like his father, he was campaigning against the Scots so could have used the Templar's dosh to finance that.'

'And?'

'Edward said he didn't believe the charges against the Templars. He demanded proof. A month later the Pope ordered him to arrest the Templars and confiscate their properties in the name of the Church. Edward again asked for proof. Why would he stick his neck out like that? A Christian king doesn't lightly disobey a Pope.

'When the Pope insisted, Edward went through the motions. He arrested some Templars, including the Grand Master William de la More, but they suffered no real hardship. He left others on their properties or receiving allowances.'

'And the Saddlescombe Templars?'

'Were left untouched. In January 1308, Edward II married Isabelle. In France, the Templars, including Jacques de Molay, were being brutally tortured. They all confessed to the heresy charges but it's assumed that was more to do with the torture than the truth of the charges.

'In August the Pope let this be known and by November 1308 Edward had been pressured by him into arresting or re-arresting all the Templars in the country. And still he resisted. Records show that he arrested less than half of them: one hundred and eight out of two hundred and fifty. Before you ask, the Saddlescombe Templars were not among those imprisoned.'

'What happened then?' Watts said.

'Over the next couple of years Edward had domestic political problems to deal with because of his relationship with his favourite, Piers Gaveston, who was his adviser and possibly his lover. His barons forced him to send Gaveston into exile and Edward needed the help of the Pope and King Philip to get him back. He bribed the Pope with jewellery and bequests of towns and castles to the Pope's nephews and he reluctantly did as he'd been commanded with the Templars.'

'Piers Gaveston – the man in the Christopher Marlowe play?'

Watts recalled Edward had come to a painful end in the play – a red-hot poker had been involved.

'Even so,' Perkins continued, 'King Edward continued to do his best to protect the Templars. He assessed the holdings of the Templars in England, as ordered, but didn't hurry to put any of them on trial.'

'But the ones he did arrest – did they confess when they were tortured?'

'They weren't tortured. Despite what people think about medieval barbarity, there was no torture in the judicial process in England. The Pope wanted to set the church's inquisitors on them but the king resisted. But in France, by 1310, King Philip was impatient with those Templars who still wouldn't confess. He burned fifty-four of them to encourage the others. It worked.

'In England and Scotland, though, after three years in custody, not a single Templar had been tortured and not a single one had admitted heresy. Then, extraordinarily, in July 1311, they were allowed to do a kind of plea bargain. As best we can gather, without admitting guilt, they abjured all heresy and threw themselves on the mercy of the church. They were forgiven and sent to monasteries to do penance. The Grand Master was one of only two who didn't feel able to do that so he remained in the Tower. He died the following year.'

'And Saddlescombe?' Watts said.

Perkins and Slattery exchanged glances again. Perkins continued, 'At the end of that same July, Edward finally gave in to pressure from the Pope to allow the church's inquisitors to do things their way. Either under torture or just the threat of it three Templars in England confessed to heresy.'

'Were any of them from Saddlescombe?' Watts said.

Slattery gave a little smile. 'All three were from Saddlescombe.'

David Rutherford, the vicar of St Michael's, answered his phone on the first ring.

'DI Gilchrist. Lovely to hear from you. Are you building your boat?'

'Excuse me?' she said.

'Noah? There was probably this same amount of rain in his day, but Noah – well, there was a man who took precautions. The first risk assessment man.'

'Two of everything,' Gilchrist said. 'But where are you going to get two unicorns in this day and age?'

'In Brighton? Just walk down Church Street.'

Gilchrist laughed. 'Your roof holding out under the deluge, is it?'

'Until the next lot of chancers get the rest of the lead,' Rutherford said. 'How can I help you, Detective Inspector?'

'It's about your colleague, Andrew Callaghan.'

'I fear I've been flippant at the wrong moment. A fault of mine.'

'Not at all. I went round to his flat yesterday and there were disturbing signs.'

She only just heard his response. 'As I feared.'

'Who were the three men who confessed their guilt?' Watts said.

Perkins gestured to Slattery.

'Stephen of Stapelbrigg, Thomas Totti and John of Stoke all said much the same thing: that there was an Inner Temple within the Templars in England,' Slattery said. 'And that's where the heresy came in. Stapelbrigg said admission to that was through a ceremony "contrary to the Faith", in which you had to deny Mary, deny Jesus was God and spit on the cross.'

'He said this heresy started with Roncelin de Fosse when he was Grand Master of Provence.' Perkins nodded though Watts hadn't made a comment. 'The man who was the signatory to the lease of the Shoreham property to William Bishop and his wife.'

'More than that,' Slattery said. 'John of Stoke said he'd been admitted in 1293 at Saddlescombe. Guess who had told him to deny Christ? Jacques de Molay, Grand Master of the European Order, on his brief visit to England in that year.'

Watts scratched his head. 'But why wasn't this used as proof of the guilt of the other Templars in England?'

Perkins shrugged. 'Maybe because Edward was still protecting the Templars – or protecting Saddlescombe – and knew the confessions were fake. All these men were vulnerable and had been free long enough to hear reports of what the French Templars had confessed to.

'Stephen Stapelbrigg had been in hiding for four years. He'd been arrested just a couple of weeks before his trial. He would have been hearing about the French confessions whilst he was lying low. Thomas Totti had been summoned to hand himself in but hadn't done so. John of Stoke had been treasurer at the New Temple in London, which merchants and barons used as a bank vault for their wealth. There were rumours of embezzlement.'

'What happened to them?' Watts said. 'Burned at the stake?'

'You'd think so, wouldn't you? If only to shut them up if there were any kind of conspiracy. But no. Like everybody else they were absolved and assigned to religious houses around England.'

'Not Saddlescombe?'

Perkins shook his head.

Watts paced over to one of the glass cabinets. 'My head is buzzing.'

Perkins chuckled. 'You wanted to know about Saddlescombe? I'm telling you about Saddlescombe.'

'There's more, isn't there?' Watts said. 'You mentioned there was another Templar who refused to abjure heresy because he hadn't committed it,' Watts said. 'Is he linked to Saddlescombe?'

Slattery nodded but it was Perkins who answered.

'When Grand Master William de la More was arrested the second time he was at the Templar preceptory in Ewell near Dover with Imbert Blanc, the Grand Commander of the Auvergne. They were waiting for one of the Order's boats to take them to Flanders, where they'd be safe from Philip of France. We know both had been to Saddlescombe. We know they went to Shoreham, possibly expecting to sail from there. We don't know why they didn't.'

'Why was Imbert in this country at all?'

'The Templar Order had been torn apart. Maybe the few

Grand Masters and Commanders who were still free were trying to salvage what they could. And that included what was held at Saddlescombe.

'Blanc, by the way, was released from the Tower into the custody of the Archbishop of Canterbury but the record doesn't show what happened to him after that. Jaques de Molay in France – who had been regularly corresponding with Edward Longshanks, you'll remember – had confessed under torture to heresy but recanted when he was supposed to confirm his guilt. In consequence he was roasted, very slowly, on the stake.'

'And what made Saddlescombe and/or Shoreham so important?'

Perkins looked up at the ceiling for a moment. 'That's the question, isn't it?' He tugged on his beard again. 'The man from Steyning who first took over the Shoreham place. Do you remember his name was Bishop?'

'Suitably ecclesiastical.'

'His wife had a very interesting first name.'

Watts waited.

'Dionysia.'

'As in Dionysus,' Slattery said. 'Pagan god of ritual madness and frenzy, a dying and reborn god, an outsider god.'

'The centre of a cult,' Perkins added. 'We know them as the Dionysian mysteries. The initiates used drugs and booze to reach a higher level of consciousness. Dionysus was Bacchus in Roman mythology. Real party boy.'

'Witches and wizards used exactly the same kind of techniques down the centuries to reach exalted states and achieve communion with the Devil and his minions,' Slattery said. 'Bacchus is usually presented as a kind of satyr with cloven hooves and horns.'

'Like the Goat of Mendes,' Perkins said. 'But Dionysus is usually represented as an androgynous youth – the literature describes him as "man-womanish". Some statues present him naked with breasts and penis.'

Watts looked from one to the other. 'And the other Shoreham tenants you mentioned forty years later?'

'You know a person's last name in those days was often

the name of the place they were most associated with?' Perkins said.

Watts nodded.

'The people who took over the Shoreham place forty years down the line were called Lot.'

'I remember,' Watts said.

Perkins smirked.

'Where's Lot, then?' Watts said.

'The Lot Valley is in the Midi-Pyrenees bordering on the Languedoc.'

'Cathar country,' Watts murmured. 'Where the heresy started.'

'Under the influence of the Cathars,' Perkins said.

'What's known about Grand Master Roncelin?' Watts said.

'Dates. Grand Master in Provence for three years before he became Grand Master in England in 1251 for two years. He's on record as being Grand Master of Provence again from 1260 to 1278.'

'The Cathars were Gnostics, right?' Watts said.

Perkins gestured to Slattery.

'They were,' Slattery said. 'But Gnosticism takes many forms. The Cathars believed in two competing gods. One, Rex Mundi, ruled the world, the other the heavens. Rex Mundi was evil – embodied chaos. The other god, the one the Cathars worshipped, was disincarnate – a genderless pure spirit, untainted by anything material. This god stood for love, order and peace. One consequence of their belief is that Gnostics deny Jesus was a god because he had a physical presence. He was incarnate, not disincarnate.'

'That kind of fits with one of the accusations against the Templars then,' Watts said. 'But how did the Cathars draw de Fosse in?'

'The surmise is that in his youth de Fosse witnessed the Albigensian Crusade massacring Cathars in southern France for forty years.'

'Massacres all that time?'

'Pretty much. First big one in the town of Béziers in 1209. Twenty thousand people slaughtered, whether they were Cathar or not. The credo was: kill them all, let God sort out the ones that belong to him. When Carcassonne, stuffed with refugees, was taken, the people were spared but had to leave naked and empty-handed.'

'That's a big castle,' Watts said.

'You've visited it?'

'Saw it from the road on the way to Homps.'

'You've been in the middle of Cathar country, then.'

'So I understand. I had other things on my mind.'

Perkins waited for more then said: 'By 1229, after much brutality, the Languedoc was under the control of the king of France. The most steadfast Cathars were burned at the stake. The Inquisition even exhumed bodies to burn them too.'

'Bloody religion,' Watts muttered.

'There was cruelty. The leader of the crusade was known for it. Prior to the sack of the village of Lastours he brought prisoners from a village nearby, had their eyes gouged out and their ears, noses and lips cut off. He left just one of them with a single eye so he could lead the others into the village as a warning.'

'Jesus.'

'In his name, yes. But at the siege of Toulouse, the crusade leader got his comeuppance when a big stone launched from a catapult crushed his head.'

'I'm pleased to hear that, but what does this have to do with Saddlescombe and Provence?'

Perkins shrugged. 'I don't have answers, just a lot of strange coincidences. Here's one. The man who led the Albigensian crusade – the man who had his head crushed at Toulouse?'

'What about him?' Watts said.

Perkins caressed his bushy beard. 'His name was Simon de Montfort.'

NINETEEN

Sarah Gilchrist stood in the foyer of St Michael's Church as the Reverend Rutherford hurried towards her.

'I have to ask you some questions,' she said.

'Of course. And I have one for you. Why did you come to the church that day?'

Gilchrist smiled, though she didn't feel it. 'Later. Do you believe in evil, Vicar?'

He gave her a long look. 'That comes with the job, Detective Inspector.' He waved his arm at the spacious church. 'If I believe in one I have to believe in the other.'

'No God without the Devil?'

'And no Good without Evil – otherwise, how would we know the difference?'

He was still looking at her.

Gilchrist looked down. 'In my job I unfortunately see more evil than good.'

'But you represent the good,' Rutherford said.

Gilchrist glanced at him. 'I may represent it . . .'

Rutherford had a lovely smile. 'I'm sure you're better than you think you are. Most people are in my experience.'

'You go looking for the good in people, Vicar, so you're going to find it,' Gilchrist said softly. 'I'm looking for the bad – and I find it wearyingly often. Especially in myself.'

She felt self-conscious as he examined her face for a long moment.

'If we've anything about us, it's in our nature to be harsh on ourselves,' he said. 'My view – hard won, I assure you – is that there are enough other people wanting to be harsh on us. We should give ourselves a break.'

Gilchrist looked at the crucifix mounted high on the wall

above the pulpit. She'd always found the idea of a religion based on an act of extreme sadism difficult.

'If only it were that easy,' she murmured.

Watts frowned at Perkins and Slattery. 'Simon de Montfort? The man who won the Battle of Lewes in 1264? That's not right. Those dates don't fit.'

'They do if we're talking about his father,' Perkins said. 'Also called Simon de Montfort. He led the Albigensian crusade. And, actually, Simon the Younger – the de Montfort who won the Battle of Lewes in 1264 – did accompany his father on his crusade campaigns when he was a child. He was at the siege of Toulouse, though not on the day his father got clobbered by that stone.'

'So what you're giving me are lots of links between the south of France and this area. You are suggesting the Templars at Saddlescombe were guarding some secret but you've no idea what it is.'

'Corrrect.'

Watts was exasperated. 'Was any of this confession stuff true?'

'Probably not. You know about confessions, ex-Chief Constable. People confess to crimes that haven't even been committed, especially if there is torture or the threat of torture. Intimidation. You know how it works.'

Watts looked again at the display cases but didn't say anything.

'Templars were often from grand families and stayed in touch with them,' Perkins went on. 'If de Fosse did start these weird inner circle things you'd think that somebody who wasn't happy about it would have told somebody in the fifty years before Philip the Fair struck.

'Also, people left the Templars. Sometimes they were kicked out because they weren't suitable, sometimes because they'd done something wrong. In extreme cases they apostasized. Now that was a serious thing to do – you were automatically excommunicated and you became a fugitive, pursued by church and state. You'd think to justify desertion some apostate would claim this stuff was going on. But nobody did. Not a whisper.

'And Saddlescombe? There was something going on but I don't know what it was. Sorry. One thing I do know. Saddlescombe was transferred to another fighting order, the Hospitallers, but the Templars joined the Hospitallers so they continued to run it. When the Hospitallers eventually got it, that is – the king hung on to it as long as he could and claimed all the movable stuff, as he did all over the country.'

'And the place in Shoreham?'

'Matilda Lot died in 1336. The Shoreham place went to Carmelite Friars with the permission of the Hospitallers.'

Watts looked from Perkins to Slattery. 'I don't know where this leaves us.'

Perkins shrugged. Watts thought for a moment.

'Nothing remains from the Templars?'

Slattery spread his hands. 'There was a chapel at Saddlescombe. It's supposedly long gone but other parts of the old structure were incorporated in the construction of the current farm some four hundred years ago – so some bit of it might still be there.'

'Incorporated in the farm,' Watts said.

'Who knows? Or something else the Templars valued might still be there.'

'Or people think it is there.' Watts rubbed his chin. 'And that valuable thing is why Crowley was at the farm?'

Perkins and Slattery said together: 'Maybe.'

Watts nodded thoughtfully, wondering whether that was why Colin Pearson chose to live there. He walked over to the display cabinet behind Perkins and pointed at a small lump of polished rock he'd been absently looking at throughout their discussion. 'What's that?'

Perkins joined him. 'Doctor Dee's crystal. He could foretell the future by looking into the depths.'

Watts looked up at the ceiling.

'So it's believed.' Perkins laughed. 'And, of course, it's what people believe that matters. If someone believes Druids worshipped stones or did sacrifices on them, if someone believes that the Templars held black masses on the Devil's Dyke and John Dee conjured up the Devil at Saddlescombe Manor no amount of rational argument or presentation of what facts we know will make any difference. We live in an irrational world.'

'Do they believe John Dee conjured up the Devil there? Did he even visit Saddlescombe?'

'John Dee lived a long life for his time – from 1527 to approximately 1608. There's no evidence Dee was ever at Saddlescombe Manor but he was definitely in Sussex for a period doing conjurations. We assume the farm was in continuous use from the Templar time – we certainly know it was being used in the early 1600s.'

'So how did you end up with the crystal?' Watts said.

'Donated sometime in the 1940s but its provenance before then is difficult to track.'

'You know John Dee's magical equipment from the British Museum has been stolen?' Watts said. 'And an attempt was made on his crystal in the Science Museum. I should keep a close eye on your rock.'

Perkins scratched his beard. 'Maybe there is some design in all this. A crude attempt was made to steal this a couple of weeks ago.'

'How crude?' Watts said.

'I was out the back for a moment and when I came in someone was fiddling with the lock of the cabinet. Pretended they weren't but asked if they could examine the crystal more closely. I might well have said yes had I not seen her behaviour.'

'It was a woman? Description?'

'I'm assuming from the voice it was a woman. No description – she was pretty much covered from head to foot in waterproofs.'

Just as Gilchrist and Heap were leaving the incident room to go to Saddlescombe Farm, Bilson called.

'As my initial tests indicated, whoever was smearing excrement on the vicar's walls and dropping it on you is the same person. And that person definitely has cancer. Not just the blood but the raised ph levels show that. If they are not already doing so, this person will need to have treatment somewhere.'

'That's a great start. Thanks, Bilson.'

She started to end the call.

'Oy!' he shouted.

She put the phone back to her ear. 'No, Bilson,' she said, glancing across at Heap, 'that doesn't mean we're going to have sex.'

'God, I'm so over you,' he said. 'But I thought you might want the rest.'

'What, you can get name and address and National Insurance number from a stool sample?'

'Pretty much. Be careful where you evacuate your bowels if you don't want your identity stolen.'

'Moving on . . .'

'People who have regular anal sex are more likely to get colorectal cancer than other people. This being Brighton and without being judgemental I'm going to start referring to the person as "he".

'He is probably a vegetarian – at least hasn't had meat for some while. Aside from missing out on all the nutritional stuff meat gives him, he's a pretty healthy eater. I'd judge he's a regular at Plenty.'

'Ha, Sherlock – there are lots of vegetarian restaurants in the city. This is Brighton, you know.'

'Yeah, I know – getting a pair of leather shoes might be problematic but getting veggie anything, you're in clover – or some other non-animal substance, obviously.'

'Might the veggie diet be a way of dealing with the cancer?'

'Could be – or the person might be a veggie anyway. I would be Sherlock if I could deduce that. However, I can say with some certainty that he ate at Plenty.'

'You found an undigested till receipt in his faeces?'

Bilson laughed. 'As good as. Plenty use seriously unlikely foods that in combination produce a certain chemical reaction – you know all cooking is chemistry, right?'

'Even in the canteen's special of the day?'

'Especially in that – though in a horribly different way.'

'Go on.'

'OK. Now hard as you may find this to believe I eat regularly at Plenty – it is one of the finest restaurants in the country, after all.'

'Which is currently closed for poisoning people.'

'I'd heard that. Well, chemistry can go wrong. Even so – I got talking to the chef last time I was there and she has a fondness for using heritage herbs and vegetables – stuff that was popular centuries ago but is almost forgotten now. In the stool sample I found undigested the seed of a pignut and some ground ivy. I can't imagine any other chef in Brighton cooking with those things in combination, if at all. Ergo, this person eats at Plenty.'

'Hang on – ground ivy sounds like something poisonous.'

'But it's not – that's not what poisoned you.'

'What did, then?'

'Give me a stool sample and I'll tell you.'

'But we've only just met,' Gilchrist tried to joke, thinking what an intimate thing providing a stool sample to someone she knew would be to do.

There was a silence, then Bilson said: 'Please yourself.'

Gilchrist cleared her throat. 'So we have someone with colon cancer eating at Plenty?'

'Sometime in the three days before he dropped the gift on you.'

'I don't suppose you happen to know if they have CCTV at the restaurant, maestro?'

'Outside my area of expertise. But I'm hoping this has won me dinner with you. Have you tried Hawksmoor? Best fillet steak I've ever eaten. Hung for twenty-one days. Melts in your mouth.'

'Whoa – I thought you said you were vegetarian.'

'No. I said I liked eating at the best restaurants in the country.'

'Thanks, Bilson.'

'Call me when you've had a chance to check your diary,' he said.

Gilchrist hung up. Great. Now she had to navigate the National Health Service. Which reorganization was taking place at the moment?

TWENTY

B ob Watts couldn't remember the last time he'd been in a church. His wedding, maybe? He'd come straight to the Church of the Rock in Brighton from Lewes for its evening service, his mind reeling from all he'd been told.

He sat at the back. What followed was not the kind of service he was used to. A choir of about twenty youngsters all had white T-shirts with 'For Christ's Sake – Give God a Chance' stencilled on the front. About half of them had guitars.

They began with the Beatles song 'She Loves You' but they had changed the words. Now it started, 'God loves you, yeah, yeah, yeah' and went rapidly downhill thereafter.

Watts knew the next song. He'd heard it once on his car radio in France. He had been so appalled by the breathtaking banality of the lyrics, delivered in this young girl's nasal voice, he'd actually looked it up online. He'd assumed the singer/songwriter was a twelve-year-old.

But, no, Joan Osborne was a grown woman and her song had apparently been a big hit. It was based on questionable theology. Osborne wondered what it would be like if God were 'just a slob' like the rest of us?

Osborne then pictured God as a stranger on a bus, just trying to get home, heading back to heaven all alone.

What had made Watts almost crash the car when he'd first heard it – and made him now bury his face in his hands so no one would see the expression on his face – was a line which proposed that this poor guy, God, didn't even have anyone to phone, although he might consider phoning the Pope.

However, the singers – they were probably too modern to call themselves a choir – were giving it their all and one girl's pure voice went right to the rafters. Watts sighed. Such a voice for such a song.

The song climaxed with another question. If you met God on the bus and could ask him just one question, what would it be?

'Can I see your ticket, please?' Watts muttered.

If this was the level of modern Christian responses to the world, he despaired. The Devil not only had the best tunes, he had the best lyricists.

As if to prove the point a thin, crop-haired man in a crumpled suit went up to the lectern and said: 'This is a song about species respect. If you want to join in the chorus it's a very simple one.'

Watts remained blank-faced as the man started to sing, a capella: 'We're superior to other species? What a load of faeces . . .'

Watts squirmed in his seat as he watched the rapt attention with which the congregation listened to the dire song. People applauded wildly, whooping, when it ended. Watts thought he might whoop *because* it had ended.

The man in the crumpled suit bowed briefly then said, 'Here's a rap about animal liberation as a means of personal liberation.'

Watts focused on the face of the tall, blonde girl with the pure voice then again at the earnest faces of the young audience around him then back at the beautiful girl, her face glowing.

He wasn't the right market for rapping but he couldn't understand why rappers got away with such terrible rhymes. Was their audience so dumb that they accepted 'cat sat on the mat' levels of poetry?

When he'd been a child he'd been singing along to John Lennon's 'Imagine' on the radio and his father had explained the terrible grammatical error Lennon had made for the sake of a rubbish rhyme that stopped the song being brilliant.

'*And no religion too* should, of course, be *and no religion either*.'

At the end of the service the vicar came to the lectern to whoops and applause. Vicar Dave, he was called.

'Thank you for coming to the Church of the Rock. The church of the rock 'n' roll.'

More whoops and high fives from the audience.

'We hope you have felt welcomed and inspired.'

Applause. The vicar looked round the congregation.

'Don't forget, though, that on Sunday we will have a more serious intent.' He frowned. 'We will be casting out demons. If you know anyone who you feel is troubled by Satan, bring them here to be saved. If you are troubled by Satan do not feel shy about coming forward.'

The service ended with a mercifully short drum solo then yet more whoops and hollers. Watts stayed seated, looking down, as the congregation filed past him. When virtually everyone had left, the visiting group of singers were still gathered before the altar. Watts raised his eyes. They met those of the beautiful young woman with the great voice. For a few seconds they looked at each other then she dropped her eyes and tugged on her hair. Bob Watts kept his eyes fixed on his daughter, Catherine.

Heading up Dyke Road in an unmarked pool car, Heap driving, Gilchrist said: 'What's with the blushing, Bellamy?'

'I just flush, I don't know why,' he replied, glancing in the rear-view mirror. 'I suppose it's a residual thing from child-hood and because I'm surrounded by men who are . . . well, you know.'

'Know what about these men?'

'I think of them and I think of Piltdown, ma'am.'

Piltdown was a village on the Downs a few miles outside Brighton. Gilchrist knew that much. She was also dimly aware of the Piltdown Man but couldn't say exactly who he was. Heap could. He glanced at her as they came out of the city on to the Downs.

'You'll remember the Piltdown Man, the scientific fraud that found a link between Neanderthal man and modern man? And women. The Missing Link? Something not quite Neanderthal, not quite human.'

'And?'

Heap gave that cute grin again though he kept his eyes on the road. 'Definition of most policemen, ma'am.'

Gilchrist didn't crack a smile, even though Heap was focused on the road passing beside the golf course. Couldn't, given her new rank. But damn if he wasn't right.

A man and a woman answered the door of Saddlescombe Farmhouse.

'We're here about the Wicker Man set alight on Brighton beach,' Gilchrist said, by way of introduction. 'And the man burned to death inside it.'

The couple exchanged looks. Heap pointed towards Newtimber Hill.

'A Wicker Man not unlike that one on the hill there. Does that belong to you?'

The man nodded.

'And the one on the beach?'

The man nodded again.

'I think perhaps you'd better let us in,' Gilchrist said.

The woman pushed the front door wide and led the way into a long, Victorian-looking scullery, high-ceilinged and tiled on floor and walls. They sat at a big table in the centre of the room. Gilchrist sat on the other side whilst Heap remained standing in the middle of the room.

Their names were Ev Johnson and Tabby McGrath and they were exactly what Gilchrist had expected. No leather in evidence about their persons or on their feet. Hair in clotted dreadlocks, man and woman both. Ev Johnson had a scrappy beard and metal hanging from ears, eyebrows, nose and bottom lip. The woman, Tabby McGrath, was nut-brown and weather-beaten with the same amount of metal cluttering up her face. Both gave off a stuffy, wet wool odour.

Once the usual regulatory stuff had been sorted Gilchrist got straight to it. 'You burned a person alive this morning.'

'What are you talking about?' Johnson said.

'There was a person in your Wicker Man and when you set fire to it you set fire to him too.'

'Now just a blooming minute,' Johnson said, jabbing his finger at the table. 'First of all there was no person in our structure and second we did not set fire to it.'

'Ev – that's an unusual name,' Gilchrist said. 'What's it short for?'

'It's short for Ev.'

'It will be Everard, ma'am,' Heap chipped in.

Gilchrist looked at the man. 'Is that right? Everard. Often misinterpreted at school, I'm guessing, young people being what they are.'

'I didn't go to school. I was home-educated.'

Gilchrist smiled and turned to the woman, who was picking at a spot. 'Tabby – that's Tabitha, yes?'

'So?' the woman said.

'So, a couple of nice middle-class youngsters – what are you doing constructing a Wicker Man on our beach? And when did you construct it?'

'Over the past couple of weeks,' Johnson said. 'We hauled it by flatbed lorry on to the beach in the middle of the night and six of us erected it in the water.'

'In the water?'

'Yes – it wasn't so difficult. Once we'd got it upright its own weight sank its base stilts deep enough into the shingle to stabilize it. But we hadn't taken account of the tide going out. We lost some impact there.'

'And there was no one inside it?'

'Of course not.' Johnson was indignant. 'What do you think we are?'

'Actually, now that you raise the question: what exactly are you?'

'We're wiccans. And the last thing we'd want to do is harm anyone. We're committed to celebrating life, not destroying it.'

'So how did the body get inside your Wicker Man?'

Tabby McGrath had been looking sullen, staring at the table, her fingers going to her spots then away again. She said now: 'Isn't it your job to answer that question?'

'That's what we're trying to do, Tabitha,' Gilchrist said. 'Why did you erect it in the middle of the night?'

'For effect. We wanted it to be there for the rising of the sun. And my name's Tabby.'

'Very feline. Was that day a significant date?'

'That evening,' Johnson said. 'Walpurgisnacht.'

Gilchrist glanced at Heap.

'Walpurgis Night, ma'am. Thirtieth of April – the night before May Day. Traditionally in Germany the night the witches met on the Brocken mountain for a sabbat. And the night the Wild Hunt can be heard but best not be seen across the Downs.'

'Best not seen?' Gilchrist said.

'If you look at it,' Heap said, 'it will take you along with it to Hell.'

Gilchrist saw Tabitha McGrath curl her lip.

'Typical male establishment distortion of a life-giving pagan ritual.'

'What's your view?' Gilchrist said.

'Paganism is a brotherhood of white magic. We believe in the light, not the dark. We believe in the spirits of the trees and the streams. We don't worship Satan; we worship pre-Christian gods.'

'And what does the thirtieth of April mean to your group?'

'Our group includes a Druid priest and a shamaness but for all of us it's the start of the celebration of spring,' McGrath said. 'May the first is a cross-quarter day coming between the Vernal Equinox and the Summer Solstice.'

'I'm no wiser,' Gilchrist said. 'But you're talking about May Day? Dancing round the maypole?'

'Dancing round the male phallus, you mean,' Ev Johnson said. 'A transgressive time, of course.'

Gilchrist looked at Heap again.

'Transgressive means men dressed in women's clothes, women in men's,' he said. 'A peasant a king for a day and vice versa. Boundaries are crossed – everything gets turned upside down.' He looked at the couple. 'Right?'

Ev Johnson gave a reluctant nod. 'More or less.'

'I understand May Day is a celebration, *transgressive* or not,' Gilchrist said. 'They make a big fuss of it over in Ditchling. But where does the Wicker Man fit in?'

'Traditionally,' Johnson said in a bored drawl, 'the celebration begins the night before with huge bonfires and ritual dancing around them.'

'So the plan was to set fire to the Wicker Man as if it were a bonfire on the evening of the thirtieth of April?' Gilchrist said.

'As the sun went down,' Johnson said. 'At the same time as we set the one here on fire. Correct.'

'So why did you set fire to it in the morning?'

Johnson shook his head wearily. 'We didn't. Why would we? The morning had no significance. Plus, we were going to do stuff around it through the day then set it alight at dusk on the thirtieth of April.'

'You haven't set the one here alight.'

'We intended to do both together. It didn't seem worth doing one without the other.'

Gilchrist was inclined to believe him but there was still the matter of the dead person.

'I repeat: how did the body get inside the structure?'

'And I repeat: we don't know. We didn't put it there.'

Gilchrist clasped her hands on the table in front of her. 'OK. How would some person or persons unknown get a body in there?'

'There was a ladder at the back leading up to the performance space we'd created in the chest of the Wicker Man.'

'Performance space?'

'We were going to do shows from in there. It was like a stage – like the staging for a giant Punch and Judy show? We were going to do readings and stuff like that.'

Gilchrist and Bellamy Heap exchanged glances.

'Go on,' Gilchrist said.

'A couple of people could have lugged a body up the ladder, I suppose.'

'What time did you finish erecting it?' Gilchrist said.

'About four in the morning.'

'How many of you?'

'Six of us.'

'What did you do then?'

'Went home. Tabby and me were going back around nine to keep a watch on it until we started doing stuff at noon.'

'Who knew you were putting it up?' she said.

'Just our group. Maybe eight people in total. Why?'

'Well, we have two possibilities. Either somebody just happened to be passing with a spare unconscious body and they took advantage of the fortuitous appearance of a Wicker Man – oh, and had fuel with them to set the structure alight. Unlikely, wouldn't you say? Or, the murderer or murderers knew it was going up and planned accordingly.'

'None of our group would do such a thing.' Tabitha McGrath was indignant.

'Then word got out from one or more of you,' Gilchrist said. 'We're going to need the names and addresses of all the people in your group. Did you tell anyone outside the group?'

'Certainly not,' Johnson said. 'We wanted to create the sense of awe such a figure brings and then double it by lighting the one here too. If word leaked out we would lose impact. That's why we didn't ask for permission from the council.'

'Now months of preparation have gone up in smoke,' McGrath said, her voice shaking. 'It's a tragedy.'

'I'm sure the murder victim who also went up in smoke agrees,' Heap said.

Gilchrist darted a look at him. He looked down, flushing. She looked at Everard Johnson. She was inclined to believe him. Even so.

'All right, Everard, this farmhouse is now a crime scene.'

'The name is Ev. What do you mean?'

'We need to examine the house for any signs that the man in the Wicker Man was here.'

'He wasn't!' Tabby said.

'We just want to be sure,' Gilchrist said. 'How do we get hold of other members of your group?'

'They all live here. We're a commune.'

'Are any of them around now?'

'Three more of us. Ellie is hard to pin down – she's gone travelling. Roger Newell is also away but you can get him at the Jurassic Museum tomorrow.'

Gilchrist had no idea what the Jurassic Museum was. She glanced at Heap. He was nodding.

'And the third person?'

'Lesley is the one who should have been guarding it. Lesley

Henderson. It's Lesley's turn to do the Brighton Farm Market tomorrow.'

'You left someone guarding it? Why didn't you mention that earlier? I'd like to have a word with the person guarding it as a priority.'

Everard and Tabitha exchanged glances.

'So would we,' Ev murmured, then looked down at the table.

'You haven't spoken to Lesley?'

'Lesley has disappeared.'

TWENTY-ONE

'How do you reach those perfect notes?' Watts said.

'Faith,' his daughter said without hesitation. 'To take a breath and hope a perfect sound will emerge is always an act of faith. And prayer. I say to God: "Lord, help me find that place as a performer where your visitation passes through me and out of my mouth."' Then, awkwardly, she added: 'Hello, Father.'

'Since when did you go God Squad?' Watts said.

'God Squad?' she said, her facial expression as exaggerated as the exclamation marks she used in her occasional text messages to him.

'It's what we used to call people like you . . .'

She laughed, eyebrows still high, face fixed in that overdone look of surprise. 'People like me? You mean freaks?'

Watts was out of his depth with teenagers. More specifically, with his own daughter.

'You're not a freak,' he said.

'Well, I have a moral compass so for you I must be a freak.'

'Now just hang on, will you?'

God, her expression was so *intense*. Now she was doing serious.

'Dad. We know what you did. OK?'

'I'm not getting this. I had a one-night stand – which is, I admit, a dreadful thing to do. But your mother had a secret affair for fifteen years with some guy in Canada – and I'm the bad person?'

His daughter looked down. 'She had cause.'

'What cause?'

She turned away, playing with her hair. 'You were a rotten husband and a rotten father.'

'I don't want to go into the whole "I was making a life for my family" spiel but, Jesus, Catherine . . .'

Her voice trembled. 'Don't use his name in vain.'

Watts resisted the urge to raise his eyes to heaven – or rather the ceiling – but it was difficult. Having seen the horrors inflicted on innocent people in the different names of God in the Balkans and elsewhere, he had nothing but contempt for any of it. And this kind of service about 'Let's Make Religion Relevant to Youth' sickened him.

Aside from anything else, Christian rock music offended his sensibilities. It was a bit like alcohol-free beer or vegetarian chicken burgers. He hated when something pretended to be something but without its essential ingredient.

A thing was what it was and rock music was about sex. Christian rock and roll was a contradiction in terms. It was about pretending. Rock and roll dancing was dirty dancing, from the hips and pelvis, and Christians couldn't dance like that and mean it.

Watts looked at his daughter. Looked at the ring on her finger. She saw him looking.

'Yes, I'm married.'

He frowned.

'To Christ.' She pointed at her ring. 'That's my chastity ring.'

Jesus H. Christ seemed an inappropriate thing to say but that was Watts' immediate response. It could be nobody but his own and his wife's fault that their twenty-year-old daughter was one of about six twenty-year-old virgins in the whole of the UK. Aaaagh.

Then he had a paranoid, Dennis Wheatley-inspired thought. That made her a valuable commodity for the kind of black magicians who seemed to be spreading their evil around Brighton. He immediately dismissed it. Almost immediately.

'How long are you in Brighton?' he said.

'Just the weekend.'

'Were you going to let me know?'

'We're on a pretty hectic schedule, Dad.'

'Have you time for me to buy you dinner?'

She shook her head. 'We're having dinner as a group and then we're going to a prayer party with Vicar Dave.'

Watts nodded.

'But why are you here, Dad?'

'I wanted to see you.'

'How did you know I was here?'

Watts looked sheepish. 'I saw it on your Facebook page.'

He'd realized months earlier that the only sure way of knowing vaguely what his children were up to was via social networking sites, though he drew the line at attempting to follow them on Twitter.

'Why did you want to see me?'

'You're my daughter.'

'OK, well.' She shrugged. 'You have. I've got to go, Dad.'

'Sure.'

'You should talk to Vicar Dave. He's great.'

Watts glanced over at the vicar, who was standing by the pulpit observing them.

'I'm sure he is.'

'He wrote a couple of our songs. He's really talented.'

'Clearly.'

Watts leaned forward to embrace her but the guitar got in the way.

She touched his face. 'God loves you, Dad.'

'I love you,' he stumbled, 'though I've not always been good at showing it.'

She stepped past him. 'Don't sweat it.'

She hurried after her friends, half-turning to shout back: 'God bless.'

'You'd think they might have mentioned Lesley Henderson's disappearance earlier,' Gilchrist fumed, stomping down the pathway back to the car, Heap hurrying to keep up.

She lowered her voice when a good-looking older woman

with long grey hair and a trim figure appeared below them on the path, shopping bags in each hand.

'What do you think, Bellamy?'

The woman gave them a quick glance and a nod as she passed them. Heap glanced back at her and watched her go for a moment.

'Too old for you, Bellamy,' Gilchrist said, also glancing back.

The woman headed towards the front door of the farmhouse. Heap glanced at Gilchrist.

'I can't see her being one of the absent three,' Gilchrist said. 'Can you?'

Heap turned and shook his head. 'I think Lesley Henderson is crucial as a potential victim, killer or witness,' he said.

'I agree,' Gilchrist said as they climbed into the car. 'But I still can't see how to link the Wicker Man with a painting of lilies.'

'I'm still looking, ma'am.'

'So what do you know about that farm?'

Heap waited until they were driving up the road before he answered. 'It was listed as a working farm in the Domesday Book. The Knights Templar were granted the land around 1228.'

Gilchrist stared at the side of Heap's face.

'When the Templars were wound up in 1308, Saddlescombe was one hundred and sixty-three acres of arable land, a windmill, two barns, an ox shed, a stable and a chapel. It was valued at twenty pounds. The rest at seventy-five pounds. The rest included farming utensils, twelve oxen for ploughing, six hundred sheep and a horse.'

'One horse doesn't sound much if they were knights.'

Heap didn't respond.

'Your research – you know you freak me out when you quote stuff off by heart.'

'Photographic memory, ma'am. I read something once and remember it forever. A blessing and a curse.'

'I can imagine – well, actually, I can't. And I suppose you got all this off the Internet.'

'Victoria County History, ma'am. Wonderful resource.'

They were nearing the Dyke Golf Club but Heap was behind a slow-moving car.

'Are you going to overtake or get back to Brighton sometime next year?' Gilchrist said.

The car turned into the golf club car park.

'Sorry,' Gilchrist said.

They drove in silence for a couple of minutes.

'Do you know how many people in Britain read horoscopes?' Heap said.

'That is not a statistic that is immediately to hand, Bellamy, no.'

'Six million.'

'That's a lot. But statistics are devilish.'

'They are. But you see my point, ma'am?'

'I'm wondering what the population of the country is.'

'Around sixty-two million, give or take.'

'So that's ten per cent. Big but not massive.'

'If six million people each gave me a penny I would be a very happy man.'

'Good point. So we have six million people who believe in this rubbish.' Gilchrist sighed. 'I see where you're going.'

'How many Christians are there? How many Muslims? How many Scientologists?'

'You want me to answer?'

'It was largely rhetorical.'

'Good – because I don't know. And I still see where you're going.'

They were dropping down into Brighton now. Seagulls skirled above them, acutely white against the black sky.

'My point is, ma'am, if you don't believe in a religion then you look around and conclude the world is full of nutcases. Nutcases who believe all kinds of unprovable nonsense. That so many do believe in unbelievable things probably means that people have some fundamental and crucial need for a faith in something beyond the real world.'

'So whatever is going on has a certain rationale from the point of view of whoever is doing it?' Gilchrist said.

'Undoubtedly,' he said.

They were heading down Dyke Road into Brighton now.

'Come for a drink,' Gilchrist said.

She saw his look.

'I'm not coming on to you so forget any screwing the boss or screwing the taller woman scenario.'

She saw a new look. God, he was as bad as she was at hiding her emotions.

'Not that I don't think taller women in general wouldn't find you attractive and not that I'm referring to your size . . .'

As she floundered she caught the look on his face. She couldn't help laughing.

'And you can piss off, Constable Heap.'

'Ma'am,' he said, a sly grin on his face. No blush.

'Hello there, Chief Constable.'

Vicar Dave had God is Love tattooed on his right forearm. The sleeve of his shirt hid whatever he had on his left. Watts had a strong urge to punch him.

'I recognize you,' Vicar Dave added. 'How can I help?'

'I'm no longer officially in the police,' Watts said. 'Call me Bob.'

'And I'm Dave, as you know. Vicar Dave, the youngsters like to call me.'

'You're pretty much a youngster yourself,' Watts said as pleasantly as he could.

'I've been doing Christ's work for fifteen years now.'

'Casting out demons.'

'Among other things.'

Vicar Dave had a piercing stare.

'Do you know the girl from the visiting choir you were talking to?'

'Yes,' Watts said. 'She has a wonderful voice.'

The vicar nodded. His eyes got added intensity from the fact they were black. Fanatic eyes, Watts thought. Charles Manson eyes.

'I heard you ask her where her voice came from,' Vicar Dave said.

'I did.'

'To analyse singing and to think of what it is like is the Devil's business. How you move from one word to another, how you connect the heart to the lyric and how you find the melodic line is for God to give.'

Watts nodded. 'I'll remember that.'

'The world is a wicked place and the Devil needs only a crack in the window to enter your home unbidden. Once inside he is a most unwelcome guest.'

'And your job is to throw him out again – but not just out of the house. You believe in possession, do you not?'

Vicar Dave nodded without looking at Watts. He spread his arms. 'Look around this city. It is filled with sin. There is madness here. Unholy madness. The Devil and his disciples assault the innocents of this city hourly with drink and drugs and lewd living. I see the debauchery on every street and it sickens me. And the only shield is the Bible and our champion is Jesus Christ.'

'How do you cast them out?'

Vicar Dave had distracted himself. He darted a look back at Watts. 'What?'

'The demons. How do you cast them out?'

Vicar Dave dropped his arms. 'The ceremony is secret, I am afraid.'

'It's in a church.'

'The first part of the ceremony is in the church then I do the actual casting out in an inner sanctum.'

Watts gave a little shrug. 'What do you do with the demons once you've got them out?'

'Pardon?'

'I'm rusty on my Bible but when Jesus cast demons out wasn't there usually a handy herd of swine nearby that the demons went into?'

'You refer to the Gadarene swine in the Gospel of Mark.'

'If you say so. I seem to remember all these pigs – a couple of thousand of them – ran into the sea and were drowned.'

'The unclean spirit when asked his name declared: "My name is Legion, for we are many".'

'There you go. But what do *you* do with them? I mean, back in New Testament times I would have been cheesed off if I'd been the owner of those two thousand pigs Christ sent off to be drowned before he went merrily on his way. Losing my entire livelihood on a passing stranger's whim – well, I might have wanted to crucify somebody myself.'

Vicar Dave gave the merest hint of a tight smile.

'But that was then,' Watts said. 'These days we live in a compensation culture. An animal-loving culture, for that matter. Send any unclean spirits the way of some local flock or herd of animals and you're going to get your ass sued. The animal liberation activists – members of your own congregation even – will be after you. I mean, Jesus might not have shown much species respect but I've just been hearing in a rap that you've yolked your church to that particular cart. Not that it will be pulled by any animals I presume.'

'Is that an attempt at levity?' Vicar Dave's eyes were fierce. 'Bob?'

'Levity? Is that like walking on water? Or am I thinking levitation?'

Vicar Dave looked for a moment at the tattoo on his forearm. 'Is there anything else I can help you with?'

'Some very strange things are happening in Brighton.'

'Harbingers of the End of Days, perhaps.'

'Do you think?'

'All the time. But, yes, the evidence seems to indicate that the End of Days approaches. It was even predicted in a calendar by the ungodly Mayans.'

'That's that then? Don't start reading any long novels?'

Vicar Dave gave his tight smile. 'Or short ones.'

TWENTY-TWO

Sarah Gilchrist phoned Watts when he was wandering along the seafront in the rain, his head swirling from seeing his daughter, experiencing the weird church service and all the talk about Crowley and Templars and the secrets of Saddlescombe Farm earlier in the day. She invited him to the Colonnade for a drink with her and a colleague.

The Colonnade was a single-room bar beside the Theatre Royal. Although not much of a theatregoer Watts liked the posters and signed actor photographs all over the walls. Plus he was a sucker for these Victorian places with their red plush and soft lights in big glass bowls.

It was chucking it down so he came through the door of the pub dripping wet. Sarah Gilchrist was sitting at a table at the back of the pub with a short, trim young man with rosy cheeks.

The pub was heaving because it was the interval at the performance of *Rosemary's Baby* at the Theatre Royal next door. However, the way parted for a man so thoroughly wet.

Sarah introduced him to the young man. 'I wanted to get you two talking about all that's going on in Brighton. Bellamy here has a big brain.'

Watts nodded as he carefully took off his dripping coat then went to the bar to order. He glanced back at Sarah. She looked tense. The return to duty, he guessed. He saw Heap excuse himself and go downstairs to the toilet.

It took a few minutes to get served but as he took the drinks the audience drained out of the pub and went back into the theatre next door.

He sat and gestured to the steps Heap had gone down.

'What's with Boy Wonder?'

Gilchrist punched his arm. 'Don't you start. He's a bright man. It's not his fault he looks like a schoolboy. University entrant but chose to come in at the bottom to learn policing from there up. Takes a lot of stick for it.'

Heap rejoined them.

'Do you know what synchronicity is?' Watts said when Heap was seated.

'The title of an old Police album,' Gilchrist said.

Watts and Heap both glanced at her.

'What? I like them.'

'Police?' Watts said. 'You were a kid when they were big.'

'I always liked the name,' Gilchrist said. She laughed. 'Not because of my future profession. It wasn't!'

'Sting got the title of the album from Jung,' Watts said. 'Jung developed this theory of coincidences that he believed had a deeper meaning.'

'I think you're about to lose me,' Gilchrist said. 'But I'm sure Bellamy understands.'

'OK, I find these books on my dad's bookshelf about the occult, signed by their authors to him with odd messages. One of them is by Aleister Crowley, the black magician. At Lewes Museum an archaeologist told me this afternoon my father was involved with Aleister Crowley in World War Two to fight the Nazis on the astral plane – don't even go there.

'He also told me some weird occult stuff about the Knights Templar at Saddlescombe Farm up on Devil's Dyke. That happens to be where Colin Pearson – one of those occult writers my father knew – lives.'

'You know the Goat of Mendes was loose on Devil's Dyke last night?' Heap said. 'He cast his shadow over the town.'

Watts frowned. 'I was up there last night.'

Gilchrist half-stood to peer at the top of Watts' head. 'Are your horns detachable?'

'Ha,' Watts said. 'Are you serious about this apparition?'

'Nobody saw him on the dyke that we're aware of, but a lot of people saw his giant shadow fall over the town.'

'I saw a ram with really big horns at the farm.'

'It was half-goat, half-man,' Gilchrist said. 'Sheep don't usually inspire terror in my experience. We were up there just now. At Saddlescombe Organics because of the Wicker Man you told me about – the commune there built it. Thanks for the tip.'

Watts spread his hands. 'There you go. I pick out this book from my dad's bookshelf and suddenly everywhere I look there's black magic. You have all this occult stuff happening in Brighton. My next-door neighbour has a sheep's heart nailed to his door. The magical equipment of some Elizabethan magician called John Dee has been stolen from the British Museum. An attempt was made to steal more of his occult stuff from the Science Museum and from the Archaeological Museum in Lewes.'

Watts took a sip of his drink. 'Oh, and a book of spells has been stolen from the Jubilee Library, which I don't think you know about. The *Key of Solomon*. Is this a zeitgeist thing or what?'

'A book of spells?' Gilchrist said. 'From the kids' section?'

'No – the real thing,' Watts said. 'It's called a *grimoire*. Pretty ancient, I gather.'

Gilchrist filled Watts in on the missing vicar, the person burned to death in the Wicker Man and the theft of *The Devil's Altar*.

'I spoke to the other vicar – David Rutherford – earlier today,' she said. 'Apparently the dead man felt under threat from Satanists. I know, I know. But he'd kind of freaked out. And certainly his flat gave every indication of that. Pentacle on the floor, all that stuff.'

'Any leads?'

'Yes, actually. Whoever threw the shit and smeared it on the walls of the vicar's apartment ate at Plenty. We're checking that out tomorrow – they're closed at the moment, having tried to poison me and Kate.'

'Revelling in your power, are you, Detective Inspector?' Watts said. 'Closing a place down because they treated you badly.'

'Fuck off – we weren't the only people they poisoned.'

'And *The Devil's Altar*?'

'We have CCTV of two people, one of whom we think is a woman. Both are swathed in waterproofs. We've traced them as far as the Imperial Arcade.'

'Most of the population of Brighton is in waterproofs in this weather,' Watts said.

'True – and it seems likely the person messing up the vicar's flat was a gay male,' Heap said.

'And in the British Museum?' Gilchrist said.

'Pass. I can maybe find out. I don't think the police have been called in about that either.'

They all took a swig of their drinks, then Heap said: 'Are you a religious man, Bob?'

'I'm quite the contrary,' Watts said. 'Religion appeals to hysteria, fear . . . ignorance. I remember my father telling me once that in its early days Christianity was not a religion – it was an epidemic. I'd go further than my father: religions are viruses. We've got to find the cure.'

'And what is that cure?' Heap said. 'Marxism?'

'That was just another sort of religion. Humanism maybe?'

'Which is based on nothing,' Heap said. 'You need a basis for a moral system: you can't just pluck an arbitrary one out of the ether.'

Gilchrist gave an amused glance at Watts.

'You a university man, Bellamy?' Watts said after a moment.

'Does it show?'

'Just a tad. Are you religious?'

'I was brought up Catholic but it didn't really take.'

'Not even the guilt?'

Heap blushed. 'A bit of that.'

Gilchrist sighed. 'People's beliefs.'

'You're not religious either, Sarah?' Watts said.

'Not in any way, shape or form. Pisses me off to tell you the truth – what people get away with in the name of it.'

The door burst open and a screeching gaggle of women tottered in wearing high-heeled boots. They took off their raincoats to reveal micro-skirts and T-shirts emblazoned with 'Laura's Hen Party'. As one they bared their teeth. Plastic vampire teeth.

TWENTY-THREE

Gilchrist's first appointment the next morning was the Jubilee Library. The rare books department was on the top floor at the rear of the imposing glass-fronted building. It looked little more than a small reading room through a set of glass doors. Subdued lighting protected twenty or so books on display in glass cases. But there were no books on shelves as Gilchrist expected.

'I thought it would look like a second-hand bookshop,' she said to the director of the collection, a nervous man with sparse black hair combed across his pate. His manner didn't seem to fit his name, which was Allcock.

'These are *rare* books, Detective Inspector – we keep them in temperature-controlled rooms. Our collection dates from the thirteenth to the twentieth century. Many are touched, if at all, only when wearing gloves but most of the collection is under lock and key.'

He led her through an enormous room, full of tier after tier of shelves, and through to a tiny office piled with papers. He cleared space on a straight-backed chair and invited her to sit.

'You lost a rare manuscript but didn't report it,' Gilchrist said. 'Why?'

Allcock looked surprised. 'That's an internal matter. We're hoping it's just misplaced.'

'That's not what we heard,' Gilchrist said.

'From whom?'

Whom. This man was another Heap.

'Is it something called the *Key of Solomon*?'

Allcock nodded reluctantly.

'How did the library acquire it?'

The librarian seemed surprised by the question. 'I don't really know but I assume it was in the George Long collection.'

Gilchrist looked her next question.

'In 1879 Long donated about three and a half thousand volumes, mostly in sixteenth-century Greek and Latin.'

'Do you really believe the *Key* has been mislaid?' she said.

Allcock shuffled papers on his desk. 'Not really.'

'Somebody broke in here? Or was it out there on display?'

Allcock looked almost sorrowful. 'I think it was probably the first time it had been out on display.'

'Aren't the display cases alarmed?' Gilchrist said.

'Theoretically.'

'Theoretically?'

'Theoretically they are locked and alarmed. But there was a week when my regular staff members and I were away on a course. Somebody not familiar with our policies turned the alarms off and unlocked the case to remove another item.'

'And they didn't lock it again,' Gilchrist said. 'And this thief just happened to be in the room?'

The man looked embarrassed. 'It appears the case might have been open for some days.'

'CCTV?' Gilchrist said.

'Yes. But our system is time-lapse. Four frames a second. Movement can be quite blurred or missed altogether.'

'You save the images though?' Gilchrist said.

'For a limited period, yes.'

'So if the thief did steal it on the day the case was first left open, the recording will probably have been wiped.'

Allcock clasped his hands. 'I would think so.'

'And nobody noticed the theft?'

'The casing of the manuscript was still there.'

'The casing?'

'It was in a silver case, very finely engraved. To be honest it was on display for the casing not the content. I doubt anyone knew what was in it.'

'Somebody obviously did.'

He looked rueful. 'Obviously. I'm just grateful the casing wasn't stolen as well.'

'Is the manuscript valuable?' Gilchrist said.

'It has intrinsic value as an ancient manuscript but it is priceless to some people.'

'Because it is a book of spells.'

'A *grimoire*, yes,' Allcock said.

'Tell me about it,' Gilchrist said. 'Pretend you're talking to a particularly stupid child and we'll do fine.'

There was a uniformed policeman hovering near the Saddlescombe Organics stall when Kate Simpson stepped into Brighton Farm Market. He was short and had rosy cheeks and people further inside the yard were giving him wary glances or whispering about him. He remained composed.

The stall had not yet opened. She stopped a couple of yards away from him. He looked at her, frowning.

'Lesley Henderson?' he said.

She shook her head. 'Kate Simpson from Southern Shores Radio. Looks like we want the same stall.'

He nodded. 'I need to take a statement from someone who should be working on this stall today.'

'Ditto,' she said. 'They provide unusual food for Plenty and I'm doing a story about the food poisoning there.'

'I didn't know about that,' he said. 'You got poisoned?'

Kate nodded. 'Me and my friend Sarah. You might know her – DI Gilchrist? Apparently among other things we ate lilies.'

'Lilies,' the policeman repeated thoughtfully. 'Does DI Gilchrist know that?'

'You do know her?'

'I work for her.'

'They were lily bulbs, actually, supplied by this place. I haven't had a chance to mention it to her yet.'

The policeman held out his hand. 'I'm Constable Bellamy Heap. DI Gilchrist brought me on to her team a few days ago.'

Kate took his hand. 'You like working with Sarah?'

'I do.'

'We've shared a flat on and off.' Kate saw a look in his eye and let go of his hand. 'What?' she said guardedly.

He flushed. 'Sorry – I think I just realized who perhaps you are.'

'And who, perhaps, am I?'

He flushed deeper. 'I think you might be the poor woman who was attacked and defended herself with DI Gilchrist's volt gun.' He dropped his hand. 'That must have been dreadful for you.'

'Yes, it was.'

She didn't want to cry but the tears came anyway. He reached into his side pocket and produced a wad of tissues.

'Crumpled but clean,' he said, holding them out to her.

She glanced around. Some of the people watching were darting angry glances at Heap, assuming he'd caused the tears.

She turned away and tried to smile. 'A man with tissues for just such an emergency. How gallant.'

She warmed to Bellamy Heap and his pink cheeks and his kind face. And at the same time she was horribly embarrassed that she'd broken down in front of a stranger watched by a crowd of total strangers.

She was even more embarrassed that she must look a

fright. She was no female *X-Factor* judge, controlling welling tears with a finger placed horizontally under each eye. She couldn't do emotional without having a make-up crisis. When Kate cried she turned blotchy and her nose ran and she made unattractive noises. Aside from that she was perfect.

She giggled at the thought. Given that she was giving some kind of tearful snort at the same time she heard the strangest sound and that made her giggle more. Heap looked bewildered. OK, so he was just a man after all.

'You wouldn't understand,' she gasped, suppressing her laugh.

'Probably not,' he said. His smile was disarming.

Kate was thinking, Oh, God, Mills and Boon. It made her laugh even louder.

'The *Key of Solomon* is probably the most famous *grimoire* in the world,' Allcock said. 'It's supposed to have been written by King Solomon – the one in the Bible? He wrote it for his son Rehoboam then ordered him to hide the book in his sepulchre when he died. The Babylonians found it during their destruction of his Temple. They couldn't understand the text until – the story goes – the Angel of the Lord came to their aid.'

'There seems to be a lot wrong with that story,' Gilchrist said.

Allcock nodded. 'That's the legend. Actually, the *Key* probably dates from the fourteenth-century Italian Renaissance.'

'And this famous book of spells was in the Jubilee Library?'

'One of them was.'

'You're losing me again,' Gilchrist said. 'He wrote more than one?'

'He didn't write any of them,' Allcock said patiently. 'As I said, it was probably written in the fourteenth century. During the Italian Renaissance ancient Greek and Roman philosophical and religious documents came from the east after the fall of Constantinople in 1451. Although some date the *Key* as far back as the Fourth Crusade's sack of Constantinople in 1204, which led to a similar transmission of knowledge long lost or unknown in the West.'

'They found the *Key* and brought it to the West?'

'No. But there were a lot of other manuscripts dealing with magic. Jewish Kabbalists and Arab alchemists put their own spin on them. One of those men probably created the *Key of Solomon.*'

'Kabbalists? Is that like the religion Madonna follows?'

'Nothing like it. That's a ridiculous modern distortion of what was a serious – if misguided – search for knowledge through the power of numbers. In this country there are a number of manuscript versions of the *Key*. This one was probably mid- to late-sixteenth century, in Latin.'

'Tell me about the spells.'

Allcock grimaced. 'The *Key* gives detailed instructions for preparing and performing acts of magic in rituals using specific materials when the planets are in certain configurations. The first part has conjurations, invocations and curses. The magician uses them to summon and control spirits of the dead and demons. It shows you how to become invisible, make someone love you and find lost or stolen items.'

'Sounds like we could make use of it now,' Gilchrist said. 'Except for the loving you bit.'

'Part two describes how the exorcist should purify himself, clothe himself and prepare the implements to be used. It also states what animal sacrifices need to be made.'

'Animal? Or animal and human?' Gilchrist said.

'I don't know the manuscript that well. I believe just animal.'

'Is it generally known the library has this manuscript?'

Allcock shook his head. 'Scarcely known at all, I should say.'

Watts had phoned ahead but there was no sign of Avril when he arrived back at the Pearson household. Pearson answered the door himself and shuffled into the living room, assuming Watts would follow.

Watts found Pearson mesmerizing but for all his contradictions rather than his powers of thought. The man's belief in his own intelligence was staggering at the same time as his self-awareness was non-existent. Had he known how ridiculous he had looked the other day in his stained tracksuit with the tea cosy on his head?

When they were settled, glass of wine beside each of them

although it was scarcely eleven, Watts said: 'Mr Pearson, what is your view of the Templars?'

'They found some secret that gave them a way to maintain their peak experiences.'

'It didn't help them though, did it? Didn't help all those burned at the stake in France.'

'Some might argue that they at least got revenge: Philip the Fair and Pope Clement the Fifth both died in agony within months of the slow roasting to death of the Grand Master Jacques de Molay.'

'And Edward II?'

'He protected the Templars as best he could. Then he let them all go.'

'How come you know all this? Have you been investigating them at Saddlescombe?'

Pearson did his teeth-baring act again. 'You've seen the books here. I know *everything*.'

'But do you live at Saddlescombe because of the Templar secret concealed here?'

Pearson's cheeks were bright red when he grinned. 'What secret?'

'The secret you were just talking about.'

'I didn't say it was located here, nor that it was a physical thing.'

'Well then, why did kings and prelates make a special point of coming here? Why did Edward II protect them?'

Pearson said nothing.

'The Templars dug a hundred and fifty feet down through chalk and flint to find water for their well,' Watts continued. 'If they had that kind of commitment . . .'

'You think there are hidden parts of the farm?' Pearson said. 'Subterranean parts? Some secret chapel containing some secret thing?'

Watts nodded. 'I'd bet money on it.'

'Their secret being what, in your view – the head of Baphomet they worshipped?'

Watts shook his head. 'No such thing.'

'You sure? It's thought the name is a transliteration of Mohamet and that they caught their strange religious beliefs through contact with the Muslim religion in the Holy Land rather than in Provence. Makes sense to me.'

Watts snorted. 'Except for one thing: if they were some kind of Muslim sect they'd know that an actual image of Mohammed is a major no-no. So they wouldn't be worshipping a head. Further – why would they renounce Christ whilst shedding blood fighting for him in the Holy Land? What kind of stupid logic is that?'

'Then what? What did they worship? What was their secret?'

Watts shook his head. 'Beats me. I was hoping you could tell me.'

Pearson rubbed his hands. 'I think the bloodline from Jesus and Mary Magdalene down to the Merovingian kings has already been pretty well covered – and proved to be rubbish, of course. The idea of Mary Magdalene and Jesus as lovers has been around for centuries – since the second and third century AD in certain apocryphal gospels. Louis Martin in his *The Gospels Without God* at the end of the nineteenth century has Jesus become an atheist and have a son with Mary Magdalene in the south of France. Kazantzakis had a similar notion in *The Last Temptation of Christ* in the 1950s – you know it? The man who created Zorba the Greek?'

'I know the Scorsese film.'

Pearson nodded. 'Statistically speaking, if Jesus and Mary actually existed and did have a child and that child had a child or children and so on down the centuries, by now half the world would be descended from Jesus. So where's the bloodline then? And if, instead, you had centuries of inbreeding between sons and daughters of a bloodline down the generations, that bloodline would probably have produced an imbecile by now.'

'Then what do you think the Templar secret was? The Ark of the Covenant?'

'Can I just clarify?' Pearson said. 'You think that whatever the Templar secret was it is presently here at Saddlescombe. What am I then? The Guardian? Have I got it underneath my desk in my study?'

'Or are you someone searching for it?'

'Do I look like I'm searching for a secret? Have I dug up half the farm to find it?'

'The Ark of the Covenant?'

'Oh, that. Well, sure, I've got that. Avril uses it as a bedding box.' Pearson shook his head. 'Why do you want to know?'

'Because I do think whatever the Templar secret is, that secret is the secret of this place – and that is the reason for all these bad goings-on.'

'Have there been bad goings-on other than the Wicker Man on the beach?' Pearson said.

Watts gave a brief outline of recent occurrences, Pearson's eyes fixed on him the whole time.

'John Dee's magical equipment and the *Key of Solomon* both?' Pearson said.

'That combination means something to you?'

Pearson was about to respond when Avril came in with a tray.

'Home-made soup – you'll try some, Bob?'

Watts stood. 'Not for me, thanks, Avril. I only popped by.'

'Made with only natural ingredients,' she said.

'Even so. But thank you.'

Avril put the tray in front of her husband.

He looked up at her. 'I thought you were at the allotment,' he said.

She patted him on his shoulder. 'I was but I couldn't let you starve, could I?'

Pearson ogled her as she left the room. Watts was amused by the man's lechery. He sat back down. Pearson contemplated the soup. He glanced in the direction of Avril's departure.

'The Ark of the Covenant resided at the very heart of Solomon's Temple,' he said. 'It contained the tablets on which God had written the Ten Commandments for Moses. But the Temple was destroyed how many times in the Old Testament? By Assyrian, Babylonian and Roman conquerors with no respect for any religious beliefs other than their own. How could the Ark have survived intact for the Poor Fellow-Soldiers of Christ and the Temple of Solomon to uncover it? I simply don't see it.'

He dipped his spoon in the soup and slurped it into his mouth.

'Anyway, I thought Indiana Jones took care of the Ark.' Pearson pointed his spoon at Watts. 'If the Ark is anywhere it's not in our coal cellar, it is in Ethiopia. The Queen of Sheba and Solomon were lovers and had a child in Eritrea. That child founded the dynasty that ruled Ethiopia until Haile Selassie was overthrown in 1974. The dynasty survived three thousand years because it had the Ark to prove its lineage.'

Watts watched Pearson take two more spoonfuls of his soup and dunk a hunk of bread into it.

'Not that anybody has ever been allowed to see it.'

Watts chewed his lip. He had no real interest in any of this Biblical stuff. Pearson leaned forward and massaged his chest then sat back, his mouth open, for a moment.

'Are you OK?' Watts said.

'No,' Pearson grunted. 'I'm old. I never know whether it's indigestion or a heart attack.'

'Have you had yourself checked out?'

Pearson sat forward again. 'Of course – despite Avril's disapproval.'

'Why does she disapprove?'

Pearson glanced at the door again. Did he think Avril was listening?

'Avril doesn't believe in doctors. Didn't you know she's a white witch? She relies on the old medicines to cure her.'

'And do they?'

'Usually,' Pearson said, rubbing his chest again.

'What do the doctors say about your health?'

'They say that when a heart attack happens I'll know it's not indigestion.' He picked up his spoon and waved it. 'Old people get sick.' He took a spoonful of soup. 'So have you finished asking me foolish questions about the Templars?'

'Maybe the Templars took something else from the Temple,' Watts said. 'What about the *Key of Solomon*?'

'Well, it can't have been here if it has been in the library, can it?'

'The original.'

Pearson shook his head. 'They stashed the original book of rituals, written in Solomon's own fair hand, down the well here? I've got news for you, Watts. The *Key of Solomon* was not written by Solomon because Solomon didn't exist.'

Watts frowned. 'He's in the Bible and the Qu'ran.'

'That may be so. But there is absolutely no other evidence for his existence. He is meant to have left a legacy of major buildings, including his Temple, but there are no archaeological remains of any of them. The odd archaeological finds that have been linked to him probably came a century later in the Omride period. This period was polytheistic so the Bible glosses over it.'

'If the Temple didn't exist how are all these conquerors pulling it down?' Watts said. 'We know the Babylonian king, Nebuchadnezzar, captured Jerusalem and destroyed the city and the Temple.'

'We don't *know* anything. The Bible is not a reliable historical source. There is no archaeological evidence although, I admit, the most likely place for the site of the Temple – Temple Mount – can't be properly explored archaeologically because of Muslim sensitivities.'

Pearson put his spoon down and moved his plate away. 'But from my perspective it's irrelevant. Leave that to the Freemasons. Don't you find it curious, by the way, that most Masons wouldn't have a clue what to do with a trowel?'

'Why irrelevant?'

'Because if you only half-listened to me the other day you will know that my life's work has been to explore the perfectibility of man – or some men – by accessing the potential within them and within their brains. And whilst I accept the probability that certain rituals can access hidden parts of the mind, I do not accept that angels or demons, gods or devils are going to show us the way. If the Templars' secret was hidden knowledge, I'm interested. Treasure wouldn't go amiss either. But if their secret was some way to raise the Devil through the so-called *Key of Solomon* – I'll pass on that, thanks.'

With an effort Pearson lifted his tray and put it on his side table.

'Now it's time for my postprandial nap. Go and pester Avril. She'll like that. She certainly liked it when your father pestered her.'

TWENTY-FOUR

Gilchrist had arranged to meet Rutherford after his Saturday service at St Michael's, although her mind was on a lot of other things.

She got the time of the service wrong. When she went into St Michael's, Rutherford was still going full throttle. His glasses were halfway down his nose and he was peering at the congregation over them. Gilchrist stood at the back.

Rutherford pushed his spectacles up his nose and looked at the papers on his pulpit.

'In his beautiful and tragic essay "God's Lonely Man", novelist Thomas Wolfe stated that: "The whole conviction of my life now rests upon the belief that loneliness, far from being a rare and curious phenomenon peculiar to myself and to a few other solitary men, is the central and inevitable fact of human existence."' He paused, presumably to let the quote sink in. 'Wolfe goes on: "When we examine the moments, acts, and statements of all kinds of people we find that they are all suffering from the same thing."'

He took off his spectacles.

'The final cause of their complaint is loneliness.'

He looked around the church. He didn't seem to notice Gilchrist.

'I think we can all find an echo in our own lives for those sentiments. But there is, of course, one vast omission in Wolfe's thesis.'

He looked up to the soaring arched ceiling. 'I speak of God's cure for that loneliness.'

That was when Gilchrist stepped back into the foyer and started fiddling with her phone.

*   *   *

Watts found Avril in the kitchen.

'Not too late for soup, Bob.'

'Honestly, no,' he said. He was finding it odd that she was acting so normally after her curious behaviour the other day. He looked at the vegetables and plants lying across the table. Saw the flowers.

'Those the lilies you cook with?'

'Calla lilies. Yes. They're poisonous.'

'All parts of them?'

She nodded. 'They contain calcium oxalate, as do rhubarb leaves. But unlike rhubarb, with the lily it makes the whole plant toxic. You haven't ingested them raw, have you?'

He shook his head.

'Good.'

'So why are they in your kitchen?'

'I cook with them.'

'You're going to have to explain that.'

'Many foods we eat are toxic if not prepared properly. Beans need soaking and boiling. Raw potatoes will give you a nasty turn. If you cook the calla leaves properly you destroy the toxins.' She smiled at him. 'All cooking is chemistry, you know.'

'So I understand,' Watts said.

'Did you come in to ask me about cooking?'

'Colin says you knew my father.'

'Does he?'

'Donald Watts.'

She squinted as she tried to remember. She shook her head.

'He wrote as Victor Tempest.'

She gave him a calculating look. 'Victor Tempest was your father?'

'You knew him?'

She started to rummage in a drawer of the table. 'Scarcely.'

She took from a drawer a small package wrapped in silk. She carefully unwrapped a tarot pack.

'These were Aleister Crowley's own design. Useless for divination because he missed out essential elements of the original.'

'Aleister Crowley gave them to you?'

'I'm not that bloody old. He died in 1947, you know.'

'Cremated in Brighton – yes, I know.'

'You know why he was cremated, don't you?'

'Cheaper?'

'They didn't want his grave to become a shrine or a pilgrimage site. Plus, it seemed the appropriate way to send him to hell – reducing him to ashes.'

'Who is "they"?'

Avril didn't hear his question. Or chose not to. 'The conspiracy theory version has it that darker fears were in play. That Crowley was a magus and a powerful one and that only by burning him could his spirit be destroyed. His Poem to Pan was recited during the service and the local newspaper reported that this made the ceremony a Black Mass. Some say they saw his spirit rise in the smoke from the chimney of the crematorium and drift away in the clear blue sky.'

'So cremation didn't kill him?'

Avril didn't respond directly. 'His ashes were taken out to sea off Black Rock and scattered by the light of the full moon. A Devil's Moon.'

'At midnight, I assume.'

She smiled. 'Naturally.'

'Who told you this?'

'Ian Fleming, I think.'

'You knew Fleming?'

She shook her head. 'He died when I was fourteen.'

'Then how did he tell you?'

'He and Colin corresponded.' She proffered the cards. 'I meant Crowley designed the cards, not that they were his. Your father gave them to me. Would you like them?'

'No, no. They were a gift to you and the Tarot is not my thing.'

'Tarot cards only do have power if they are a gift. If you purchase them for yourself they are useless.'

'Did my father ever talk to you about Aleister Crowley?'

'I don't remember. So many conversations with so many men whilst taking so many drugs.'

'Tell me about your children.'

Avril looked cautious rather than surprised at the abrupt change of subject. 'What about them?'

'Do they still live at home?'

'They flew the nest years ago, Mr Watts.'

'Bob, please.'

'Why do you ask about them? Bob.'

'I noticed on my last visit that one bedroom, underneath all the books, still seemed to be used. And there is that second chalet in the garden . . .'

Avril frowned. 'I didn't know you'd been poking around in our home.'

'I observed in passing. Colin was showing me around.'

'If you must know,' Avril said. 'Colin snores. I occasionally find it necessary to leave his side for the sake of my beauty sleep.'

Watts spread his hands. 'I just wondered if one of them still lived at home, that's all.'

Avril shook her head. 'They stay over occasionally.'

Watts smiled. 'Colin also said you don't believe in doctors.'

'He's been quite gabby, hasn't he?'

'Do you?'

'Most modern medicines are plant-based in one way and another. I prefer to go to the source.'

'How do you know how to identify the source?'

She walked over to a table by the sink and picked up a book. She held it in front of her, cover out. 'Culpepper's Herbal Remedies. My Bible. And these Downs are my chemist's shop.'

'I imagined it was mostly grassland,' Watts said.

Avril smiled, showing her sharp incisors. 'It's a paradise. The whole of the valley is carpeted with orchids in June. There are many rare things here. The silver-spotted skipper butterfly, burnt orchid, even juniper trees. And there are many medicinal herbs and plants to be found.'

'Great.'

'In the autumn you see a purple blanket of flowers. Know what they're called?'

'I don't.'

She laughed a pleasant laugh. 'Devil's bit scabious.' Then picked up a long, oddly-shaped root from the table. 'Do you know what this is?'

'It looks a bit like a human figure.'

'*Mandragora officinarum.* Common name: the mandrake.'

'Mandrake – that's in Harry Potter, isn't it? And not in a good way.'

'It's been associated with witchcraft since the Middle Ages. It's because the roots are bifurcated they look a bit like the human figure. Legend has it that when you pull the plant from the ground it shrieks in pain.'

'Did this one?'

'The seeds are used medicinally. The flower has five points.'

'Like a pentacle?'

Avril looked at him for a moment. 'Indeed. This root can grow up to two feet in length. It has narcotic properties if you get the proportions right. If you don't you can fall into a coma.'

'You use it as a narcotic? Or have done?'

'Long ago and far away, Bob. In another life, it seems.'

She waved at the things on the table.

'Greater burdock – when the root is a year old, boil or steam it as a vegetable. You can cook the leaves and the stem tastes like asparagus. Angelica here has a liquorice taste – you can eat it raw. The stem is a good substitute for celery – and since it grows six feet there is a lot of it. This is Good King Henry – cook the leaves as an alternative to spinach.'

'Do you provide ingredients for Plenty, by any chance?'

Avril didn't answer. She picked up a bell-shaped purple flower with a long stem.

'This is my queen of plants, my beautiful lady.'

'What is it?'

Avril tilted her head and peered at it. 'As I said – my beautiful lady. In Italian: *belladonna.*'

'That's a poison, isn't it?'

'Haven't you got it yet, Bob? All the best medicines are poisons too if used in the wrong doses. It's all about duality, Bob. And harmony.'

She raised the flower. 'It's called *belladonna* because beautiful ladies in Italy used to apply it in a dropper to their eyes to make their pupils dilate and make themselves more beautiful. It is extremely poisonous. Especially the berries. That is why it is also known as the devil's cherries – and deadly nightshade, of course.'

'But you say it's a medicine.'

'In the right proportions. Extract the alkaloids from the leaves or the root and they can be used for asthma, colds and fevers, gastrointestinal disorders, migraines and arthritis and even motion sickness.'

'They're tropane alkaloids?' Watts said.

'They are – atropine and scopolamine.'

Avril put the flower down and picked up the tarot pack again. 'Are you sure you won't take this?'

He hesitated. 'If you insist.'

'I do.'

Their hands touched as she passed the pack to him. Watts examined her placid face. Something was nagging at him but he couldn't say what.

'Should I say goodbye to Colin?'

She shook her head. 'I'll say it for you. He'll be sleeping.' She picked up a lily. 'Take this too. I heard you talking about Solomon. In the Song of Solomon this is the hosanna – the lily among the thorns.'

TWENTY-FIVE

'Sherry, Vicar?' Gilchrist said, smiling at David Rutherford. They were sitting in a booth of a stylish bar at Five Dials where Rutherford had suggested they have their conversation.

He smiled at the cliché and looked at the waitress. 'My usual, please.'

When she had gone he turned to Gilchrist. 'My own ritual after the ritual of the service.'

'I heard some of your sermon,' she said.

He didn't ask what she thought. Instead, he said: 'There are some people so lonely and self-obsessed that they think God must have been the same as them once, all alone and therefore lonely in the vastness of the cosmos. And that is why he created us from clay.'

'He wanted company.'

'They assume. It is massively arrogant because what they are doing is creating God in our likeness rather than us in God's. How dare we put our own petty feelings on to God?'

'It makes some sense in one way,' Gilchrist said. 'He wanted company and then either he got bored or he decided he didn't like us. Which is why he's been ignoring us ever since.'

Rutherford scrutinized her then turned to the waitress as she returned with their drinks. Gilchrist had ordered a white wine but Rutherford's drink came in a V-shaped glass with three olives in it speared on a plastic stick. He contemplated it.

'Dry martini. Gin not vodka. Shaken. Olives, not a slice of lemon. Light on the vermouth. What was it Buñuel said? In the perfect dry martini you should just wave the vermouth bottle over the gin in the glass.'

'Buñuel?'

'Great Spanish-Mexican surrealist filmmaker. Made *Le Chien Andalou* with Salvador Dali – the one that starts with a woman having her eye sliced open with a razor.'

'Ugh,' Gilchrist said, smiling uncertainly.

He relished the first sip of his cocktail. He popped one of the olives into his mouth.

'He was anti-church and religion. Right up your street, I would have thought. You should watch his *Veridiana*. A masterpiece.'

'I'm not anti-church,' she said. 'Just sceptical.'

Rutherford popped a second olive into his mouth and started talking as he chewed it.

'If I may venture, in that regard you have the fierceness about you of someone who has been disappointed in your faith. Perhaps even wounded by it.'

She sipped her wine and considered how to answer. 'My father was a vicar,' Gilchrist said. 'At your church, briefly.'

'Ah,' Rutherford said, watching her. 'Did the day you came have any significance for the two of you?'

She shook her head. 'I came on impulse.'

'Is he still alive?'

Gilchrist nodded. 'But we don't speak.'

'I'm sorry to hear that.'

'You should try being a kid and having a religious nut giving you advice over the breakfast table every morning.'

Rutherford leaned in. 'You should try looking in the mirror every morning and *seeing* that religious nut.'

He held her look and smiled. Gilchrist couldn't quite make the smile but she touched his arm.

'You're not a nut.'

'I hope you're right but from a certain perspective – a non-believing perspective – my faith makes me one.'

She took a sip of her wine. 'If I may say so, Andrew Callaghan sounds like he was a nut.'

'Emotional intensity is always difficult to cope with – for everyone. Andrew was passionate about his beliefs. He believed Evil is a palpable reality in the modern world.'

'Do you?'

'When you look around at all the cruelty it's hard to believe otherwise. But he believed in possession – he wanted us to do exorcisms and cast out demons.' Rutherford spread his hands. 'Mine is not that kind of church. I fear that had he lived there would have been a parting of our ways.'

'He seemed full of fear towards the end,' Gilchrist said. 'Judging by his flat.'

'And that is the perplexing thing. I don't know what he experienced to turn him into that frightened soul.'

'There's nothing you can think of that triggered it? No encounter?'

Rutherford shook his head.

'I haven't asked you about a significant other,' Gilchrist said.

'There was no one,' Rutherford said. 'And if the subtext of your question was whether he was gay, I'm afraid I can't answer that either.'

'It wasn't, but thank you.'

She swirled the wine round in her glass. 'What do you know about the *Key of Solomon*?'

'I know that, according to your account, poor Andrew adopted at least one of its rituals to try to protect himself from Satan.'

Gilchrist frowned. 'The pentacle on the floor?'

'Indeed. I'm guessing there were silver bowls at each point of the pentacle containing salt and mercury. Effective against the dark forces.'

'What dark forces?'

'Black magicians, wizards and witches.'

'Hang on – we're back in Harry Potter land, aren't we?'

'It's more serious than that.'

'Excuse me, Vicar, but magic is a load of baloney.'

He examined his drink for a moment. 'Whether you believe it or not there are people who believe absolutely in such things. Just as people believe in a Christian God. And if they feel someone has put a spell on them then it's true to them. People have died from believing they are bewitched. Accounts of anthropologists around the world are full of such cases.'

Gilchrist nodded reluctantly. 'How do you know about the *Key of Solomon*?' she said.

Rutherford smiled. 'My guilty pleasure the other week was to watch at the Theatre Royal a play called *The Devil Rides Out*. The *Key of Solomon* features. The heroes take refuge within such a pentacle from a powerful magician based, I believe, on Aleister Crowley. Crowley was, you may know, cremated in Brighton.'

'An odd play for a vicar to watch,' she said.

Rutherford looked over the rim of his glass. 'Good triumphing over evil? Surely not.'

He smiled his gentle smile. 'Besides, I like to know what the other side is up to.'

He watched her drink her wine. 'Why do you ask about the *Key*?' he said. 'Aside from wishing to deflect from comments about yourself.'

'A copy of it has been stolen from the Jubilee Library.'

'I didn't realize the library had a copy. How interesting. But you think it may somehow be linked to Andrew's persecution and murder?'

'It seems an odd coincidence.'

Rutherford had almost finished his cocktail. 'Indeed. But don't fear that it will give the thief magical powers. Not straight away, anyway. Serious occultists say a spell needs to be handwritten by the magus who wants to make use of the magic in it. A handwritten spell is the only thing with potency. That combination of the magician's mind with the spells.'

'I don't believe we are in danger from any magical powers at all. What I find dangerous are those people you mentioned who do believe in them and will do vile things to acquire them.'

Rutherford drained his glass.

'Another?' Gilchrist said.

He shook his head. 'One is my limit. But I am in no hurry for you to finish your wine.'

'Do you believe in magic texts then?'

'Perhaps in the one we have not yet found.'

He saw her puzzled look.

'Every library in the world has collections of catalogued and un-catalogued or mis-catalogued manuscripts. Every great house and palace has attics full of old documents, also un-catalogued. Half the world's knowledge has been forgotten and is lying around waiting to be rediscovered. For all I know the God particle was discovered in some non-quantum physics way thousands of years ago and then the knowledge lost with the disappearance of a civilization and its language.'

'God particle?'

'The Higgs Boson? The particle that existed some infinitesimal moment after the Big Bang that gave mass to matter and made the world possible. It gave us life and quantum physicists at CERN think they've found it.'

Gilchrist shook her head. 'I'm just a plod, Vicar. I'm having enough trouble with all this black magic stuff without having to deal with physics – quantum or any other sort.'

Rutherford smiled. 'As you say. For what it's worth, the scientific view of magic is that it is a pseudo-science in which people wrong-headedly suggest a direct cause-effect relationship between the magical act and the desired effect.' He clasped his hands. 'You might say I'm in the same business.'

Gilchrist started to rise. 'I need to get on,' she said.

He stood. 'As do I.'

Gilchrist extended her hand. Rutherford took it in both of his – but lightly.

'If you need to talk more about your faith – lack of faith . . .'

Gilchrist smiled and turned away as she realized she was about to cry.

TWENTY-SIX

Kate Simpson wanted to leave the Church of the Holy Blood in Hove almost the moment the service started but she was hemmed in. She clutched tightly in her hand the order of service she had been given when she entered. She couldn't see anything remotely Christian about what was happening.

The vicar was naked except for a thong and, frankly, he didn't have the body for it. He was middle-aged and sagging in most of the places she'd rather he didn't sag. He was also extremely hairy.

He was standing at the front of the room with a narrow table beside him. On the table were spikes and needles. As he gave his sermon he pierced himself with them. Every time he did so the congregation moaned. Kate winced.

Actually, it wasn't so much a sermon as a monologue about his upbringing in a fiercely Pentecostal hamlet in Texas. It had the only church in the State where they handled snakes and scorpions, a practice common in the Appalachians and Georgia and Tennessee – the last his state of birth.

'You know the Devil made Texas. He scattered tarantulas over the roads, put rattlesnakes under every rock. He made sure the rattlesnake bites and the scorpion stings. He put thorns on the cactus and on all of the trees. He made the heat in the summer a hundred and ten – too cool for the Devil but too hot for men. The Devil did all that. Still does.

'So we needed to defend ourselves from the Devil. We all fell into ecstatic raptures, as you will shortly do, and we all spoke in tongues. Glossolalia they call it now. I don't mind telling you that I was a holy child. The spirit entered my mouth when I was so young. When I shed tears of ecstasy they were gathered on kerchiefs and passed around as blessings.'

He took out a scalpel and held it up beside his shaved head.

'I can't shed tears now.' He pointed with his other hand to a teardrop tattooed under his eye. 'That's the only tear I've shed for fifteen years.'

He set the scalpel against his forehead. 'So instead I shed my blood.'

As he said this he cut his forehead with the scalpel then made other rapid cuts all about his shaved head. Blood spurted and flooded in a sheet down his face. Kate cowered away, even though she was nowhere near the front of the church. No one else cowered away. On the contrary.

The vicar held out cloths in both hands to catch the blood.

'Bathe in my holy, blessed blood,' he shouted, passing the cloths to two people in the front row.

He started down the central aisle, shaking his head as he did so. People leaned towards the spray of blood. Kate leaned away, feeling nauseous.

As he walked the vicar was talking rapidly. The congregation was wailing and moaning at increasing volume and attempting to repeat the vicar's words, which, as best Kate could hear, were gibberish.

People were grabbing for the rags or rushing out into the aisle to dab their own cloths in his blood. The people to her left pushed by her to get to him, allowing her to retreat against the side wall. All around were raised, nonsensical voices; blood-smeared people writhing or tearing at their clothes.

In the bedlam Kate felt increasingly giddy and the vicar strutting back to the front of the church, his bare, flabby buttocks wobbling, making Kate even more nauseous.

He raised his arms and a semblance of calm came upon the congregation, although some were still delirious and babbling.

Kate saw that one man had ripped all his clothes off and was hunched naked in the corner, alternately grimacing and grinning. A woman was blowing a feather in the air. The man next to her, his face distorted in fury, tried to snatch it.

Other people were plucking at imaginary objects on their bodies. A number were staring with a strange intensity at a hand or foot or scrutinizing one of the bloody cloths. Some were licking their lips or thrusting their tongues out and panting like thirsty dogs. A few were simply reeling, others clutching at their hearts. A worrying number were convulsing.

Kate held down panic. Was this mass hysteria and, if so, was she catching it? She felt that if she moved away from the wall she too would overbalance.

The vicar, blood still streaming down his face, laughed, showing expensive dental work. He fixed his eyes on Kate and gestured round the room.

'The important thing is having a witness to your insanity to make sense of the madness of it.'

Kate looked down at her hand, still clutching the order of service tightly. Order of service? What bloody order? A laugh bubbled up in her throat but she daren't let it out.

She jammed the paper into her bag, pushed herself away from the wall and squeezed past a comatose woman lying on a pew, a flip-flop dangling from her right foot. She staggered out into the rain.

Watts drove from Saddlescombe to Nicola Travis's house in Lewes to take her to Glyndebourne. He'd said yes to her invitation but he was nervous. He recognized she found him attractive and he certainly found her so but he had been pretty much celibate since the breakdown of his marriage.

He had wondered about prolonging his brief affair with Sarah Gilchrist but neither of them seemed to know how to take it forward. She was clearly as bad as him at developing a relationship. He liked and admired Sarah a lot and was pleased to have her as a friend. Perhaps it was easier to leave it at that. But what about Nicola?

She was in her front garden with a pair of secateurs and a trowel. She was wearing wellingtons, short shorts that showed off her strong, tanned legs and a T-shirt with the logo 'Wind in my hair, men at my feet'. Whilst reading her chest, Watts deduced she was wearing no bra.

She grinned when she saw him, his dinner suit on a hanger draped over his shoulder.

'Mr Watts, I know you're going to scrub up well.' She tilted one hip and angled one knee in towards the other. 'Though I was intending to go as I am.'

'There'd be no men watching the opera if you did,' he said, leaning down to kiss her on the cheek.

She moved her head and they were kissing on the mouth. When he pulled away she gave him a look and led him round the side of the house.

The kitchen door was open. She put the secateurs and trowel down on a table beside the door then went to the sink and washed her hands. She dried them off quickly, turned and hoisted herself on to the kitchen table. She stuck a leg out. 'Help me with my wellies, will you?'

He took hold of her heel and pulled at the rubber boot. As he did so he was aware of her raising her arms. He put the first wellington on the floor and looked up as she dropped her T-shirt on the table behind her and leaned back. He was right about the bra.

It was some time before the other boot came off.

Kate Simpson walked unsteadily into Hove Park and sank on to a bench. She was facing a huge rock with stones around it and a fence outside that. There was a sign but she was too far away to read it. She felt drunk – no, different to that. Spaced out. She wasn't a drug user but when she had smoked mari-juana the effect had been similar. Except here her limbs didn't seem to belong to her.

She stretched her hand out in front of her and examined it for any sign of familiarity. She turned the palm up and started. It was scarlet. She brought it close to her face. There was a scarlet line going up her arm.

She looked at her other hand. Normal.

She was aware she had started to sweat.

She speed-dialled the radio station's taxi firm. She stayed

on the bench, breathing slowly for a few minutes, then tried standing. She walked over to the rock.

An old sign read: 'Goldstone tolmen or the Holy Stone of Druids.'

Kate found she was mouthing each word she read. Goldstone. That was the name of the old stadium for the local football club. She looked blankly at the big rock. It was twice her height, probably three times her length. She walked round it slowly.

She came to another plaque.

'On 3 June 1929 the Ancient Order of Druids (Brighton and Hove Royal Arch) planted an oak tree nearby. There was a ceremony and a banquet afterwards attended by many important figures in Druidism.'

She was wondering which of the trees around her was an oak when a car horn sounded. Her taxi. She glanced at her hand again then grabbed her bag and made her unsteady way out of the park.

A part of her felt she should go to A&E but the main part of her thought she should just get back to the flat and calm down.

She closed her eyes in the back of the taxi then immediately opened them as her head whirled. The streets going by also made her dizzy. She focused on the back of the taxi driver's head. He was bald but he seemed to have dandruff. The thought made her start to giggle but she forced it back down.

Back in the flat, finally, she lay down on the sofa, dropping her bag beside her. The scrunched-up order of service from the Church of Blood fell out on to the rug. She closed her eyes without feeling quite so giddy. She drifted away.

Gilchrist was thinking about her father on her way to meet Heap. Her relationship with him – there was a story. Her mother, Sylvia, had died when she was six. She had only vague memories of her. Perhaps because of her mother's death, her father became more rigorous about his religion as she got older. Not what these days would be called a fundamentalist, perhaps, but certainly extreme.

He shovelled religious shit on her until she was old enough to know better. Some of it stuck. The worst part was the guilt about perfectly natural human desires. The best of it – maybe the only good thing about it – was the morality. That morality led her to become a copper because she wanted to do good things in life.

Of course, her affair with the married Bob Watts tipped her own moral scale over to bad. And her guilt was probably what screwed that relationship even before it got going. She was a moral person, although the morality had long been disengaged from its religious source, and, well, she didn't approve of people like her.

She was still unsettled by the events of the past few days. She didn't feel fully recovered from the food poisoning she'd experienced. Occasionally she found herself going into a kind of trance. She intended to get herself checked out – just maybe not yet.

In charge of men like Donaldson she was also getting a familiar feeling she usually tried to keep away from. Old stuff welling up. Stuff to do with her father.

Heap gave her a little wave. He was standing in a narrow alley in front of a black door. 'Welcome to the Jurassic Museum of Technology, ma'am.'

'What is this place?'

'A museum of curiosities. Madame Tussaud crossed with Barnum and Bailey. It's quite something.'

'Jurassic Technology? I thought Jurassic was a period in geology. Jurassic Park – dinosaurs and stuff. Is this like the Booth Natural History Museum?'

'Stuffed birds and foxes about to pounce? Not exactly. Nor is it dinosaurs. I don't really know what it is. There's one in Los Angeles.'

'And?'

Heap looked down at his feet. 'That's weird too.'

'Weird how?'

'They have this stuff that's . . . weird.'

'Weird. Barnum and Bailey, whoever they are. Thanks for explaining. Linked to Devil worship in some way?'

'Probably not. It's more that it's . . . weird.'

Gilchrist tilted her head and touched his arm. 'You're being unusually inarticulate, Bellamy. This is Brighton, you know. Weird is the norm.'

'Ma'am.' He pushed open the door. 'Just a reminder: we're looking for a Roger Newell.'

It took a moment for Gilchrist's eyes to adjust to the dark. Gilchrist saw a black-bearded man, soberly dressed in a black suit and shirt behind a narrow black counter. She waited whilst Heap went over to ask for Newell. He gestured for Gilchrist to come over.

'He'll be back in fifteen minutes, ma'am. This gentleman suggests we look round.'

Without speaking the man handed them each a floor plan of the museum. It was laid out in a series of dark rooms, each one hidden from the next. As they walked through Gilchrist was aware of ambient noise filtering in from hidden speakers. In the first room it was breathing. The only light in the room came from the glass boxes on pedestals.

Gilchrist peered into a glass box containing an insect on a leaf. 'It's an ant with a tie-pin sticking out of its head,' she said.

Heap read the card. 'The stink ant of the Cameroon. *Megaloponera foetens*. Because it's so big, it's one of a very few ants whose cry can be heard by humans. It's a floor-dweller in the rain forests. And sometimes it inhales a spore from a fungus and the spore grows in the ant's brain.'

'Do ants have brains, Bellamy?'

'Indeed, ma'am. Tiny ones. An ant naturally has far fewer brain cells than a human but when you put ants together a colony of ants has the same size brain as us.'

Gilchrist gave him a look. 'How do you know that?'

Heap shrugged. 'Swot at school.' He carried on reading. 'So this ant's behaviour changes as the spore grows in its brain. It climbs to the rain forest canopy and dies up there as the fungus eats into it and produces this spike—'

'Tie-pin.'

'When the tip of the spike bursts the spores rain down on the rain forest floor to get other ants.'

Gilchrist frowned. 'That has to be a gag, doesn't it?'

Heap shrugged again.

The next room had odd barks of laughter coming out of the hidden speakers. There was a glass box containing, according to the label, the Horn of Mary Davis of Saughall. It was indeed a horn, some five inches long. According to the card it had grown out of the back of Mary's head.

'In Cheshire,' Heap added.

'Do you think the fact it was Cheshire is significant?' Gilchrist said.

'You mean something in the soil? It seeds football million-aires now.'

'This can't be right,' Gilchrist, reading, said. 'Men grew horns in front and women behind.'

For the next five minutes they wandered through more rooms. There was a scale model of Noah's Ark. A plan of a sixteenth-century battle.

They moved into a room of Victorian photographs. There was whispered conversation just below their aural threshold although there was no one else in the room. Indeed, they seemed to be the only two visitors to the museum.

Gilchrist looked at the first two photographs then looked more closely. The first photograph was of a stocky, muscular man standing facing the camera, legs apart. He was naked except for a pair of thigh-high white women's stockings. He had bushy pubic hair and a long penis.

In the second photograph the same man was lying on his back with his knees bent, his legs apart and his feet flat on the ground. Beneath the penis, where his testicles should have been, there was a vagina.

Embarrassed, she glanced at Heap, but he was reading the card beside the first photograph. The next photograph had an anonymous hand pulling back the foreskin of the penis. In the one after the same hand was spreading the vagina.

'The celebrated French photographer Nadar took these photographs of a hermaphrodite in 1860,' Heap read. 'Possibly the finest examples of medical photographs ever taken, he took them at the request of Armand Trousseau who told him this patient had a "strange malady".'

'Armand Trousseau?' Gilchrist said.

Heap was examining the photographs. It was too dark to
see if he was blushing.

'God, they're weird,' Gilchrist said.

'I think they're rather beautiful,' a male voice said from
behind them.

Gilchrist flushed at being overheard and turned.

An androgynous young man with a pale face framed by a mass
of curly hair gave a small smile. 'I disagreed with the word
"hermaphrodite" when they wrote the card but that's what such
people were known as then. Today the term 'intersex' is preferred.'

He held out his hand to Gilchrist.

'I'm Roger Newell. I understand you want to speak to me.'

TWENTY-SEVEN

'It's an opera by Gluck,' Nicola Travis said.

Watts was driving along a country lane just a couple of
miles from Glyndebourne. Travis lounged in the passenger
seat, head back, dreamy smile on her face.

She was wearing a black cocktail dress that showed off her
toned arms. Watts glanced at her bare bicep.

'No patch today. Are you OK in the car?'

She tilted her head towards him. Same dreamy smile. 'I'm
very OK.'

He looked back at the road. 'Gluck the lesbian artist?'

'Different person. This is Christoph Willibald Gluck and
we're seeing his best-known opera: *Orfeo ed Euridice.*'

'The Orpheus in the Underworld story,' Watts said.

'That's right. Orpheus goes to get his dead wife from the
Underworld but can only succeed if he doesn't look at her.
She thinks he's ignoring her so gets upset. He's obliged to
reassure her by looking back at her and she dies again. Which,
frankly, is her own stupid fault.'

Travis laid her hand on his thigh. 'How are you with ballet?
There's quite a lot in this version.'

'I'll endure.'

She gave his thigh a squeeze. 'Orpheus is traditionally sung by a woman. A contralto like Josephine Baker or Kathleen Ferrier. But in 1760 Gluck did a version where it could be performed by a soprano castrato.'

'Which is it going to be tonight?'

'That remains to be seen,' Travis said, that same dreamy smile on her face.

Gilchrist and Heap interviewed Newell in a storeroom at the back of the museum. Newell indicated the boxes around them.

'We're still unpacking exhibits.'

'Tell us about the Wicker Man,' Gilchrist said.

'Nothing to say, really. I was one of the half dozen who took it down from the farm on to the beach in the middle of the night. I drove the truck, actually – I'm the only one with an HGV licence from a gap-year job. We unloaded it at the water's edge and once we were sure it was secure we left someone on guard, the rest went back home for a bit of sleep and I came down here.'

'Bit early for work, wasn't it?'

'We've been against the clock trying to get the museum open before the festival so I thought I could get a few hours in.' He looked sheepish and indicated a couch in the corner of the storeroom. 'But to be honest I was knackered so I had a kip on there.'

'And there was nobody in the Wicker Man.'

'Of course not.'

'Who stayed to guard it?'

'Lesley Henderson – but I don't know what happened there. I've not seen Lesley since.'

'Do you know where Henderson is?'

'I assumed at Saddlescombe?'

'Did you tell anyone about your plans?'

'Of course not – that would have defeated the object as I understand it. I wasn't directly involved in constructing it – they just needed me to drive it down there. As I said, this museum has been my main focus of attention.'

'Are you a Druid or a wiccan or a wizard?' Heap said.

Newell laughed. 'Basically a pagan. But, you know, a lot

of gays are interested in the pagan and the occult. That's why it's so popular in Brighton.'

'What's the attraction?' Gilchrist said.

'Well, at a basic level, it's the link between queers and the freedom of nature – and of the night. In the years when homosexuality was illegal queers operated clothed in darkness – as do witches and sorcerers. They operated in nature, where there are no restrictions – as do magicians and pagans. Darkness may be a negative cultural meme but it is central to both the queer experience and to black magic – and has been for centuries.'

Gilchrist glanced at Heap to see whether he understood the word 'meme'. He appeared to.

'Black magic and homosexuality have always been linked. Take the Knights Templar – when they were broken up the accusation that they had been practising black magic was linked to charges of homosexuality – sodomy and anilingus.' He saw Gilchrist's look. 'Rimming?' Still incomprehension. 'Well, never mind. Then there's Joan of Arc – a cross-dresser who was burned as a witch.'

'I think there might have been more to her than that,' Heap said mildly.

'Not in queer history,' Newell said. 'At the end of the nineteenth century all these gay French writers were interested in the occult. The decadents? Huysman wrote *A Rebours* which influenced Wilde's *Dorian Gray* but he also wrote *La Bas* – essentially a novel about black magic.'

'What about the link between gays and paganism?' Heap said.

'In California back in the seventies there were big attempts made to make gayness central rather than an add-on to a preexisting spiritual tradition. Among the pagans, the Faery Circle, the Reformed Druids of America, the Radical Faeries all rejected hetero-imitation and redefined queer identity through spirituality.'

Gilchrist glanced at Heap. His face was expressionless.

Newell caught the look and smiled. 'One meme in LGBT culture is a passionate need to forge an identity free of hetero-oppression. Whether they are pagan or Christian they want some deity who isn't linked to gender or sexuality. They look for a non-inclusive model of a deity. A deity who transcends gender.'

Gilchrist frowned. She knew the lesbian, gay, bisexual part of LGBT but had to think whether the 'T' stood for transgender or transexual. 'Give me a moment to absorb that,' she said. Transgender, that was it.

'It makes sense if you think about it,' Newell said genially. 'Does a planet have a gender? Then why should its creator? Yet Christians think in terms of God as a he. Pagans think often in terms of goddesses, which feminists love. LGBT Christians want a god who is neither; LGBT pagans want one who is both.'

'A bisexual?' Gilchrist said.

'Quite literally,' Newell said. 'Androgyny and – to a degree – sexual confusion is important both in world myth and in pagan beliefs.'

'Is that why those photographs interest you?' Heap said.

Newell nodded. 'Don't forget intersex people have great potency in the occult.'

'You know a lot about this,' Gilchrist said.

'I did my dissertation on it,' Newell said. 'But Lesley may be the person you need to speak to for greater insight.'

'Why?' Heap said.

'Because there's a certain amount of sexual confusion surrounding Lesley.'

Heap frowned. 'As in gay or straight?'

Newell scraped his hair back off his forehead. 'As in male or female.'

Gilchrist was out of her depth, yet again. She could think of only one thing to say. 'What's a meme?'

Travis had packed an ice box but they left that in the boot and headed for one of the marquees in the gardens surrounding the old house.

Usually, people would be sitting on rugs all over the grounds drinking their pre-opera champagne. They would dine al fresco during the long interval in the middle of the opera.

But the constant rain had reduced the gardens to a quagmire so aperitifs and the subsequent dinners would all take place in marquees, at tables on duckboards.

Watts bought a bottle of the house champagne and he and Travis found a corner of a table by the entrance to the marquee.

Travis's dreamy smile had been replaced by a sardonic one. She leaned into Watts. 'It's always the same at these posh dos. The men soberly, smartly dressed in dinner jackets; the women dressed like dog's dinners.'

Watts glanced around. There were certainly a lot of unflattering dresses on display.

'You probably don't know exactly what tulle is,' she murmured. 'But you're seeing a lot of it.'

Travis chinked his glass and took a sip of her drink.

'They're all here – wives of politicians, of captains of industry, of the country's business elite done up like Christmas trees and looking like Christmas turkeys. Giant polka dots, oversized bows, unfeasibly high heels.'

She took another sip of her drink.

'When it comes to female fashion the rich are different,' she said. 'They have money but no taste. I've always thought women with more money than fashion sense should be obliged to wear the female equivalent of a standard dinner suit, as men do – mostly. Men wearing ties not bow-ties with dinner jacket – what's that about? Those idiots aside, women should dress as soberly as men.'

'To avoid making spectacles of themselves?' Watts said.

Travis shook her head. 'To save the rest of us from embarrassment.'

Watts laughed. He liked this woman.

'Never have I felt so out of touch,' Gilchrist said as she walked with Heap down to the seafront. The rain was holding off for the time being. 'What's a meme again, big brain?'

'It's like a concept or an idea shared by a culture.'

'I'm not sure I'm any wiser. When he mentioned Joan of Arc was a cross-dresser who was burned as a witch – could that artist Gluck's cross-dressing be part and parcel of why she called her painting *The Devil's Altar*?'

'It is possible, ma'am, but I don't know. However, I think I might have found a link between that painting and the Wicker Man, thanks to your flatmate Kate.'

'Kate?'

Heap flushed. 'I met her at the farmers' market this morning. We were both looking for someone to talk to at the Saddlescombe Organics stall. She's doing a story on the food poisoning at Plenty.'

Gilchrist felt odd that one of her staff had met her friend, even if it was Bellamy.

'And what did Kate tell you?'

'Did you know you ate cooked lily bulbs as part of your meal the evening you got food poisoning? Provided by Saddlescombe Organics.'

Gilchrist stopped.'Lily bulbs and the home of the Wicker Man. OK, let's get down to the restaurant and then tomorrow it's time for another trip to the farm.'

'What about Lesley Henderson, ma'am?'

'Man or woman, you mean? Well that's going to be an interesting line of enquiry. Interesting choice of first name though, don't you think? Lesley could be man or woman. Do you want to see if you can get anywhere with a birth certificate?'

'With only the name to go on?' he said.

She smiled. 'I have utter faith in you, Bellamy.'

Travis was almost exhaustingly vivacious. During the opera, Watts was mildly embarrassed as she kept making comments in a voice far too loud. He was aware of a dichotomy in his personality. He had no problem, back in the day, addressing large audiences or doing radio or television, but he was also quite shy. He preferred to be unobtrusive when out in public.

Travis was wriggly, constantly shifting in her seat. He assumed that was because she wasn't enjoying it but wondered too if it was the booze. She wasn't obviously drunk but there was something off-kilter.

At the interval, as they were getting the hamper out of the boot, he asked if she was enjoying the opera.'

'You kidding?' she said, her voice ascending on the last syllable. 'I'm adoring it.'

She pressed her body against him. 'That said: what say we skip dinner and get in the back seat of the car?'

Watts couldn't help but look around the car park, at the same time chiding himself for being a coward. He was clear on his thinking. Earlier, she had expressed her pleasure loudly. Extremely loudly. His ragtop had very little soundproofing. Assuming they got in the back of the car, and she enjoyed herself, most of Glyndebourne would know.

He looked down at her. To hell with most of Glyndebourne.

TWENTY-EIGHT

The restaurant was closed with no sign of life inside. Gilchrist telephoned the number on the door and left a message asking the manager to call her as a matter of urgency. She looked at her watch.

'Enough for today, Bellamy. I'd invite you for a drink but I wouldn't want you getting the wrong idea.'

'No, ma'am.'

They parted and Gilchrist cut up across the Pavilion Gardens to New Street. She was turning right at the statue of Max Miller but looked left and saw a familiar figure walking towards the Colonnade. She watched the figure go into the pub and headed that way herself.

She ordered a drink at the bar, aware that Danny Monaghan, the person she had seen, was sitting in the corner at the far end of the room. He was trim, fit-looking, hair perhaps a bit greyer than the last time she'd seen him.

Their paths hadn't crossed since the aftermath of the Milldean Massacre. As the most experienced armed response officer in the force, Monaghan had been supposed to lead the armed raid that went wrong. He'd stood down because he'd been drinking earlier in the day. A couple of months later he'd left the force – an act that immediately made Gilchrist suspicious.

Gilchrist didn't really trust any of her colleagues – a mix of paranoia and experience – but Monaghan was a man she would have entrusted her life to. Then.

She took her drink over to his table.

'I was over the limit,' he said as she sat down.

'Did I ask?'

He smiled. 'You wanted to. From what I hear that flipping massacre is all you want to talk about.'

Gilchrist took a swig of her drink. 'Well, this is going rapidly downhill.'

'I'm just saying. I know there was a lot of dodgy stuff going on but I wasn't part of it.'

'Fair enough. I believe you.'

'In that case . . .' He raised his glass and chinked hers.

'Why'd you retire then?' she said.

He lowered his glass. 'Offered more money elsewhere. The force was keen to get rid of us on favourable terms.'

'Money isn't everything,' Gilchrist said.

Monaghan gave her a look. 'You should have gone,' he said.

'I hadn't done anything wrong.'

'Nor had I but the time was right. You hung on. A month ago I would definitely have said you should think about getting out. Nothing for you in the force any more.'

'Thanks a lot.'

'I was just being realistic. You know how these things work. The Milldean thing is a mark against you, even though you were cleared. And then the volt gun.' He spread his hands. 'But, as I say, that was a month ago.'

'The evidence disappeared,' Gilchrist said. 'No volt gun in the evidence room, no case to answer.'

Monaghan grinned. 'Yeah. I heard.'

Gilchrist bristled. 'It had nothing to do with me.'

Monaghan put his palms up in a placatory gesture. 'I know. You weren't even in the country when it happened. Still . . .'

He shook his head then gave her a sideways look. 'Good old Reg Williamson – God rest his fat arse.'

Gilchrist thought Monaghan was changing the subject but there was something in his tone of voice. She leaned forward. 'What do you mean?'

'Your partner was a busy boy on his last day of service.'

'And what does that mean?'

'You don't know?' Monaghan looked at her face. He

shrugged. 'OK, then: you don't know. Reg lifted the volt gun from the evidence room. It's somewhere in the briny deep off Beachy Head in all likelihood.'

She clenched her jaw. Reg Williamson, in the middle of all he was going through, on the day he drove his car off Beachy Head, had thought of getting her off the hook.

'How come you know this and I don't?'

Monaghan drained his beer. 'Another reason you should maybe still think about leaving. The seaside is the last place you want to be in a leaky vessel.'

Gilchrist made a face. 'I don't trust anyone in the force anyway after Milldean.'

He ignored that. 'Buy you another before I go?'

She shook her head. Monaghan stood.

'You watch out,' he said. 'You've spent more time on suspension than working the last few months. You must be tired working a full week.'

She laughed. 'Fuck off.'

He leaned down to kiss her on the cheek. 'Just saying.'

He put his glass on the bar as he walked out and didn't glance back.

Travis talked non-stop for the remainder of the dinner period. Watts nodded and grinned and smiled, chewing his food slowly and sipping his wine. He knew people were looking at them. He knew his clothes were a bit askew. She was sitting with her legs open, her cocktail dress riding up on her thighs.

He couldn't figure out if she was high from life, from the sex, from the drink or from something she might have taken earlier. But high she certainly was. It was compelling but also unnerving.

Arm in arm, they went back into the opera house for the second half. Travis was vivacious; Watts was wary.

The phone signal wasn't great in the Colonnade so Gilchrist was surprised when her mobile rang. It was Bellamy Heap.

'What are you up to, Bellamy?'

'Sorry to disturb you, ma'am. I've got something else for you. I've been in touch with Gluck's biographer.'

'That was very punctilious of you.'

'I thought so, ma'am.'

'Go on.'

'The painting is not of lilies. The flowers are datura. The plant was a favourite of Constance Spry, Gluck's lover at the time Gluck did the painting.'

'Where does that get us?' Gilchrist said.

'I'm not sure. Datura is used medicinally. You can smoke the leaves and the roots for asthma. In low dosages it's a useful medicine for travel sickness on transdermal patches.'

'Doesn't sound particularly diabolical then.'

'Well, in the States it's called jimson weed or loco weed because it sends horses mad if they eat it in the wild. And it's always been a "magic plant" wherever it grows. The Aztecs used it as part of human sacrifice rituals.'

'Nice.'

'But here's the thing, ma'am. In Europe, datura is linked to witchcraft – like henbane, mandrake and deadly nightshade, which are roughly in the same family. It's an essential ingredient of love potions and witches' brews.'

'I'm guessing witches' brews aren't good but what bad stuff, specifically, does datura do?'

'Pretty much all parts of the plant are hallucinogenic because they are toxic. The line between use as a hallucinogenic and as a poison is a fine one. A lot of people tried it as a recreational drug at the end of the last century and died or went psychotic. One person's hallucination is another person's delirium. Doctor Gonzo in *Fear and Loathing*—'

'*Fear and Loathing*?'

'You really should get out more, ma'am.'

Gilchrist smiled to herself. 'So my flatmate keeps telling me. So, this *Fear* thing?'

'Hunter S Thompson? Gonzo journalism? His book *Fear and Loathing in Las Vegas* is pretty much a cult classic, a textbook for every druggie and slacker student. Johnny Depp played him in the movie—'

'OK, Bellamy, I sense you're gearing up here – can we get back to datura?'

'Doctor Gonzo is a friend of Thompson. He's given a datura

bulb as a gift. Now datura grows from seed but some sorts do have tubers so I guess that's what he means.'

'Bellamy . . .'

'Sorry. He eats the whole thing at once. He goes blind and is carted home in a wheelbarrow where he starts making noises like a raccoon.'

'So there's a risk it can turn you into a raccoon but the greater danger is that it's an hallucinogen that can kill you,' Gilchrist said.

'In a nutshell – but that's also true of most hallucinogens,' Heap said.

'What makes datura particularly dangerous then?' Gilchrist said.

'It's full of tropane alkaloids: scopolamine, hyoscyamine and atropine. It's probably one of the most dangerous plants on sale in garden centres. In some countries it's illegal to buy, sell or cultivate datura plants. It can be lethal for children. If they get atropine poisoning, they're going to die.'

'If the kids eat it, you mean?' Gilchrist said.

'It doesn't have to be eaten. It can be ingested in various ways – even through the pores.'

'Scopolamine, you said – truth drug, isn't it?'

'Sometimes thought to be,' Heap said. 'The Czech secret police used it when quizzing political prisoners. If you know your Raymond Chandler he used it in *Farewell My Lovely.* It's in Graham Greene under another name.'

'The patron saint of Brighton crime,' Gilchrist said. 'Might have known he'd figure. Is Pinkie a junky then?'

'It's not in *Brighton Rock*; it's in *The Ministry of Fear.*'

'Don't know it,' Gilchrist said.

'The protagonist in *The Ministry of Fear* uses a drug called hyoscine, derived from the scopolamine in henbane, for the mercy killing of his wife. Later someone else tries to poison him by putting it in his tea.'

'Bellamy – did you know all this before or do you swot things up when the rest of us are asleep?'

'Sleep, ma'am?'

She heard the rustle of paper.

'I printed it all off the Internet. It's used as a poison for suicide and murder. Crippen used it to kill his wife way back when. Between 1950 and 1965 in India there were almost three thousand deaths caused by ingesting datura.

'These days in Thailand they slip scopolamine to tourists to rob them. In Bogota, Colombia, one in five emergency room admissions for poisoning have been attributed to scopolamine. It's used to rape as well as rob.'

'Where does this take us in the investigation of a murder, a theft and a church desecration?'

Heap coughed. 'Presumably Gluck knew something of the potency of datura when she named her painting. But the thing is, ma'am, these datura look like lilies to anyone who isn't a gardener and even to people who are. I wondered if someone mixing up datura tubers and lily bulbs is what poisoned you and Kate. And that takes us right back to Saddlescombe.'

'Good thought. But tell me you've figured out if Lesley Henderson is a man or a woman and I'll be truly impressed.'

'I would like you to be so, ma'am. I'm working on it.'

TWENTY-NINE

For the remainder of the date Travis's off-key exuberance irritated the hell out of Watts. As he drove back to her home he was trying to think of an excuse not to go in. Nothing had come to him by the time he pulled up behind a *deux chevaux* parked in front of the house.

But Travis surprised him. Leaning close, her perfume wafting over him, she said: 'I'm not going to invite you in, Mr Watts. You've quite tired me out.'

Watts probably should have made a token effort to persuade her. Relieved, however, he simply said: 'Of course. I'm pretty tired too.'

She gave him a quick look then kissed him on the cheek.

'It's been such a day,' she said.

Watts didn't say or do anything when she got out of the car. He watched her sashay to her front door. She gave him a wave and blew a kiss before she went inside. He put his car in gear, pulled round the other car and drove away.

Gilchrist found Kate sprawled on her sofa bed, her handbag on the floor beside her, things spilling out of it. Gilchrist thought she might be drunk but couldn't smell alcohol.

'Kate?' she said, shaking her gently.

Kate didn't respond at first then opened one bleary eye. 'What's happening?'

Her voice was croaky.

'You tell me,' Gilchrist said.

'It was like the other evening but I haven't eaten anything today.'

Gilchrist glanced down at the contents of her bag. She picked up the scrunched-up programme. 'What have you been doing?'

'I went to church.'

Gilchrist opened out the programme and saw it was actually a service sheet. As she read the first page she was aware her fingers were beginning to tingle. She glanced down at Kate's half-open hand beside her head. She reached down and opened it. The palm was scarlet.

Gilchrist dropped the service sheet and rushed to the kitchen sink. She grabbed TCP from the cupboard and poured it over her hands then scrubbed at them. When she had dried them on kitchen towel she called Heap.

'Emergency, Bellamy, so no pissing about. Ingesting datura – did you say you can ingest it by touch?'

'Transcutaneously?'

'By touch, Bellamy.'

'Sure, ma'am. It gets into your system through the pores. In South America and some Asian countries they saturate business cards or publicity flyers with burundanga – that's what they call scopolamine. They hand the impregnated paper out to tourists then follow them until the drug takes effect. Then they attack them. There is talk they do the same in the US.'

Gilchrist glanced back at the service sheet and down at her friend. 'What happens if you overdose on it?' she said, glancing at Kate, who was still pretty much comatose on the sofa.

'Drowsiness, dizziness, agitation, fever, excitability.'

'That's it?'

'Seizures, convulsions, hallucinations, coma and death.'

'Better get an ambulance round here, Bellamy. I think Kate's OK but best to be sure. And get someone over to the Church of Holy Blood with a search warrant. I want to talk to the vicar and the staff about impregnating their service sheets with scopolamine.'

'I'm on it, ma'am. One more thing about scopolamine. In Colombia it's known as the Devil's Breath.'

She frowned.'Because it smells bad?'

'No, ma'am. Because it steals your soul.'

Watts was in his poky Brighton house, sprawled on the sofa, shoeless, drinking a black coffee when his mobile rang. It was a landline number he didn't recognize, except that it was a Brighton code.

It was Nicola Travis.

'It seems like only a moment,' he said.

'Bob, I'm so sorry I sent you away. Too much excitement in one day for a Sussex girl. Quite exhausting, actually. Please forgive me.'

'Nothing to forgive,' he said. 'Probably as well I didn't come in.'

She laughed throatily. 'Well, I'm not so sure about *that*.'

He gave a quick laugh.

'I left my purse in your car, I think,' she said abruptly. 'I hope. It has my phone in it.'

'I can go and look. Do you want me to bring it over tomorrow?'

She was silent for a moment, then: 'How gallant. I wonder if you would first mind checking that my purse is actually in your car? If it isn't I need to phone Glyndebourne. But no peeking now.'

Watts was already on his feet. 'I'll call you back in ten minutes.'

He found his shoes and went out into the night.

Her purse was in the pocket of the passenger-side door. He saw her cold box too, sitting in the back seat.

He phoned her from the passenger seat. 'Got it.'

'Thank goodness.' She sounded more than relieved. 'And my phone is in there?'

'I don't like to pry,' he said.

'Don't be silly. I'm not asking you to scroll through my texts. Just see if it's in there.'

'OK. Hang on.'

There was actually little in the bag. Watts groped around in the bottom and touched something hard and oblong. He pulled out the latest iPhone. He was using the same one himself. The screen was dark but he touched something by mistake and it lit up. There was an image of a flower as the screen saver. He dropped it in his jacket pocket.

'It's here,' he said. 'Shall I bring it over tomorrow? The ice box is here too.'

'How sleepy are you?' she said.

'You'd like me to bring it over now?'

'I know it's a horrible imposition but a girl without her mobile . . . Would you?' Her voice was throaty again. 'It doesn't have to be a return trip.'

Don-Don was sitting in the interview room with a bald-headed man who had nicks all over his head. The man was sitting back, legs apart, a kind of sneer on his face. Gilchrist thought he had his hands together in his lap in prayer until she saw the plastic restrainer on his wrists. She could tell the sneer wasn't going down well with Donaldson, who was leaning across the table, clenching and unclenching his fists. He jerked to his feet when Gilchrist entered the room.

'Ma'am, this is Nick Cropper, the vicar of the Church of the Holy Blood. He was just pointing out that tropane alkaloids come under no illegal drug classification. I was pointing out that forcing them on unsuspecting members of his congregation probably was illegal. He was disputing that point.'

'Why is he wearing restraints?' Gilchrist said. 'Have we arrested him?'

'He has been charged with assaulting a police officer, ma'am, yes.'

'You?'

Donaldson grinned. 'Not likely, ma'am. The officer sent to collect him. He apparently doesn't like being disturbed when he's with one of his parishioners.'

Cropper grimaced. 'Bursting in on a man doing God's Holy Work.'

'That's a bit of a highfalutin way to describe sex with someone young enough to be your son,' Donaldson said.

'A friend of mine might have died because of you, Mr Cropper,' Gilchrist said, taking the chair beside Donaldson. 'She's spending the night under observation in hospital.'

'Reverend Cropper. My church just gives people a bit of a high. Some people can't handle it.'

'Reverend – buy that title on the Internet, did you? Do *any* of your congregation know what you're doing to them?'

'Enhancing their lives? I would think so.'

'Where did you get the scopolamine you impregnated the order of service with?' Gilchrist said.

'None of your business,' Cropper said. 'It's not an illegal substance. I have a patch on my arm impregnated with it at this very moment.'

'You suffer from travel sickness?' Donaldson said with a frown.

Gilchrist glanced at him.

Cropper bared big white teeth. 'Hardly.'

'If it's legal there's no harm in telling us who supplied it, is there?' Donaldson said.

'Saddlescombe, by any chance?' Gilchrist said.

Cropper just looked at her.

'There's a lot of religion going around,' Gilchrist said. 'What do you know about recent events in Brighton?'

Cropper leaned forward, his face suddenly intense. He raised his hands and pointed as best he could with the first finger of each. 'Here, in your sleepy town, Lucifer has risen.'

'Early riser, is he?' Donaldson said. 'Because he'll need to be to get a hold here.'

Gilchrist glanced at Donaldson. He really wanted to punch the vicar.

'Tell me about the murder of a vicar committed not by the Devil but by some real-life individual.'

Cropper shrugged. 'Can't help you there,' he said, and leaned back again.

'He was murdered in a barbaric way,' Gilchrist said. 'He lived in fear of his life.'

'He was afraid of the Devil?' Cropper said. 'A wise man.'

'He was afraid of the Devil because some human had put the idea in his head,' Donaldson said.

Cropper looked intently at Donaldson. 'I know many vicars. All are wary of the Devil if they are true to their faiths. But which one has been murdered? Vicar Dave?'

'Who?' Gilchrist said.

'He casts out demons and writes Christian songs – very, very bad Christian songs.'

'That's enough to be killed, in my book,' Donaldson muttered.

'Not him,' Gilchrist said. 'A real vicar: Andrew Callaghan.'

Cropper nodded and jerked both hands up to put his finger on a bloody scab above his ear. 'A real vicar indeed.'

Donaldson produced the only photograph they'd been able to find of Callaghan. It was some ten years old.

'You know him?' he said.

'Don't be so eager,' Cropper said. 'Do you think I'd admit to knowing him if I'd done something to him?'

'It's been known,' Donaldson said.

'Nothing is known,' Cropper said. 'A lot is presumed.'

'OK,' Gilchrist said. 'Did you know him?'

Cropper levelled a look at her. 'I did.' He turned his mouth down. 'Liberal sort. Which doesn't mean I would kill him. Why would I? I didn't even know he'd been killed.'

He looked back at the wall.

'Why would you think vicars would be killing each other?'

'To avoid a plague of them?' Gilchrist said.

She looked away as Cropper picked at the scab on his pate with a horny fingernail, his other hand hanging from the restraints in front of his face.

'That's very funny,' Cropper said.

'How did you know Andrew Callaghan?' Gilchrist said.

'He came to ask my advice about someone who'd come to him for help.'

'Who?' Gilchrist asked.

'Well, he didn't name names. Someone who caused him concern because of his sexuality.'

'What was it about this person's sexuality?' Gilchrist said.

'What does it matter?' Cropper said.

'Let us decide what matters,' Donaldson said. 'What specific advice was he looking for?'

'I've known Andy many a year. A little straight for my tastes but he has his depths. Had his depths.'

'How did you meet?' Gilchrist said.

'A conference of vicars. He was a good listener. I'm a great talker.'

'You're mesmerizing, I believe,' Gilchrist said. 'With a little help from hallucinogenic substances.'

'An enhancement of my effect and not the cause of it, I assure you.'

'OK – why did he think you could help him with this person?'

Cropper gestured at his scarred and sutured head. 'He thought I might have experience of such a person since I go to the dark places of my religion.'

'What was dark about this person's sexuality?' Donaldson said. 'I thought the church had pretty much every kind of sexuality covered these days.'

Cropper bared white teeth in a grin but said nothing.

'And had you experience of such a person?' Gilchrist said.

'In fact not.'

'What was your advice?' Donaldson said.

'In Brighton? Are you kidding? My advice was: embrace the difference.'

'Are you going to stop dancing around the maypole and tell us what this person's problem is?' Donaldson said.

Cropper looked at his cuffed hands; held them up for a moment as if in prayer. 'A confusion about sexual identity.'

'Swings both ways?' Donaldson said.

Cropper shook his head.

'This person *is* both ways.' He guffawed abruptly. 'Lucky person has a penis and a vagina. Both fully functioning.'

'Lucky?' Donaldson said, grimacing. 'Poor sod might have the worst of both worlds: might be frigid *and* impotent.'

Gilchrist was thinking about the photographs she had seen in the Jurassic Museum.

'This person wasn't called Lesley Henderson, by any chance?'

Cropper shrugged.

'All I know is it was a hermaphrodite,' he said.

'Intersex,' Gilchrist said.

Donaldson turned to her. 'Sorry?'

Before Gilchrist could explain there was a tap on the door and Heap came in.

'I'm hoping you're not here to spoil the broth, Chef Heap,' Donaldson said, leaning in to the recording machine to add: 'Detective Constable Heap has just entered the interview room.'

'I am a lousy cook, Detective Sergeant, so I probably would if we were cooking. However, I'm here with information.'

'Before you give it,' Gilchrist said, 'just explain to the DS and Vicar Nick Cropper here about intersex people.'

'Ma'am,' Heap said. 'The term "hermaphrodite" is considered misleading and insensitive. Now such people are DSD and we refer to their status as intersex.'

Donaldson laughed. 'What the fuck's DSD?' He glanced at Cropper. 'Excuse my language, Vicar.'

'Disorders of sex development,' Heap said. 'It acknowledges a discrepancy between the external and the internal genitals – testes and ovaries. Medical science has no idea what the underlying cause might be.'

'Both lots of kit apparently work in this case,' Gilchrist said. 'So "discrepancy" doesn't quite cover it.'

'I was quoting the technical description, ma'am,' Heap said. 'But what you describe – true gonadal intersex – is extremely rare.'

'This is all getting on *my* gonads,' Donaldson said. 'DSD. Intersex. Jesus.'

'Like you, Detective Sergeant, I do prefer the old name,' Heap said. 'Hermes and Aphrodite conjoined.' He looked at Cropper. 'Does the person under discussion have breasts in addition to a penis and a vagina?'

Cropper nodded. 'I believe so.'

'How old is he/she?' Heap said.

'Mid-thirties, I believe,' Cropper said.

Heap turned to Gilchrist. 'It's unheard of for someone of that age not to have been assigned a gender. In the days when this person was born, gender was assigned within days, sometimes hours. Usually the gender assignment was based on a quick look at the external genitals – which sex looked more developed – totally ignoring the chromosome gender.'

'You mean how big the willy was?' Donaldson said.

Heap ignored him. 'It was easier to reconstruct female genitalia rather than functioning male genitalia so the child was often assigned to be a girl. That could cause problems later for the individual if, as frequently happened, the chromosome gender was male. Female body, male brain. But not doing any surgery, not assigning a gender at all – unheard of.'

Gilchrist was, as usual, impressed with Heap's knowledge.

'No sleep again, Constable Heap?' she said.

'Do you need me any more?' Cropper drawled. 'You three seem to have it sorted.'

They all ignored him.

'Ma'am,' Heap said. 'These days chromosomes, neurons, hormones, psychological and behavioural factors are all taken into account. Surgery is delayed for as long as possible – but not as long as twenty or thirty years.'

'Snails and slugs are functioning hermaphrodites,' Cropper said abruptly. 'In the absence of a male, slugs self-fertilize.' He smirked at Gilchrist. 'One slug – the banana slug – has such a big cock in relation to its overall size it sometimes gets stuck inside another slug. If that happens, they bite off the cock and the eunuch only mates as a female thereafter.'

Cropper winked at Donaldson. 'Doesn't bear thinking about, does it?'

THIRTY

It had been a long day for Watts but it was still relatively early in the evening when he headed for Lewes. The rain had let up for some time now but he almost missed the comforting swish of the windscreen wipers.

The lights were against him at Five Dials. He was sitting twiddling with the car radio when his daughter walked in front of his car, draped over a man. She was taller than the man so leaned down against him, her long hair spilling on to his shoulder.

For that reason it took him a moment to realize the man was Vicar Dave.

Anger had been an abiding problem for Watts – well, one of them – but he felt helpless as it surged over him looking at this horrible man with Watts' lovely daughter.

He hurled himself out of his car, bellowing: 'What the hell do you think you're doing?'

His daughter whirled as if attacked, stumbling against the kerb. Vicar Dave steadied her and brought her on to the pavement. He kept his arm protectively around her as he gave Watts a cold look.

'I assume you're addressing me rather than your daughter in such an aggressive way,' he said quietly, his voice almost lost in the blare of a car horn as the lights changed and Watts' car blocked the way. 'But whatever I'm doing has nothing at all to do with you.'

Watts looked at his daughter. 'What are you doing with this charlatan?' he said, aware even as he said it that this was absolutely the wrong way to go.

His daughter, flushed with embarrassment, looked beyond Watts at the impatient driver honking his horn. 'It's none of your business,' she said.

He took a step forward. His daughter stepped in front of Vicar Dave.

'You're making yourself ridiculous, Father.' There was scorn in her voice. 'It's a bit late to show parental concern for me.'

'You told me you were married to Christ,' he said.

'Which is why you are being ridiculous,' she said. She glanced at Vicar Dave. 'Dave respects the sanctity of that marriage.'

Watts looked at the vicar, who held his gaze. 'Yeah, right.'

There was a renewed blast of a horn and an inchoate shout as the car behind Watts' veered round it to get through the lights. Other cars followed. More hoots and jeering calls.

Watts pointed at Vicar Dave. 'Your card is marked, Mister.'

Vicar Dave shrugged.

'Let's go,' Watts' daughter said. She took a couple of steps away from Watts and Vicar Dave. She looked at her father with something like disgust, something like pity. 'Goodbye, Father.'

Fuck it. Watts had wanted to hit the vicar the first time he saw him. He'd fucked this up with his daughter. He might at least get something out of it. He took a swing at Vicar Dave's enticing face.

Watts would have laughed if it hadn't been so damned pathetic. Vicar Dave was handy, handy enough to dodge Watts' fist and use the momentum to up-end the former chief constable.

Watts heard everything from his pockets clatter to the floor a second before he did. At least, he thought afterwards, he remembered how to hit the ground without breaking anything.

His daughter looked at him, unconsciously tossing her hair. Vicar Dave walked off with a shake of his head. His daughter came over and helped him to his feet. She picked up some things and handed them to him.

More drivers blared their horns at him as they navigated round his car. She shook her head and said in a tiny voice, 'Goodbye, Dad.'

He nodded at her then turned and went back to his car. The light was on green. She was still standing on the pavement as he drove off. She called something and gestured but, feeling foolish and angry and pitiful, he drove on.

There had been an abrupt change in Cropper, as if a switch had been flipped. He stretched his hands out and pointed his fingers at Gilchrist.

'When God brought me to town the Devil came with me.'

Gilchrist looked into his fierce eyes. To use a technical term, the guy was definitely a nut-job.

'Let me guess,' she said. 'You can't have one without the other.'

Cropper burned a look into the wall and tilted his head. 'I'm not so sure. When I look in the mirror, I don't see God at all. All I see is the Devil.'

'You believe you're the Devil?'

'I believe the Devil is within me and works through me.'

'Can't you cast him out of you as you cast him out of others?'

Cropper looked at her intently. 'Why would I want to? Besides, those I cast out of others are the Devil's minions.'

'Not the Big Man himself?' Donaldson said.

'The Devil is no mere man, big or otherwise.'

'Well,' said Donaldson, 'except that, according to you, he's inhabiting your body and you're a mere man.'

Cropper rolled his shoulders.

'How's he look?' Gilchrist said. 'The Devil.'

Cropper grimaced. 'Like me.'

'No horns, yellow eyes, sulphur coming out of his nostrils – none of that stuff?'

'Don't be absurd,' he said, and indicated his plastic hand restrainers. 'If I wished to break these shackles, I could do so.'

'That I'd like to see,' Donaldson said. 'Even if I had to pay for the cost of replacement. Try it, why don't you? Demonstrate to us that you really are possessed by the Devil.'

Cropper gave a secretive smile. 'The Devil is above party games.'

'How's he going to feel about being under arrest?' Donaldson said. 'You and him both.'

Cropper laughed then, almost good-naturedly. 'You amuse

me. You think you have the Devil by the tail? If you had captured the Devil you would wish you had not done so.'

'What about God?' Gilchrist said, though she wasn't sure why.

'God?'

Cropper suddenly fisted one hand and hit himself, hard, against the side of his head, his other hand flapping. 'God is the Alien. The Abyss. The Non-Existent.'

Gilchrist shuddered.

'What does that make the Devil?' Donaldson said.

Cropper massaged his temple with meaty fingers. 'Why, Rex Mundi, of course.'

'The Ruler of the World,' Heap said.

Cropper's sleeve had rolled up above his bicep. Heap pointed at the patch on Cropper's arm. 'Are you by any chance bipolar, Mr Cropper?'

THIRTY-ONE

Nicola Travis's garden was lit with white Christmas lights strung across the trees and leading round the side of the house. Watts parked behind the *deux chevaux* that had been there before. A clapped-out old thing, it seemed familiar but perhaps that was only because it was typical Lewes.

Carrying the ice box and purse, he followed the trail of lights. In the garden there were tall shrubs with hanging, trumpet-shaped flowers.

Nicola Travis was waiting for him at a metal table. She had changed into jeans and a T-shirt. There was a teapot and two mugs on the table. He put the ice box on the floor beside the table and handed her the purse. He gestured round the garden.

'Exotic flowers.'

'Angel trumpets mostly. Mixed with their cousins, the thorn apple. *Datura stramonium.*'

'Lovely,' he said.

'They are. My favourite plants and flowers only bloom cloaked in darkness.'

Watts didn't know what to say to that.

'Datura is associated with Saturn and Venus. Saturn is of the night. Venus? I'm guessing because of these big, lush, flowers – like a woman's sex. Georgia O'Keefe painted the blossoms of the Sacred Datura, you know. But Venus has her darkness too. Like many beautiful things, all parts of these plants are poisonous.'

Travis was rooting in her bag.

'I thought O'Keefe painted calla lilies,' Watts said.

'She painted those too. Where's my phone?'

Watts smiled. 'Sorry – put it in my pocket for safe-keeping.' He put his mug down on the table and felt in his jacket pockets.

'I hope you haven't been peeking,' Travis said.

'I wouldn't dream of it,' he said, switching to his inside pockets. He pulled out an iPhone and she reached for it. He pressed the indent to illuminate the screen. 'No, that's mine,' he said. He rummaged through all his pockets whilst the smile slipped off her face.

'Listen, I'm really sorry,' he said. 'I took a tumble earlier and it must have fallen out of my pocket.'

'My phone fell out of your pocket?'

'At Five Dials.'

'What was it doing in your pocket?'

'I – I don't really know. When I found it I just dropped it in there for safe-keeping.'

'Safe-keeping.' Travis's voice was chilly.

Watts remembered his daughter calling after him and waving. He'd assumed she was either cursing or forgiving him – those were the two options for Christians, weren't they? But now he wondered whether she had found the phone in the gutter and had been trying to bring him back.

'It's OK,' he said. 'I think my daughter might have it.'

'Your daughter? Why on earth would she have it?' There was ice now in Travis's voice.

'She was there when I took a tumble,' Watts said. 'I'll text her.'

Under Travis's intense scrutiny he clumsily tapped out a message and sent it off.

'Why don't you try phoning her too?' Travis said.

Watts dialled his daughter. It went straight to voicemail. He left a message then shrugged. 'I'm sure your phone is safe.'

Watts could almost see the immense effort of will it took for Travis to smile and nod.

'Well,' she said, expelling air. 'Why don't we sit out here until she gets back to you?' She indicated the teapot. 'I've made a kind of mulled wine.'

They sat, she poured and handed him one of the mugs. She chinked hers with his. He took a sip of a lukewarm, heavily spiced drink.

'That tastes exotic.'

'Just stuff from the garden.'

'Not the toxic stuff, I hope,' he said.

She ignored his remark but she seemed to relax. Indeed, she recovered some of her earlier vivacity as she gabbled.

'I like sitting out here after dark, watching my flowers come to life. Datura is so potent. The hawk moth feeds off it and takes its poison to keep it safe from predators. The plants are not often used for recreational drug use but some-times – you can go deep, deep inside yourself, into a visionary state.'

'Nicola – you sound as if you've tried it.'

She ignored him again, speeding up, her eyes moving rapidly from side to side.

'Some people feel like an alien or that they are dissolving – the kind of oneness that Buddhists seek, I imagine. Other people suffer terrible anxiety because they are frightened they are going to lose control and that they will go insane – the very things the anxiety, rather than the datura, causes.

'Waking dreams, hallucinations of objects and beings that aren't there. A common belief is that you have turned into a bird. Inexperienced users might believe they can fly from the highest rocks. They come down to earth pretty promptly, although they may die still believing they are flying. Even so, it used to be an ingredient in flying ointments – you know, witches on their broomsticks?'

Watts watched her face and her expressive, waving hands in fascination. He shifted in his seat, wondering if drug use was what made Nicola manic, hoping his daughter would text soon.

Cropper was taken to a holding cell and Gilchrist led Donaldson and Heap back into the crime room. She stifled a yawn as she said to Heap: 'What's with the bipolar question?'

'I discovered new medical uses for scopolamine. Most relevant: it's used for colon and intestinal problems.'

'Like cancer?' Gilchrist murmured.

'For those who don't believe in conventional medicine,' Heap said. 'Formerly it was used to control heroin and cocaine withdrawal symptoms and to combat depression. And it's still used on patches to control bipolar disorders.'

'Bipolar – we're back to two things not one – there is a word for that, isn't there?'

'Duality, ma'am.'

'Always to be relied on, Bellamy.'

'Didn't you say you had important information for us, Heap?' Donaldson said tetchily.

'Yes, sir. Two things.'

'Take your time,' Donaldson said.

'Sir – do you know the full name of the Knights Templar?'

'That would be a no, Heap. I live in the modern world.'

'Sir. It's the Poor Knights of the Temple of Solomon. A conspiracy theory type would have a field day. Poor Knights of the Temple of Solomon ran Saddlescombe, on the outskirts of Brighton, hundreds of years ago. A copy of the *Key of Solomon* – obviously linked to the Temple of Solomon – resides in and is stolen from the Jubilee Library in Brighton.'

'What's your point, Constable?' Donaldson said. 'Or are you auditioning for the History Channel?'

'I took a call from someone called Allcock.'

'From the Jubilee's rare books collection?' Gilchrist said. 'What did he have to say?'

'He said he was mistaken about the provenance of the *Key* that was stolen from the library.'

Donaldson sighed. 'Provenance . . .'

Gilchrist was also impatient: 'It wasn't centuries old? So what?'

'Not that, ma'am. He said it wasn't part of the George Long collection. He checked. It was only donated in 1947.'

Gilchrist frowned. 'I don't see . . .'

'It had belonged to Aleister Crowley.'

Gilchrist thought for a moment. 'Who died that year. Was he the donor?'

Heap shook his head.

'Jesus, Heap,' Donaldson said impatiently.

'The donor puzzled Allcock,' Heap said.

'It wasn't Gluckstein, was it?' Gilchrist said.

Heap laughed. 'That would have been good. I hadn't thought of that. But not her. It was Ian Fleming.'

'The James Bond bloke?' Donaldson said.

Heap nodded.

'Bloody hell,' Gilchrist said.

'As you rightly say, ma'am.'

'He was friends with Victor Tempest – the father of Bob Watts. We need to call him. I need to call him.'

'With respect, ma'am, we have more immediate issues,' Donaldson said. 'What was the second thing, Heap? Was it to do with what's happening now?'

'I've traced Lesley Henderson.'

'His present whereabouts?' Donaldson said.

'His or her past.'

Donaldson sighed. 'I asked for something immediately relevant.'

'If we assume she's the person who went to see Andrew Callaghan she is our main suspect,' Gilchrist said. 'So any information is immediately relevant. What did you get, Bellamy?'

'Yes, come on, teacher's pet – spit it out,' Donaldson said.

Gilchrist gave Donaldson a hard look but said nothing. Heap flushed but ignored him.

'He was registered as a male at birth. He has lived at Saddlescombe all his life, though for most of it in a cottage on the estate. His mother's name is Avril Henderson. Avril

Henderson is the wife of Colin Pearson, the writer on the occult.'

Gilchrist jumped to her feet. 'Let's get going.'

The phone on her desk rang. She snatched it up. 'Desk sergeant here, ma'am. Young lady just come in with what she claims is evidence that she is willing to hand over only to you.'

'OK – we're coming down – I want a car and driver waiting at the front door, please.'

'Ma'am.'

They clattered down the stairs as the lifts in this building took forever to arrive. Gilchrist led the way into the foyer. A familiar blonde-haired girl was standing near the door, an intense-looking man with burning eyes sitting on the bench seat behind her.

'You have something for me?' she said to the girl.

The man stood.

'So,' the girl said. 'You're the woman who broke my mother's heart.'

The Goat of Mendes returned at the edge of the night, alone on the rim of the world, to salute the rise of a Devil's Moon. The Goat stood in a circle of blazing candles on Newtimber Hill, looking out to the sea from which all came. The Goat of Mendes, shaggy head and curling horns above broad shoulders and naked human body, arms outstretched before it.

Ten yards away a crumpled form lay in a wheelbarrow between the legs of the Wicker Man. Kindling was stacked against those legs. Someone was crouched over the kindling. A smell of petrol was in the air.

THIRTY-TWO

'And you would be who?' Gilchrist said to the girl with the long blonde hair.

'You mean *whom*,' the girl said. 'And I would be Catherine Watts, the daughter of Chief Constable Watts, the man whose marriage you wrecked when you had your sordid affair with him.'

Gilchrist flushed and clenched her jaw but was momentarily speechless. Heap stepped halfway between Gilchrist and Catherine Watts.

'I believe you have some information for us, miss,' he said.

Catherine glared at Gilchrist. 'I haven't finished what I want to say,' she said.

'I'm afraid that whatever you want to say will have to wait,' Heap said. 'We're in the middle of a murder inquiry which you would be wise not to impede.'

Catherine flashed an angry look at him. 'I'm hardly impeding it when I've brought in evidence,' she said sharply.

'You are if you don't tell us what it is, Miss Watts,' Heap said.

Catherine looked back at Gilchrist then fixed her attention on Heap. 'It's a mobile phone,' she said. 'It has something horrible on it.'

'Where did you get it?'

Catherine looked at the intense man beside her as if for support. He nodded.

'Who are you, sir?' Heap said.

'My parishioners call me Vicar Dave.'

Heap and Gilchrist exchanged glances.

'Go on, Miss Watts,' Heap said.

'It fell out of the pocket of my father, Bob Watts.'

Gilchrist frowned. What was going on here?

'And what disturbs you?' Heap said.

Catherine handed him the phone. 'See for yourself. Look on the video.'

Gilchrist and Donaldson pressed in close to Heap as he turned the phone lengthways and touched the video icon. Catherine Watts never took her eyes off Gilchrist.

Gilchrist watched the video again with Heap in the back of the car heading for Saddlescombe. She had quickly ascertained, with some relief, that it wasn't Bob Watts' phone but she was puzzled about why he had it. Donaldson was back in the office finishing off the interview with Bob's daughter and tracing the owner of this phone.

The video was filmed in low light in Callaghan's flat. The camera panned across the wall with the scriptures on it to Callaghan, sitting on a stand-up chair in shirt and trousers, trussed with tape. There was tape over his mouth. The camera moved in on his eyes, wide and fixed.

A woman's voice, indistinct. 'You refuse to see what's going on? Well, soon you will see.'

A Stanley knife was waved in front of the camera.

'I'm going to cut your eyelids off,' the woman said.

The camera pulled back to show a figure leaning over Callaghan, almost obscuring him. The elbow of the right arm moved as the figure presumably started to work with the knife.

The woman started to talk again. 'Did I just nick your eyeball? Sorry. I don't know how to do this really. Who does? I know it's important you keep still so I've made sure of that. Ugh – that stuff coming out of your eye doesn't look good.'

There was a muffled voice from somewhere else in the room.

'Is that so? It's your vitreous humour apparently. Sounds quite alchemical, doesn't it? It's the gunk between the lens and the retina.'

She got to work again.

'Did you ever see that Salvador Dali film? He made it with Luis Buñuel. Starts with a moon and then someone holding a woman's eye open and then a razor and then – ugh. Horrible. Of course, it wasn't really her eye. They used a cow's eye. Or did they? Maybe the cow's eye substitution was just a story they put around to cover what really happened. Maybe the woman was never seen again. Maybe they killed her and disposed of her body. She might have been the woman in that trunk at Brighton station. Well, no. That was years later, I think.'

The woman held up to the light something papery and thin between long fingers and thumb. She put it in her pocket. 'Just so you know: I probably will dice your eyeballs anyway. I don't believe it will hurt. I'm told eyes feel no sensation. But even if they did there's nothing you could do about it. "Dark, dark, dark, amid the blaze of noon." That's Milton. *Samson Agonistes*. "Eyeless in Gaza" and all that. Listen to me – the literary allusions just keep flowing. A bit like all this blood going into your eyes. Who knew eyelids bled so much?'

The other voice came from somewhere in the room again.

'No, not like Oedipus,' she said. 'Oedipus put out his own eyes. Samson had it done to him. Philistines with swords or hot pokers or hot coals did it.'

The video ended there.

'Samson – you know he pulled down the Temple on the heads of the Philistines?' Heap said.

'We're back in the Temple of Solomon, are we?'

'Who are they, do you think, ma'am?'

'I assume the other voice in the room was the camera person,' Gilchrist said.

Heap shook his head. 'That voice would have been the clearest because it was nearest the phone.'

'So you think three people?'

Heap nodded.

'Lesley Henderson, her mother Avril and Colin Pearson?'

'Maybe,' he said, as the car pulled into Saddlescombe Farm.

'Look at that moon, Bob,' Travis said. 'A true Devil's Moon. There'll be some dark deeds tonight under that cold light, for sure. Here's a trivia question: from what stage and film show does the song "Old Devil Moon" originally come?'

'Musicals aren't my thing,' he said.

'*Finian's Rainbow*. Fred Astaire is in the film. Don't usually associate him with the Devil, do we? Well, I don't. He's associated with Brighton too. In *The Gay Divorcee* he comes to

Brighton for a quickie divorce, you know. The film was released in 1934, same year as the Trunk Murders.'

Travis was standing when she started to sing. She had a pretty good voice. She did a twirl or two on tiptoe, giving him exaggeratedly arch looks.

'Something in your eyes I see . . .'

She leaned in.

'. . . wanna laugh like a loon.'

She touched his cheek with her finger.

'. . . that old devil moon in your eyes.'

She stopped in front of Watts and shook her head.

'Oh, Bobby, Bobby. Your beautiful eyes.'

Watts shifted in his seat again. Or tried to.

Tabby McGrath answered the door.

'Is Lesley Henderson here?' Gilchrist said without preamble.

'We haven't seen him for a couple of days.'

'Why didn't you tell us Lesley Henderson's mother lived nearby?'

McGrath bridled. 'I didn't know,' she said indignantly. 'Who is his mother?'

'Avril Pearson,' Heap said.

McGrath looked surprised. 'None of us know that. But then we don't know Lesley well.'

'Do you know him as a man or a woman?' Gilchrist said.

'As a person.' McGrath was smug now. 'We don't judge people here.'

'We're not judging anyone either,' Gilchrist said. 'We're trying to solve a crime.'

'We also respect each other's privacy.'

'So you never noticed anything unusual about Lesley?' Heap said.

McGrath chewed her lip. 'Sometimes Lesley dressed as a woman; sometimes as a man. Either way was cool with us.'

'How well do you know Avril Pearson?' Gilchrist said.

'Avril cultivates a lot of the particularly unusual produce we provide local restaurants with.'

'Produce that goes to Plenty?' Gilchrist said.

'Among other restaurants.' McGrath was defensive now.

'The produce that got the restaurant closed?'

'That was a mix-up. We thought we were supplying lilies but we took something else by mistake.'

'Datura, wasn't it? What was that batch for?'

'You'd need to ask Avril about that.'

'But you know,' Heap said.

McGrath looked cagey.

'Was it to do with Avril's cancer?' Heap said.

Gilchrist kept her face expressionless.

McGrath nodded. 'She was trying to cure herself using datura.'

Gilchrist was remembering the shit smeared on Callaghan's walls and dropped on her. 'Is she with you?' she said.

McGrath shook her head. 'She never comes in here. Try the gardens or her house.' McGrath pointed. 'It's that one there. If she's not there, try her daughter.'

'Who is where?' Heap said.

'Who is who?' Gilchrist said.

McGrath shrugged. 'I don't know the answer to either of those questions.'

Gilchrist and Heap thanked her and turned to leave as she shut the door pretty much in their faces.

'How the hell did you know about the cancer?' Gilchrist said.

'Educated guess,' Heap said. 'I figured Avril Henderson would be anti-conventional medicine.'

He opened the gate to Avril Henderson's cottage. There was no answer at the front door. Heap got out his torch and they walked down the side of the house into the back garden. The torchlight caught a clump of tall white flowers.

'What are they?' Gilchrist said. 'They're beautiful.'

'Bell lilies or trumpet lilies.'

'And Avril Henderson grows them.'

'As well as the datura that features in the painting.'

The kitchen door was locked and there was no reply to their knocking. Heap swept his torchlight around and beyond the garden.

'Ma'am.'

The beam of light had landed on a chalet out towards the end of the garden with light spilling from the window.

They made their way between half-a-dozen garden sheds to the chalet. Heap knocked on the door. No answer. No sign of movement. Gilchrist tried the handle and was a little surprised when the door opened.

'Hello?' she called, then stepped inside.

The room was sparsely furnished. A single bed in one corner; a Welsh dresser against the wall. There were candles in abundance on each of the shelves of the dresser. Leaning against the wall beside the dresser was *The Devil's Altar*.

Heap pointed at a wax disc and a black object laid out on the dresser. 'John Dee's paraphernalia, I would guess,' he said.

Gilchrist picked up a book. 'And the *Key of Solomon*.'

'Lesley Henderson or his mother stole these things, do you think?'

'Both,' Heap said. He was peering out of the window towards Newtimber Hill. 'Ma'am? I think the Wicker Man is on fire.'

THIRTY-THREE

Watts seemed to be stuck in the chair. His limbs didn't obey his brain's instruction. In fact, he couldn't remember how he had ever been able to move his limbs. His brain felt disconnected from his body.

Nicola walked over to him. She tilted his head back to look into his eyes, kissed him slowly on the lips, breathed into his open mouth.

'The Native Americans of the desert regions used Sacred Datura as a medicine. They'd make a paste to use it as anaesthetic for bone-setting or toothache. You're experiencing the numbing effects in a rather different form now. Of course, ingesting it can be a bit kill or cure. If you get the dose wrong people can go psychotic, suffer permanent physical disability or have a lethal heart attack.'

She walked behind him.

'But you looked sturdy enough to ingest *datura stramonium*. That's what I've given you. Your sturdiness is what attracted me to you all that time ago. A lifetime, really. If you only knew the journey I've been on since then.'

She reappeared in front of him.

'*Datura stramonium* is popular in Haiti. I wonder if you can guess what for?'

Watts could guess. He believed he said it but didn't know if any sound had emerged from his lips.

'Zombies!' She clapped her hands. 'Isn't that great? All those wonderful Hammer horror films with coffins in graveyards breaking open, spewing out the dead – and the undead. Well, of course, they've been doing that here lately because of the floods. The dead, at least. The colloquial name for *datura stramonium* over there is *concombre zombi*. Bit of a giveaway, really.

'So voodoo practitioners use datura to put people into the zombie state. The part I don't get is how you get from paralysing someone to getting that person to do your bidding. I'd love you to do my bidding but if I commanded you to get up out of that chair to serve me – or do I mean service me? – I don't see how you could, since I've paralysed you.' She chewed her lip. 'Difficult one.' Then looked up. 'Lot of stars out tonight. Beautiful sky. I love the night.'

Something moved in the little peripheral vision Watts had. Another person was in the garden.

As Gilchrist and Heap crunched up the path to Newtimber Hill they could see the legs of the Wicker Man ablaze. In front of the figure a circle formed of hundreds of candles cast a softer light. In the middle of the circle, silhouetted against the flames, stood the Goat of Mendes with erect penis and full breasts.

'Jesus,' Gilchrist muttered as she approached the circle. Heap moved off at an angle to come up beside the circle of light.

Feeling foolish, Gilchrist called: 'Lesley Henderson?'

The Goat of Mendes put its hands to either side of its head and pulled the head off. It had concealed a bearded person with long flowing hair. Gilchrist looked from beard to breasts to penis. She was sure there would be a vagina beneath the penis.

'Are you Lesley Henderson?'

'He is Dionysus.'

A woman with long grey hair was standing near the Wicker Man, a wheelbarrow in front of her. A body was slumped in the wheelbarrow.

Gilchrist sighed. Here we go.

'I wasn't aware Dionysus had a goat's head,' Heap said.

Henderson put the head on the ground and straightened.

'That was for revelry,' the woman said. 'You know the Dionysian rites have been carried out on this site for centuries?'

'Are you Avril Pearson?' Gilchrist said.

'And if so, who is this person?' Heap called. Gilchrist saw Heap take possession of the wheelbarrow and roll it a few yards away from the woman.

'The rites are sacred frenzy,' Avril Pearson said to Gilchrist.

Gilchrist looked at the goat's head then back at Lesley Henderson. She echoed Heap's question: 'Who is that person in the barrow?'

'His name is Colin Pearson,' Avril said.

'Your husband?' Heap was down on one knee now, feeling for a pulse in the neck. 'You were trying to set fire to your husband?'

'Is that Lesley Henderson?' Gilchrist persisted.

'I gave him that name, yes. But the name has nothing to do with what he really is.' Avril Pearson pointed at her husband. 'And that man is nothing to do with him.'

'Because his father is a god?' Heap said, stepping towards Henderson and shaking his head at Gilchrist. Pearson was dead.

Gilchrist looked from the mother to the son, wondering exactly what to do.

'Mum knows a lot more about datura than I do, of course,' Travis said. 'We use it to hex and to break hexes. You can commune with birds.'

She leaned forward and kissed Watts on both cheeks.

'We use it to produce sleep and induce dreams. Did that happen to you, darling, when you stayed at my mother's that night? Did you dream?'

Her mother? Avril Pearson was her mother? Was that why the car outside had seemed familiar? Was she the other person in the garden now?

'My mother is putting things to rights because she's dying. She hates Colin, my stepfather. He's in his own world. Or was. He's probably in the next world by now.'

Watts remembered the soup Colin Pearson had drunk earlier in the day that Avril had tried to press upon him.

'Colin is antediluvian. She went along with that at first – all women of her generation did. Then she got resentful. Then she got angry. Then she got ill and then she got vengeful.

'He's not my dad so I don't care,' Travis said. 'He tried it on with me once but I slapped him down and he didn't pester me after that. But it changed things between us, of course. He didn't try it with Lesley. Didn't go anywhere near Lesley when he found out. Mum had Lesley during a bit of a muddled period of her life.'

All very interesting but Watts was mostly thinking: *what are you going to do to me?*

'Have you read *Middlesex*?' Travis asked. 'A hermaphrodite grows up thinking she's a girl until puberty hits and he realizes he's a boy. Lesley chose to remain both. It gives her power. Sometimes he grows a beard. A beard, breasts and a penis: it's quite disorienting.'

She stroked his cheek.

'I'm blessed too. I have two personalities. They would have worshipped me in the past but today they try to control me with drugs.'

Henderson spread his arms. Gilchrist couldn't help but notice his penis had drooped.

'There is no one on earth like him,' Avril said. 'So where does he come from? His existence must have some other meaning.'

'Meaning that you tried to access through magic ritual?' Heap said, now only a couple of yards from Henderson's flank.

Henderson lowered his arms.

'He's beautiful, isn't he?' Avril said.

Gilchrist nodded. In a way she didn't want to explore just

at that moment, she did find Lesley oddly beautiful. No, not oddly – just beautiful.

'The vicar found him disgusting. He told him he must be born of the seed of the Devil and I should have destroyed him at birth.'

'So you burned him to death in the Wicker Man on the beach,' Gilchrist said. She pointed at Colin Pearson. 'And you were about to do the same with that man. Why did you kill him?'

Henderson had crossed his arms across his breasts.

'He killed neither man,' Avril said. 'He is a bringer of life not death.'

'Then who?' Heap said, stepping into the circle of candles.

Henderson spoke for the first time. 'Kali has always protected me.'

'Who?' Gilchrist said, also stepping into the circle.

'Do you mean the Indian goddess?' Heap said. 'Getting your mythologies mixed up, aren't you?'

Avril nodded towards Pearson's body. 'That man convinced me that all myths are one myth.'

'And he told you about Kali, the Hindu goddess of Destruction?' Heap said.

Before Avril could reply, Henderson said, though with some uncertainty: 'I am the god died and reborn in every culture.'

Gilchrist said, 'Did you carry out some kind of ritual with John Dee's equipment using the *Key of Solomon*?'

'Was there some secret here at the farm that you made use of?' Heap said.

There was a sudden whoosh of fire and the flames from the legs of the Wicker Man rushed up the torso. Gilchrist could feel the heat.

'He made himself a god,' Avril said. 'He is Dionysus, the secret and the mystery.'

'A dying and reborn god,' Heap said. 'Yes, you told us.'

The whole of the Wicker Man was now ablaze. Gilchrist took a step back. 'Bellamy, let's move them away.'

She moved out of the circle and over to Avril Pearson. She took her arms. Avril resisted but Gilchrist started to drag her away from the blaze.

Heap stepped behind Henderson. 'Put your arms behind your back,' he said.

Henderson looked puzzled.

'You think you can chain a god?' Avril called.

'We seem to be doing a lot of that this evening,' Heap called back.

Henderson didn't move.

Gilchrist pulled Avril Pearson away to one side as one of the legs of the Wicker Man gave way at the knee. The figure tilted.

'Bellamy!' Gilchrist called.

Heap grasped Henderson's arm. 'Let's get away from here, sir.'

Henderson shrugged him off. 'I am to be reborn through fire.'

He turned to face the blazing, crackling Wicker Man. Flames were now leaping high into the sky, smoke blotting out the Devil's Moon.

The other person in the garden stepped in front of Watts. A man. He wore a paint-splattered jumper and held an asthma inhaler in one hand and a roll-up cigarette in the other. Watts remembered now where he'd seen the car outside before. It was regularly parked near his father's house in Barnes.

'You know Nick,' Travis said.

Nick Brunswick nodded at Watts and took a drag on his cigarette. 'Your daughter has Nicola's phone. That's unfortunate. We have something on that phone that is private.' He picked up Watts' phone from the table. 'Your daughter's name isn't Sarah Gilchrist, is it? She's the only one who's been phoning you. Several times. No message though.' He put the phone down and puffed on his inhaler. 'What to do with you?'

Brunswick looked at Travis. 'Have you heard from your mother?'

Travis shook her head. Brunswick nodded.

'Nicola and Avril and I tormented the man who had tormented Lesley. We filmed it. I put him in the Wicker Man. I set it alight. And later tonight, we will set the rest of the world alight. Lesley will be reborn.'

Brunswick dropped the cigarette and trod on it. 'You were asking about the AA. I lied to you at Caspar's house. I lied to him. My mentor did not disappear. My mentor died and willed to me the AA. Why me? Because I have His blood flowing through me.'

Watts didn't know who Brunswick meant by He. Brunswick was eager to tell him.

'Aleister Crowley was my grandfather. He had a number of children – some he knew about, some he didn't. The promiscuity during sex rituals made it difficult to keep track of paternity. His mistress, Ninette, bore my father and three other children.' He puffed on his inhaler again. 'I have created Crowley's moonchild for a great mission.'

Heap grabbed Henderson's arm again but Henderson half-turned and, showing surprising strength, hurled Heap bodily out of the circle of candles.

Heap fell almost at Gilchrist's feet.

'Get out of there,' Gilchrist cried. 'You're going to be burned alive.'

Gilchrist bent to help Heap up, her eyes on Henderson. Henderson took a step back as the other leg of the Wicker Man gave way and the whole fiery edifice started to topple. Avril cried out something Gilchrist couldn't make out.

Henderson raised his arms to the heavens and looked up to the moon, his face exalted in the flickering light from the flames. Then the Wicker Man engulfed him.

'I thought Lesley beautiful the first time I set eyes on him and her,' Brunswick said. 'I didn't want to change anything. The most perfect creation. We thought we had made him but couldn't be certain. Avril was going through a troubled time.

'Neither Avril nor I suffer from a hormonal imbalance so there was no natural reason for us to create someone so special. Unless it was meant to be. She was urged to assign gender but I encouraged her to wait. It seemed like dithering to Avril but I persuaded her.'

'Mum wants to make Lesley a god now,' Travis said. 'That's why I stole the John Dee things from the British Museum and the *Key of Solomon* from the library. The theft of the painting was a little more whimsical.'

She stroked Watts' face again. Was he imagining it or could he feel her fingers this time? Was the drug wearing off?

Gilchrist and Heap watched in horror as the fire roared and surged around Lesley Henderson. Gilchrist started forward but Heap grabbed her arm.

Henderson made no sound from within the fire but nor did he rise up, reborn. Avril sank to her knees and covered her face with her hands. Heap phoned the emergency services. Gilchrist's own phone rang. It was Donaldson.

'Sylvia has tracked down an address in Lewes for that phone and we're on our way.'

'Give it to me,' Gilchrist said. She repeated it aloud for Heap's benefit. 'Who does it belong to?' she said.

'One Nicola Travis.'

'Who is she?' Gilchrist said.

'We're trying to find out.'

Gilchrist and Heap turned to Avril Pearson, kneeling at their feet.

'Let's go, Mrs Pearson,' Gilchrist said.

'Nick here was the only man who treated my mother kindly,' Travis said. 'The pill was meant to liberate women of my mother's generation but it meant they weren't allowed to say no to men. Free love and all that. And then all the other stuff followed. "Don't be square, Avril. You've got to open yourself to all experiences, Avril. Just turn over, Avril."'

Travis spat full in Watts' face. 'You don't know what you're doing when you're that age,' she said. 'What damage you're doing to yourself. That men are doing to you.'

Brunswick took her arm and moved her away. He squatted in front of Watts, examining his face. 'What are we to do with you, *mon semblable, mon frère*?'

Watts felt his left hand twitch.

Brunswick stood, his knees creaking, and went into a huddle with Travis. Then they moved out of Watts' vision and into the house. Watts tried to figure out how to make his limbs respond to his brain. What was it Pearson had said about perception being like a javelin?

A barrel-chested man appeared in front of him. He glanced at Watts and walked out of his line of vision.

DS Donaldson sat hunched on a straight-back chair in the corner of Watts' cramped, low-ceilinged cottage beside the sorting office. Gilchrist, Heap and Kate Simpson were all crammed in there too.

'Crikey, Bob, how do you function in here?' Gilchrist said.

He shrugged. 'Badly.'

'Is your daughter joining us, sir?' Heap said.

Watts shook his head. 'Not this time.'

'So what's happening?' Donaldson said, to no one in particular. 'Case concluded, isn't it?'

Donaldson had been accompanied by half-a-dozen beefy policemen when he'd arrived at Travis's house. The arrests had been boringly anticlimactic. An ambulance had collected Watts. He still felt a bit spaced out but, a day later, at least he was more or less functioning normally.

'Pretty much,' Gilchrist said. 'Everybody and his dog seemed to be trying to find a way to fulfil his or her potential.'

'Maybe not the dog,' Kate said. Then: 'What did Avril Pearson have to say about killing her husband?'

'She said: "Because he killed me",' Gilchrist said. 'Her colon cancer is well-advanced.'

'It's the same thing that killed Farrah Fawcett,' Kate remarked.

After a moment Watts said: 'The one loose end is what the secret of Saddlescombe is or was,' Watts said. 'It didn't seem to figure in what Avril and her family were up to.'

Gilchrist gestured to Heap. 'Bellamy's your man. He knows everything.'

'I do know that Travis misled you, sir,' Heap said to Watts. 'With regard to the zombie thing. Although datura did paralyse you, in Haiti the agent used is actually tetrodotoxin. It doesn't come from a plant but from the pufferfish.' Heap flushed as he saw all eyes on him. 'Just saying.'

'Detective Sergeant Donaldson,' Watts said, 'I'm not saying you're a Freemason but if you were to be you might be able to shed light on what the Templars might have guarded at Saddlescombe.'

'How so?' Donaldson said. 'If I were a Mason.'

'I went through all the things that might have been there and came up with nothing.'

'There is the Ring of Aandaleeb.'

'Sounds like something from a computer game for teenage boys,' Donaldson said scornfully. 'Wizards and Sorcerers?'

'The ring is also known as the Seal of Solomon,' Heap said. 'It has magical powers.'

'We *are* back to a teenage computer game,' Gilchrist said.

'No, no,' Heap said. 'It's what the Templars took from Solomon's tomb in the Temple. Except there's little proof of Solomon's existence and less of the Temple's.'

'Tell that to the Freemasons,' Donaldson said. He spread his hands. 'Not that I can help you with this ring.'

'I think all this is rubbish,' Gilchrist said. 'There was no secret at Saddlescombe, just a lot of coincidences.'

'It's not necessarily rubbish just because it's weird,' Watts said. 'A fish fell on your head, didn't it?'

Gilchrist laughed.

'Didn't it?'

'Conger eel,' she said.

'That's still a fish.'

'What's your point?' Gilchrist said.

Watts shrugged. 'No point really. I guess we're fated never to know the true story about Saddlescombe.' He looked around. 'It's only in fiction that it all has to make sense at the end.'

EPILOGUE

'It's someone for you, Dad,' fifteen-year-old Bobby Watts said, coming into the garden from the family house.

Victor Tempest glanced at his wife and heaved himself out of his chair. She carried on reading her book. He looked up at the woman's face at the window of the sitting room. 'I'll take care of it,' he said, patting his son on the shoulder as he walked past him.

She was still standing by the window when Tempest came into the sitting room.

'Avril – I'm surprised to see you here.' He offered his open hand. 'Come out of the sunlight so I can see you.'

Avril Henderson walked over to where he was standing in the middle of the room. She put her arms around his neck and kissed him on the lips. He looked beyond her into the garden. Bobby was looking up at the window; Tempest's wife was fiercely intent on her book.

Avril stepped back. 'You wrote to Colin about that ritual you did with Aleister Crowley, Ian Fleming and Dennis Wheatley in Saddlescombe,' she said.

'Load of nonsense,' Tempest said.

'You say,' Avril said. 'Your letter left a lot unexplained.'

'For instance?'

'Why there?'

Tempest took a couple of steps and looked out of the window at his family in the garden. 'The Templars,' he said.

'What about them?'

'They had a powerful secret.'

'I don't know much about the Templars.'

'They found a ring.'

'A *Lord of the Rings* type ring?'

Tempest laughed. 'Probably the same ring. At least, it's where Tolkien got the idea for his ring. From Crowley, actually, in a pub in Oxford called the Eagle and Child over more than a few brandies.'

'What was this ring?'

'Solomon's ring. The Templars found it in Solomon's tomb and they brought it to Saddlescombe.'

'Why?'

Tempest laughed again. His son was still staring up at the window. He looked at Avril and smiled. He could see why his pubescent son was staring. In her thirties – and, therefore, ancient as far as his son was concerned – Avril was a very sexy woman.

'I don't know. But it got here via a circuitous route through Provence. It came with the kings and reached Sussex with Simon de Montfort in hot pursuit.'

'But why Saddlescombe?'

'It's true that London or Paris were the obvious places. But maybe a small place – a quiet place – made more sense. Kings, princes and prelates all came down. Some believed in its power and hoped to share it. Some didn't. The De Montforts, father and son, were tenacious in trying to find it. The younger Simon, the one who won the Battle of Lewes in 1264, then dismissed it as nonsense. The king – Henry III – had stayed with the ring the night before and it did him no good. Then the king's son, Edward Longshanks, defeated Simon de Montfort at Evesham, so who was laughing then?'

'What? You mean Edward had this ring?'

Tempest shrugged. 'Or the power of the ring. The ring never left Saddlescombe – theoretically, its power is still there.'

'That's what he told me.'

'Colin?'

Avril nodded. 'But is the ring still there?' she said.

Tempest looked down at his hands and smiled. 'At Saddlescombe? Maybe.'

She shook her head vehemently. 'I don't want to know that unless I know where.'

'Finding a ring on a farm sounds a bit like a needle in a haystack scenario. And I can't believe for a minute it has any power.'

'Why but for this do you think we're living in a freezing house in the middle of nowhere?'

He shook his head. 'I think you're probably searching in

vain. I was at Crowley's funeral in 1947. The service at the crematorium.'

'And?'

'A lot of his stuff was burned with him.'

'This ring of power?'

Tempest shrugged.

'But such a ring would survive a fire, surely?'

'If it has the power that is claimed for it.' Watts put his hands on her shoulders. 'It's all nonsense, Avril.'

She pulled sharply away from him. 'No. I won't believe that.' She thrust her face towards him. 'You know why they cremated Crowley?'

'Of course. So his grave could not become a shrine or place of pilgrimage.'

'That – and to be sure he couldn't return. Fire destroys any chance of return. They didn't want Crowley to be a died and reborn god.'

'He wasn't a god, Avril. When I knew him he was a drunken, drug-addicted old man wearing rouge and a wig that looked like it belonged on a mop.'

'He had the power.'

'He was self-deluding. The cremation ceremony included his own Hymn to Pan so one local rag described it as a black mass. It wasn't.'

'They say you could see his spirit rising out of the crematorium's chimney in the smoke.'

'You couldn't.'

She turned away.

'Why did you come, Avril?' he said, remarkably softly for him.

'I'm on a long journey,' she said.

'I hope it's leading somewhere,' he said. 'Excuse me a minute.'

He walked back into the garden. 'I'm just going to give our guest a lift,' he called. 'I'll be back in half an hour.'

Tempest had recently purchased one of the first Saab convertibles.

'You OK with the roof down?' he said as he closed Avril's passenger door.

She nodded but said nothing, looking straight ahead. Tempest intended to have sex with her somewhere but no layby seemed appropriate. He drove into Richmond Park.

There was certainly tension in the car. He couldn't work out whether it was the right tension. He pulled into the car park.

When he put the roof up she seemed to know what was expected of her.

They were having sex when the first blackbird hit the canvas roof. He didn't know it was a blackbird. He thought it was some pervert who'd sneaked out of the bushes. The timing couldn't have been worse. The last thing he wanted to do was make her pregnant but, startled, he lost control.

A couple of moments later he glanced up and saw hundreds of black objects plummeting from the sky.

A blackbird came through the passenger window and landed beside Avril's head. Her eyes were closed but she turned her head to see this bright orange beak and dead eye beside her. She started to make guttural noises that were not screams but weren't to do with the sex.

Blackbirds rained down on the car. Two more came through the open window and landed in the driver's seat. It took them a minute or so to disentangle then another minute for him to close the windows. A bird struck Tempest a glancing blow on the side of his head.

Birds were splattered on the windscreen and on the hood. As birds thudded against the canvas above their heads and continued to rattle on the bonnet and boot Tempest was trying to remember his schoolboy physics.

Galileo had figured out that all free-falling objects fall at the same rate of acceleration. Didn't he drop a couple of cannon balls off the Leaning Tower of Pisa? Tempest couldn't recall if anyone had been standing underneath.

Anyway, a beach ball, an aircraft or a bloody blackbird starting from the same point would all hit his car at the same time. Or was that only in a vacuum?

And what happened about the weight? Couldn't a peanut crush your skull if it had fallen far enough before impact? He knew it was something to do with Newton's second law of motion and the object's terminal velocity.

He heard a rip – the very reason his mind was racing around these questions. In practical terms, what chance did a stiffened canvas roof have of withstanding the direct impact of a blackbird that, at the point of contact could, for all Tempest knew, weigh half a ton?

Then again, the blood dripping into his eyes reminded him, his skull had survived the impact of a blackbird. Perhaps they weren't falling very far? He grimaced when he realized he was wondering how far they were falling without asking the more fundamental question: why were they falling at all?

Another ripping noise, directly above his head. A yellow beak poked through. He immediately thought of the Hitchcock film *The Birds*. Was this a scene from that? If not, it should have been. He looked at the mound of birds in the driving seat and the back seat, realized several others were crowded round his ankles and one – ugh – lay by his head, a glistening black eye staring up at him. He pushed it to the floor with the back of his hand.

The difference between what he was experiencing and the film was probably that all these blackbirds were dead. Didn't seem to help his Tippi Hedron though: Avril had gone into a rigid state of shock.

Tempest remained protectively hunched over her as the bombardment continued. He didn't know how long it actually went on – he hadn't looked at his watch when it started – but by the time it slowed down the roof was pretty much shredded and his windscreen was splintered in a dozen places.

He and Avril sat in the car a good five minutes after it seemed to have ceased, squashed together in the passenger seat. He could see in the vanity mirror that he had a deep laceration down the side of his head and a bloody gouge in his scalp.

When the sky was clear of flying objects he opened the car door and stepped out, squelching birds as he did so. The car park was littered with broken-winged, broken-backed birds. It was a dizzy collage of colours – the black of the birds, the yellow of their beaks and the crimson of their blood. Most of them had burst open on impact with the tarmac.

He helped Avril out and put the back of the passenger seat

up. He helped her sit in it. For as far as he could see in the park there were smudges of black. Halfway along the road, a car, dented and buckled, had its windscreen wipers sluggishly smearing the smashed remains of the screen with blood and feathers. A dazed-looking driver stood beside the vehicle, his head tilted back to look up at the sky.

Tempest glanced at the Saab. A dozen broken birds lay on the remains of the car roof; a dozen more were piled on the buckled bonnet. He looked up. Fluffy white clouds drifted in a turquoise sky. The sun was big and bright.

He looked at the ring on his finger. He hardly ever wore it. He'd put it on today on a whim. It was among the stuff Crowley had bequeathed to Ian Fleming in 1947. Fleming had passed it on to his friend. It had been in his cufflinks box most of the time since. It looked like brass but he'd never bothered to check.

Avril was staring straight ahead when he leaned into the car and said, 'It will take more than the AA to sort this out.'

They both burst out laughing.

AUTHOR'S NOTE

I am grateful to Diana Souhami, author of *Gluck: her biography* (Pandora) for advice about Gluck's *The Devil's Altar*. My characters' views on Gluck do not, of course, reflect hers. The painting is in Brighton's Museum and Art Gallery, where the security system is far more robust than I suggest, as it is in the Jubilee Library (which does not possess a copy of the *Key of Solomon*).

The Lewes Archaeological Museum does not possess anything belonging to John Dee. The British Museum does have some of John Dee's magical paraphernalia on display in its wonderful Enlightenment Room (Room One). The Museum of Jurassic Technology really exists in Los Angeles and contains all but the photographs as exhibits. It has no plans to open a branch in Brighton so I created a facsimile.

I have invented all employees of Brighton police, Brighton Museums, the Royal Pavilion, the Jubilee Library, Lewes Archaeological Museum and the British Museum. No character is based in any way on any real employee of those institutions. Ditto Saddlescombe's tenants.

The curious history of Edward II's shielding of the Knights Templar in Britain is true, although Saddlescombe's part in this history is my invention.

Aleister Crowley's involvement with Ian Fleming during World War II is based on anecdotal evidence, although the rituals are said to have taken place in Ashdown Forest not Saddlescombe.

Birds, fish and other creatures fall from the sky in large numbers more often than you might think . . .

Peter Guttridge, 2013